Morgan Spade

Help! My Boss is a Cowboy Billionaire

Morgan Spade

Help! My Boss is a Cowboy Billionaire

by Sophie Devon

Help! My Boss is a Cowboy Billionaire by Sophie Devon

Published by Thady Publishing.

Copyright © 2022 Sophie Devon

More books in this series by Sophie Devon

Buck Spade - Never Date a Cowboy Billionaire

Morgan Spade - Help! My Boss is a Cowboy Billionaire

Carson Spade - A Fake Wife for the Cowboy Billionaire

Follow Sophie on Tiktok:

www.tiktok.com/@sophiedevonbooks

Get notified when new books in this series are published here:
www.writtenbysophie.com

Chapters

Chapter 1

Red and bronze autumn leaves danced in the wind as they twirled across the proud front entrance of a luxury hotel. Or at least, the building's cobbled courtyard, gleaming, three-story-high glass wall, and rustic stone sides resembled a resort hotel; but it was in fact a private home, the main house of the Seven Spades Ranch complex. If a bystander had glanced up from the courtyard just then, he might have caught a glimpse of two tall, dark men dimly visible on the second floor: Buck Spade, the eldest of seven brothers, and his next-youngest brother Morgan.

The two men stood at the window for a moment in frowning silence, then disappeared back inside.

Buck sat down beside his brother on the couch, clasped his hands in his lap, and stared at Morgan in frowning concern.

His brother shot him a look of wintry gratitude. "Thanks for coming down here, Buck. I hate to interrupt you and Kate's honeymoon."

Buck adjusted a pillow behind his back and settled in. "It's all right," he rumbled. "Kate and I are going to be on our honeymoon for a month at least.

"I came as soon as I got your message. Something bad must've happened to make you want to talk, Morgan," he added, in a gentle attempt at humor. "What's wrong?"

Morgan looked away from him, and Buck could tell that he was struggling to contain himself. He shook his head bitterly and waved an impatient hand in the air.

"I just got a text from Cece," he rumbled.

Buck frowned. "Cecily? I thought you and her weren't talking any more. What did she want?"

Morgan rubbed his long hands over his face. "What does she always want," he mumbled bitterly. "She wants to make my life a living hell. But this time, she's really outdone herself." He turned to pin Buck with an angry stare.

"Do you know what she told me, Buck? She texted me to tell me that Kit wasn't my son. Just like that." He waved an angry hand in the air. "I know she's a nightmare, but even I didn't see this coming!"

Buck's frown deepened. "Has she given you any proof of—of what she says?" he stammered.

Morgan shook his head. "Well, I know Cece's cheated on me with just about every man in Texas," he grumbled. "So it is possible Kit might not be my son."

Buck stared at him, then sputtered, "No, that can't be right," he objected. "Kit's the spit and image of you. He looks just like you did at that age. He's yours all right."

Morgan shot him a smoldering glance. "Well, it makes no difference to me either way," he growled. "Kit is my son in all the ways that count, and I'm not giving him up." He rolled a shoulder angrily and added, "Cecily's just mad that the court awarded me custody after the divorce. This is her way of getting even."

Buck put a hand on his shoulder briefly and coughed, "I'm sorry, Morgan. You're right, this is just Cecily getting payback for you fighting her in court. Kinda the last twist of the knife. Forget it. You won custody of Kit. There's nothing more she can do."

Morgan tilted his dark head, as if to concede the point, but muttered, "If she can prove that Kit's not my son, the biological father might sue for custody."

Buck leaned toward him and muttered, "Not likely. He's not likely to win, anyway, since if he was the father, he sure didn't step up before now. Forget it, Morgan."

His younger brother rubbed his face with a brown hand and mumbled, "I'll try, but I didn't get a wink of sleep last night. All I can think about is somebody coming over here to take Kit away from me."

Buck put a hand on Morgan's shoulder. "You want to call Eugene?"

Morgan shook his head. "I don't see the use of calling a lawyer right now," he replied reluctantly. "If Cece tries something, then it'll be a different story."

"Well, if she does, we'll be ready for her," Buck replied in as bracing a tone as he could muster. "Don't pester yourself about it, Morgan. It's just one last little trick to make you sweat. Don't let it work. Come on down to breakfast."

Morgan grumbled and looked away. "No, I couldn't eat anything."

Buck stared at him in sympathy. "She's lying, Morgan," he said softly. "And it wouldn't exactly be the first time, would it? Seems to me that if you weren't Kit's father, she'd have hit you with it before now."

"That's a fact," Morgan agreed glumly. "She sure didn't care what she said to me when we fought." He sighed and shook his head.

Buck looked away uncomfortably and glanced around his brother's big living room. Morgan's apartment suite was warm and homey, with its paneled walls and hanging Indian blankets, but there was no little boy playing in it.

"Where's Kit?"

Morgan followed his glance. "Aw, I sent him downstairs," he confessed, and rubbed his brow as if it hurt him. "I don't want him to see his daddy like this. I'm a wreck, Buck."

Anger whisked up in Buck's heart as he stared at Morgan's haggard face. He'd known when Morgan had married Cecily Cooper that she was a gold digger. Everybody in the family had seen it except Morgan, but they'd all known better than to tell him. It wouldn't have done any good.

But seeing Morgan's strained eyes still made Buck suffer a flick of guilt. Maybe he should've sucked it up and told Morgan the hard truth when it might've helped.

Maybe it would've been better to let Morgan hate him, than to see his brother like this. Buck frowned and looked down at his hands, and Morgan glanced at him.

"You go on down to breakfast, Buck," he rumbled. "There's nothing you can do. I just needed to get it off my chest."

Buck shot him a stricken glance. "You're sure you don't want to come down and eat?"

Morgan shook his head. "I'm sure. You go on."

Buck sighed deeply and stood up. "Come on up to my place if you want to talk, Morgan," he said quietly. "Anytime. And if you need help, I got your back."

Morgan glanced up at him. "I know it, Buck," he replied softly. "Thanks."

Buck gave him a crooked smile and walked slowly to Morgan's front door. He paused there with his hand on the knob and looked back over his shoulder.

"I'll keep Kit busy for a while downstairs," he promised.

Morgan nodded. "I appreciate it, Buck."

Buck gave his brother one long, last glance before he opened the door and walked out into the hall of the big ranch house that he shared with his brothers. It was the hub of the Seven Spades Ranch, and it was probably what had first attracted Cecily Cooper to Morgan.

That big hotel they lived in all but shouted, *We have money. Come and get some of it.*

Buck bit his mouth into a hard, straight line. Cecily was a greedy little leech, and she'd never loved anybody but herself: not Morgan, not even Kit. The day Morgan had divorced her had been the best day he'd had in years.

And as Buck descended the big staircase, he made up his mind that he wasn't going to let her come back and haunt them, not if he had to spend a fortune on fences, firewalls, or legal fees.

As the eldest, Buck considered himself the protector of his family; and now that Morgan had divorced Cecily, he was free to do more than just sit back and watch her antics.

Chapter 2

Morgan Spade pulled his long brown hands over his face and stared at the paneled walls of his living room in dull resignation. His little five-year-old son Kit was the only good thing that had come from his marriage to Cece. But now she was trying to take him away, too.

Morgan closed his eyes in frowning shame. *Why didn't I see it at the time,* he wondered, *why didn't I see what she was?*

It's not like she was subtle.

Morgan's memory replayed the first time he'd ever seen Cecily Cooper. It painted her in all her blonde, bronzed glory as she lounged under a pool umbrella at Padre Island. Her hair had been bleached almost white, her skin had been tanned a deep, smooth brown, and she'd been wearing a pretty white cotton caftan and jewelled sandals. Cece had a lot to show off, and staring at her had been his first mistake.

The second had been to convince himself that there was such a thing as love at first sight.

Morgan closed his eyes. He'd lied to himself long before Cece had lied to him. That 'love at first sight' fairy tale had been the lie that he'd built all the other lies on. Fairy tales like, 'I can make her love me,' and 'If I'm patient, she might change.'

And when reality had come knocking, when he'd finally had to admit that Cece didn't want to change, when he'd finally had enough of her lying and cheating, their marriage had crashed and burned in an ugly divorce.

The Lord only knew that he'd tried, but he'd finally had to admit that a man couldn't save his marriage all by himself. That the old saw, 'Marry in haste, repent at leisure,' had been coined for men like him.

Morgan sighed and shook his head. The divorce had been the most painful thing he'd ever had to endure; but once he got it, he'd believed he was shut of Cece. He hadn't heard a word from her since she'd walked out of the courtroom a year before.

So her surprise text that morning had been like a punch to his gut. He felt chewed up and spit out, and Cece was counting on that.

It'd be easier to soak him for money if he was scared she was going to take Kit away. Because this new lie wasn't a thing in the world but Cece trying to get back in his wallet, even after their divorce. She knew that if she threatened to mess with Kit, if she hit him where it really hurt, he'd pay her to go away.

And the bribe would work until she ran out of money and called him again. With Cece, it was always about money.

Morgan muttered under his breath. If he'd been fresh and rested, he would've told her where to go and how fast to get there; but after their messy divorce and two long, bitter custody battles, he was tired.

Maybe he was willing to play her game to get a little peace.

Morgan stood up slowly and drifted over to the glass wall. His apartment suite overlooked the front courtyard, and when he glanced down, he saw Buck playing catch with Kit.

Morgan's eyes glistened as he watched his little dark, curly-haired son. Buck was right; Kit did look like him. He was a tall boy for his age, and dark: black-haired and brown as a nut.

But Kit was like him in other ways, too. He was a quick study, he didn't talk a lot, and he loved horses.

Morgan's expression softened as he watched Kit jump up and snag the ball out of the air. Kit was a good kid with a good heart.

He wasn't at all like Cece.

Anger flared in Morgan again as he scanned Kit's laughing face. Cece had never given a rip about their little son. She'd only sued to keep Kit because he was her last link to the Spade family money.

Morgan's dark eyes followed Kit as he missed the ball, then turned to scramble into the grass after it. His son was only five years old. So far he'd been able to hide from Kit that he was nothing but a meal ticket to his mother.

But Kit was a smart kid, and he was starting to suspect.

Morgan's face contracted in pain. Kit was starting to ask questions like, *Why doesn't Mommy ever come to visit us*, and *Why wasn't Mommy at my birthday party?*

Morgan rubbed his jaw. He wasn't an especially good liar, but he'd had to learn fast. He'd made up all kinds of new fairy tales to shield his son from the painful truth.

Your Momma's way over the ocean right now. She went to visit her family, she's too far away to visit us.

Your Momma called to tell you she's sick, and she can't come to your party, but she sent you this nice birthday present.

Morgan winced to think that he was telling fairy tales about Cece to his son now, instead of to himself; but the time was coming when those fairy tales wouldn't work any more, and his heart broke for his son.

Morgan pulled his long hands over his face. If he let himself think too much about that, he'd lose his mind, so he decided to focus on the present. He ran a hand through his black, shoulder-length hair, rubbed his moustache, and shuffled off to the bathroom to shower the shock and worry off him. He wanted to show his little son a calm, smiling face when he came back inside.

Morgan walked through his living room to the side opposite the glass wall. The big room was wood paneled on three sides and was decorated with historical Indian artifacts, most of them displayed under a spotlight and encased in glass: brightly-colored blankets, intricately woven baskets, painted pottery, even a beaded and fringed leather tunic dating from 1865.

The sight of them reminded Morgan of his weekend plans. He'd promised to take Kit up to the Standing Bear Powwow in Oklahoma. Native American culture and history had always fascinated him, and it was a love he wanted to pass down to his son.

The colorful costumes and music and dancing would captivate a little boy; and it would be good for him, too. Maybe all the sound and color and motion would take his mind off Cece and the threat implied in her message.

The threat of another custody battle.

Morgan drifted down the long, paneled hall to the second door on the right. He turned in and flicked a switch to reveal a cavernous bathroom.

The bathroom walls were made of natural stone and bright green moss was growing in the gaps between their rough brown rows. Massive potted ferns and palms created the illusion of wild undergrowth.

It was as relaxing and luxurious a space as money could buy, but as Morgan shrugged out of his shirt and walked over to flick on the water, he wasn't seeing the rough stone walls of the shower.

He was seeing his little son's innocent face, and praying that his ex-wife's threat would prove an empty one.

Chapter 3

Heather Weston braked in front of the Seven Spades Ranch to allow a big green jeep to exit the huge main gates. The sturdy four-wheeler exited the ranch in front of her, and the driver threw up a hand in thanks as he passed. Heather got a glimpse of a dark, handsome man with shoulder-length hair and a bristling black moustache. The two of them made eye contact for a split-second, and then he was gone.

Heather shot a startled glance in the rear view mirror, but the jeep was already far down the road as it zoomed toward the interstate.

Heather lifted a cup full of steaming coffee to her lips. Coffee tasted especially good to her on a cool, foggy morning. She took a long, slow sip, gave herself an instant to relish it, then set it down, flicked her turning signal and passed under the huge iron archway.

Her blue sedan had barely cleared the ponderous gates before they began to swing closed; and as she watched, they locked behind her with a heavy *clang*.

Heather brushed a tendril of her sandy blonde hair back from her face and stared at them in the rear view.

Wow, she thought with a touch of awe. *I must be on a security camera.*

Heather sighed, smoothed her long hair back from her brow, and pressed her ballerina flat a touch deeper on the gas. Arthur had told her that the Seven Ranch was huge, and that it felt like forever to get from the gates to the first crossroad in the drive. She glanced at her watch. She was supposed to meet him at the ranch vet office by eight.

Arthur was the Seven's retiring veterinarian, a colleague of hers, and the man who'd recommended her to the Spades as his replacement. Heather shook her head in wonder. Working veterinary medicine at the Seven Ranch was a dream job, and it had been very kind of the older man to recommend her.

Heather glanced at the crumpled piece of paper on the passenger seat. Arthur had drawn her a crude map on the back of a drug insert.

Turn left at the first crossing, his scrawled note read, *and go straight for about a half mile.*

She glanced at the long, straight driveway ahead. There was no crossroad that she could see; just green Texas pastureland, and what looked like a stable complex far in the distance, off to the right of the drive. She glanced at the map.

That would be the thoroughbred complex, she thought to herself. She was keen to see it, but it wasn't what she was looking for at the moment. Arthur had told her that the vet office wasn't far from the main stable complex, the ones that housed the working stock.

Heather glanced off into the green distance and marveled that she still couldn't see the main house. She was a relative newcomer to the area, having moved to Dallas from Wyoming, but even she had heard that the Spade family was fabulously wealthy.

To be fair, most of her ranching clients had been. It took a lot of money to maintain cattle and horses, and especially to run a ranch like the Seven; but by all accounts the Spades were the one-percenters. The *ne plus ultra* of Texas cattle barons.

She had to admit that she was curious to see what they were like. Arthur had told her that the Spade brothers were surprisingly down to earth. That they were mostly nice, reasonable people.

Her affable, white-haired colleague had laced his fingers together on his desk and had stared at her over the rim of his glasses. "You'll be dealing mostly with Morgan Spade. He runs the day-to-day work on the ranch. Real hands-on guy. Up before dawn and out on the range most every day. He knows his stuff, about horses especially, so you won't have to educate him."

"That sounds ideal," she'd told him in wonder. "Thank you for recommending me, Arthur."

The older man had waved a hand in the air. "It wasn't a favor, my dear," he'd drawled. "As charming as you are, it was pure business. I consider you the best qualified to replace me here. And even though the Spade boys are nice enough, be aware: they expect nothing less than the best from their vet. One hundred and ten percent effort."

She'd blinked at him. "Of course."

Arthur's face had crinkled into a smile, and he'd risen from his desk. "You'll be perfect here," he assured her. "You've got the education, the credentials, and the gray matter." He tapped his head and grinned. "But you have something even more important, Heather. You've got the gift of healing. The intuition, the feel for it." His hand moved from his head to tap his chest. "You've got it *here*. No one can be a really great horse doctor without heart."

Heather blinked as she remembered Arthur's touching words. They never failed to move her, and she was determined to do her best to justify his faith in her.

"You can drop by on Friday," he'd told her. "I'll have all of my things moved out of the condo by then, so I'll give you the keys and a walk through."

That had been another of the perks of working at the Seven Spades: the position included housing. The Spades provided not just a state of the art vet office and animal hospital, but also a very nice condo for the vet, right on the ranch.

She was expected to be available at all hours of the day and night, so it made sense to live on the premises.

The sight of a crossroad up ahead snapped Heather out of her reverie, and she slowed to turn the sedan to the left, then down the new drive.

The big main barn was now visible, a huge red structure off to the north; and to her relief, she could see the vet complex now. It was made up of a spacious, fenced pen, a cinder-block stable, a warehouse-like metal building, and then, a stone's throw off, a trim, two-story clapboard condo.

Her new home.

Chapter 4

Heather pulled her car up into the gravel lot outside the metal building, and to her relief, the door opened and Arthur ambled out and threw up a hand. She smiled, waved, and climbed out of the car to greet him.

"Did you have any trouble finding us?"

"Not at all," Heather assured him, and leaned over to give him a quick peck on the cheek. "I can't wait to see the hospital."

The older man turned to open the door, and he beckoned for her to follow. "You'll love it," he promised. "The building may not be fancy, but they spared no expense on the equipment. Everything in here is state of the art."

Heather walked into the office behind him. The office was modest, with the usual accoutrements: bland carpet, generic office furniture, a few potted plants in the lobby, a desk, and amateur paintings of animals hanging on the white walls.

But she noted, as they moved further in, that there was a big hall behind the lobby, opening onto a huge main office with a big desk and a big, sleek, brand-new computer.

Arthur gestured toward it from the doorway. "I had them buy that toy for you," he muttered. "I'm a dinosaur and I hate computers, but I expect you'll want one."

Heather took the room in at a glance, then turned to ask, "What about the examination room? Are there any animals here right now?"

"Nope. I finished up with all our patients. And I can't remember the last time that happened," Arthur chuckled. "As for the exam room, it's down the hall," he went on. "It's all stocked up. The x-ray room is at the end of the hall next to the surgery. There's a kennel just outside the building for the smaller stock, and of course you saw the stables."

Heather opened a door to peer into the exam room. "I'm impressed, Arthur," she murmured.

Arthur sighed and gazed down the hall. "Yes, the Spades believe in doing things right," he nodded. "It makes good business sense to provide everything your vet needs."

"Everything and then some," Heather echoed in wonder.

Arthur inhaled sharply and suggested, "Come and have a look at the condo. I'll show you the place, and then I have to scoot. I'm moving to a retirement community down the road, and I have to meet the movers in an hour."

"Of course."

Heather followed him out a side door, and they walked across the parking lot and down the road a few hundred feet to the white condo. It was shaded by a pair of big, spreading oak trees, and bordered front and back by a neat picket fence. Arthur opened it and led the way across the front lawn, up the porch steps, and across the porch to the front door.

He unlocked the front door, and Heather followed him across the empty foyer. Heather's eyes flicked over it. The floors were gleaming hardwood, as was the staircase. An antique brass chandelier hung from the foyer ceiling, and the ceiling was stamped tin.

She drifted into the front room, and their footsteps echoed across the empty floor. A huge picture window faced rolling meadows on the west, and another bank of windows framed the shaded lawn under the oaks to the south.

Arthur glanced at his watch and murmured, "I'm afraid I'm not going to have time to give you the full tour. I'm going to have to run." He dug into his pocket and produced a ring of keys. "Here's the keys to the house and office. If you have any questions, you can call me."

Heather stared at him in baffled gratitude as she took them. "Thank you, Arthur," she replied softly. "Really, you've been so kind."

"Talk to me when you've been here a few weeks," he laughed, "You're going to earn every one of these perks." A more thoughtful look dawned on his face, and he added, "But it's the best job in the world. I loved it. I think you will, too."

"I know I will," Heather agreed, and leaned over to give him a parting peck on the brow. "I want you to come back when you've settled in. We'll have lunch together."

"It's a date," he laughed, and waved to her.

Heather followed him out to the porch and watched as the older man stumped across the lawn and back to the office. She waited until Arthur's car had pulled out of the lot and disappeared down the road, then turned back inside the house with a sigh.

She glanced around at the blank, beautiful rooms, imagining her own things inside them. Her wry conclusion was that her place was going to look almost Amish, because her furnishings were simple and few.

She didn't need much in the way of furniture, because she'd never spent much time inside a house. Not even her own. She'd lived most of her life outside on horseback, or inside big, drafty barns, helping a mare to foal or tending a sick calf.

So the condo, as big and pretty as it was, was almost beside the point. What she really wanted to see was that big red barn: and she turned back outside to go get her car.

Ten minutes later, Heather pulled her car off the drive and onto the green shoulder a little below the outer pens ringing the Seven's main stable complex. At its center was the biggest barn she'd ever seen. It was massive in size, old-fashioned in style, but still new. When she opened the door and stepped out of the car, the air smelled of grass and fresh hay and pine resin even from the road.

Heather closed the car door and slogged through the grass. It had rained recently, and her ballerina flats sank down into the water with every step, but she kept going. She had to be careful, because she'd been invited to a luncheon at the main house later, and she was wearing the nicest dress she owned.

As she passed, a couple of horses in the pen pricked up their ears and came trotting over to stare at her over the fence. Heather turned to walk over and stroke the nearest on the nose.

"Hi there, gorgeous boy," she murmured. "I wish I had an apple for you."

She ran a hand over the horse's gleaming neck. The stallion was bright eyed, alert, and had a smooth, shiny coat. It looked like a healthy animal, and knowing Arthur, she was sure it was.

But it wouldn't hurt to have a little look-see.

As she stroked the horse, a young man came walking up from the barn side of the pen and rested his arms on the top of the fence rail.

"Morning, ma'am," he drawled, and grinned at her.

Heather glanced over at him as she stroked the horse's neck. "Good morning."

The man pushed his hat back from his brow and stared at her. "Can I help you?"

At this, Heather looked up at him. "It's more like, Can I help you," she replied. "I'm Heather Weston. I'm the new vet. I came over to have a look at your horses."

Her words wiped the smile right off the fellow's face, and he stood up straight and tilted his head to one side. "Did Morgan hire you?" he demanded.

Heather shook her head. "Arthur did," she murmured. "He told me Mr. Spade left the hiring decision for his replacement up to him."

The young man stared at her for a long moment, then shook his head. "Ma'am, I think you better talk to Morgan before you start," he mumbled, and rubbed his nose. "He's not here right now, but he'll be back in a few days."

"Yes, Arthur told me," she replied. "I'm sure he won't mind if I have a look at the horses. I'd just like to have a quick peek."

"Well, um—"

"I'll meet you around the front." Heather smiled at him, turned and picked her way through the soggy grass toward the front entrance of the barn.

Chapter 5

Buck settled into the softest leather chair in his apartment and stuck his big bare feet out to warm them in front of a crackling fire. As he stood there, his new bride, a redheaded beauty swathed in a pink satin dressing gown, came walking out of a nearby doorway and glided across the room to join him.

Kate sat down in his lap and snuggled onto his chest as Buck draped his arm over her shoulders. She looked up at him and murmured, "We need to go ahead and get dressed, because we have to get everything ready for the luncheon today."

He looked down at her. "Luncheon?"

"Yes, of course. Have you forgotten? We're having a welcome party for the new vet."

Buck sighed. "Isn't that Morgan's job?" he grumbled. "I'm no good at those kind of things."

Kate took his chin in her hand and turned it to face her. "Yes, we're *all* going," she insisted. "Everybody who can be there is going to be. We want to make her feel welcome."

Buck raised an eyebrow. "Her?"

Kate nodded. "Yes. Arthur called for Morgan last week, but Morgan wasn't—well, he didn't take the call, so I picked up. Arthur told me all about the lady. He said her name is Heather Weston, and she's very qualified."

"Well, I know one thing," Buck retorted. "Morgan's going to have a cow when he finds out it's a woman, and so will the hands. I've never heard of a woman vet on a ranch. It's rough work. Hard work. It's dirty, and it can be dangerous."

"I'm sure she's used to that, or your vet wouldn't have recommended her," Kate replied, and kissed his ear. "Come on and dress now, Buck. We have to get finished if I'm going to have the porch room ready in time."

"We should've postponed it until Morgan was here to welcome her," Buck muttered, as he stood up. "He's gonna be gone for days. He just left to take Kit up to Standing Bear."

"What's that?"

"Oh, it's an Indian powwow up in Oklahoma," Buck mumbled. "Morgan wanted to get away for a few days to spend time with Kit." He shook his head.

Kate took his arm and pulled him gently. "Well, then we'll just have to stand in for him," she replied. "Think of it as a way to take some of the pressure off Morgan."

Buck fell quiet as he followed her. "There is that," he muttered. "All right, then."

Buck drifted down the hall and into their bedroom. Kate had already laid out a nice shirt and slacks on the bed for him, and he sighed as he picked up the shirt.

"It was easy to dress myself before I married you, Kate," he reminded her. "Just a white shirt, jeans, and boots. What's this thing made of?" he complained, and rubbed the new shirt with his fingers.

"It's raw silk," Kate called from their bathroom. "Casual, but elegant."

Buck sighed and shouldered out of his housecoat. "Does anybody know this woman?" he wondered aloud. "Has anybody met her?"

"I haven't," Kate's voice murmured. "All I know is what Arthur told me on the phone. But it's common courtesy to make a newcomer feel welcome. I'm sure she's a bit nervous. This place can be intimidating when you're new."

Buck glanced toward the open bathroom door in surprise. "Were you intimidated?"

"Very," she murmured.

Buck raised his brows in dismay. "You never showed it."

"And I'm very proud of that," she retorted, and breezed out of the bathroom, buttoning the cuff of a sleek, caramel-colored wool dress. Buck looked up and grinned.

"*Wooo-ee*," he whistled softly, and Kate beamed and twirled around for him. "I don't want to go anywhere now! Come over here and kiss me."

"You'll get your kiss after the luncheon," Kate told him. She kissed her finger, then pressed it to his nose. "Get dressed."

An hour later Buck allowed Kate to lead him down the big staircase to the first floor, then down the long main hall all the way out to the back of the house. The back wall was made of glass, and it slid aside to admit them to a huge outdoor patio room paved with slabs of gray slate.

The northern pastureland of the Seven lapped right up against that patio, like a green ocean, and it rolled away to the top of a high hill just beyond. A massive fire pit stood between them and that view, and there was already a mighty blaze roaring in it.

Carson and Luke looked up as they entered, and Carson drawled, "Well, here are the last arrivals. Looks like this is it."

"Well, I know Will's in Virginia, but where's Jesse and Chance?" Buck demanded.

Luke rubbed the back of his neck and gave him a sheepish look. "I called Jesse, but he told me to"—his eyes flicked to Kate's face, and then back to Buck's— "Um—I mean, he told me he was busy and couldn't come."

"What about Chance?" Buck frowned.

Carson chuckled into his glass. "He's in New Orleans. He says it's a sales trip."

Buck pinched his mouth closed, then shot a worried glance at Kate. "Well, I guess this is it," he replied reluctantly, then glanced around at a big table to one side of the fire. It had a beautiful fall arrangement in the center and was ringed by dozens of platters and bowls. A faint whiff of grilled steak and ham overcame the scent of burning logs, and Buck grinned.

"Kate, you sure do make a pretty table," he told her proudly, and Carson and Luke chimed in.

"Sure enough, Kate."

"You always outdo yourself."

To Buck's amusement, Kate went pink with pleasure. She wasn't above a little preening now and then, but she'd earned the praise. The table was beautiful, and the food smelled delicious.

He glanced down at his watch. "When does the guest of honor arrive?"

"Any minute now," Kate replied with a worried frown. "I hope she didn't get lost on the way here."

The words had hardly passed her lips when two newcomers approached down the hall. Buck turned and saw that one was Miss Ada, their stern, disapproving, ramrod-straight housekeeper; and the other was a young woman he assumed to be Heather Weston.

She was a dainty-looking thing, with long, wavy, sandy-blonde hair spilling over her shoulders and eyes like big blue marbles. She was dressed up in a long, foofy-looking cotton dress and little flat shoes, but Kate gasped under her breath; and when his eyes drifted down, he could see that the whole hem of Heather's dress and her shoes were caked with mud.

And something else.

The newcomer smiled apologetically and tucked a long spiral of blonde hair behind one ear. "I'm afraid I'm not exactly ready for the party," she confessed. "I couldn't resist a trip to the stables."

Buck raised an eyebrow, and his opinion of Heather Weston's chances went up a notch; but Kate surged forward instantly.

"I'll take you up to our place," she offered, "and you can wash up."

They all watched as Kate swept their guest out of the room and away; and they were left to stare at one another and draw their own conclusions.

Chapter 6

"Did you have a good time at the powwow today, buddy?"

Morgan pulled a blanket up around Kit's chin and gazed down at his son's sleepy face. He'd chosen a camping site whose tents were made to look like teepees, and the lantern turned the canvas walls to gold and glowed in Kit's eyes.

Kit's eyes widened in one last flare of excitement before he dropped off. "It was the best day ever," he nodded and lifted the bear tooth necklace he'd been clutching to his chest. "I want a hat like the dancers had, with a hundred feathers!"

Morgan sputtered and brushed his son's smooth check with a forefinger. "You want a headdress, huh?"

Kit's head bobbed. "I want to come back next time," he murmured. "And eat fried bread and Indian tacos."

Morgan's eyes gleamed with amusement as he gently pried the necklace out of his son's grip. "We'll put your necklace here next to your cot," he rumbled, as he set it on top of a folding table.

"I liked the Pawnee dancers best," Kit mumbled, as his eyelids drooped. "They were the coolest of all."

"The Pawnee are sure enough the coolest," Morgan agreed with a slow smile. "You remember why?"

Kit yawned, and his small hands clutched the blanket. "Because Big Russ's grandma was Pawnee," he sighed.

"That's right," Morgan murmured, and leaned down to plant a peck on Kit's smooth brow. "Sleep tight, buddy."

"Night, daddy," Kit yawned, and closed his eyes.

Morgan sat gazing down at his little son's face, then twisted to turn down the lantern. The inside of the teepee went dim, but he didn't go to bed himself. He walked outside in the star-spattered darkness of an Oklahoma night and stared up into the sky.

There was always something about the stars that was like a hand on his shoulder. Something that reminded him that he wasn't alone. That the Lord was watching over him and Kit.

Morgan stared up at the night sky for a long time in peaceful silence before he sighed and reached for his phone. Its small blue glare was in garish contrast to the soft night all around him, and its first message was garish, too.

It was from a friend of his back in Sandy Creek.

Hey Morg. When you got the time I'd like to come over and take a look at some of your stock. I need a good working horse.

You need to come by my place sometime this fall and we'll get some hunting in.

Travis

P.S. I saw your ex in town today. Thought I'd give you a head's up. Ha ha.

Morgan straightened up in alarm and frowned at the screen. There was only one reason Cece would be in Sandy Creek. She had visitation rights, and that meant she had free access to the ranch as long as she claimed she wanted to see Kit.

Morgan glanced back at the teepee. He could imagine how confused and hurt Kit would be if Cece told him that his father wasn't really his father. That Kit wasn't a Spade, that he didn't belong to him and the rest of the family after all.

He pulled a hand over his face. He already knew what Cece was going to do. She was going to hold that over his head. She was going to threaten to tell Kit a pack of lies that would break his heart if she didn't get a bunch of money.

Morgan lowered the phone, then raised his face to question the stars. The answer he got, after gazing silently at the black deep, was that there was only one way to fight a lie, and that was with the truth.

He hated the idea of getting a paternity test—but if Cece was going to challenge his paternity rights, he needed to prove he was Kit's father.

A DNA test would be the first thing their attorney Eugene would ask for, if he ended up having to call him.

How to protect Kit from Cece wasn't as easy to figure. She was his mother, even if she didn't act like it, and it would be hard to keep her away.

A gust of anger shook him, and Morgan's jaw tightened as he frowned up at the starry sky. *So help me,* he vowed, *I'll never let another woman make a fool of me again. I'll never put Kit through this torment again.*

I'd rather live the rest of my life alone, than to be dragged through court, and live in constant turmoil, and have to pay out a fortune, just to have a few days of peace with my son.

Maybe there are still a few good women out there amongst the bad ones, but I've proved that I can't tell which is which.

He sighed and glanced down again. His phone was still glowing blue, and when he scanned it, there were other messages—something about a new vet, but he was in no mood to do any more business that night. The news that Cece was in town was more than enough for the end of a busy day.

He'd deal with all that when he got back.

Morgan flicked the button and tucked the phone back in his pocket, then stared up at the stars once last time before turning in.

Lord, I need help, he prayed. *Show me what to do.*

I can't keep Cece from lying to Kit; so help me to be here for him.

Chapter 7

Heather closed the door of her car and trudged to her new house with a knapsack in her arms. She crossed the lawn of the condo, climbed the porch, and pushed through the front door. Once she pushed it shut behind her, she kicked off her shoes and padded across the pristine floor in her bare feet.

She climbed the stairs to the second floor, found the bedroom, then set the knapsack on the floor and knelt down to unzip it. She had to say one thing for the Spade clan: they were a sociable bunch. She'd been surprised and touched by the warmth of her welcome, especially considering that she hadn't had time to clean up before she met them.

She giggled at the memory of the horror in Kate Spade's eyes when she looked down and saw her muddy shoes. It was completely understandable that mud wasn't a part of Kate's world; but for a horse vet, mud was an inescapable fact of life.

Mud was inevitable; and she'd had to slog through so much of it in her career that it didn't bother her at all any more.

Of course, she probably shouldn't have gone to that barn on the same day as her welcome luncheon; but she hadn't been able to resist, and she believed they understood.

The men there, especially. Arthur had told her they were all avid horsemen.

Heather pulled a couple of blankets and a pillow out of the knapsack and tossed them across the empty floor. Her furniture, such as it was, was still in a storage unit back in town and the movers weren't due until the weekend.

Lucky for her that she was used to sleeping on pallets.

She pulled a couple of little plastic carry bags out of the knapsack and carried them to the master bathroom across the upper hall. The walls were covered in white beadboard and there was a big oriole window overlooking the back yard.

Heather opened up the medicine cabinet and began stocking it with a few essentials; then she tossed her hairbrush and her makeup bag into the bathroom counter drawer.

She glanced over to check out the shower. To her relief, it was big and sturdy, with a rainfall shower head and even a shower radio. Heather flicked the radio on as she peeled her dress off and sang along with the music.

There's a love out there for me

Sure to be

It may seem like they'll never be

But you see

I know what I know

Though it may seem slow

One day he'll show

Off we'll go

And we'll flow, yeah

Just flowww

Heather turned to grab a bar of soap off the counter and stepped into the shower stall, singing to herself.

Her thoughts returned to the past few hours. The Spade family had all been nice enough, but she was getting the vibe that maybe Arthur hadn't told the family about his choice to hire her.

They'd all looked surprised to see her.

She rubbed the bar of soap between her hands. They all kept mentioning a man named Morgan, and to judge by the tone they'd used, she might have a bit of a problem with him. She wasn't sure what *kind* of problem.

But if past experience was any guide, he was likely going to balk at the fact that she was a woman. She'd had to prove herself to just about every rancher she'd worked for; and to be fair, she couldn't really blame them for being skeptical. She weighed 120 pounds soaking wet, and she didn't look like she could handle an angry horse or a cow protecting its calf.

She always had to prove it; and so she did.

She turned her face to the water and sputtered into the spray, wondering if the man she'd seen at the gate for an instant had been Morgan. They all told her he'd left the ranch.

Maybe she'd seen him go.

She hummed a bit and rubbed her arms. She'd only got a glimpse of him, but what she'd seen had looked good. And now that she thought about it, he looked like the other men she'd met that day: Kate's big husband and his brothers.

It probably had been Morgan.

She switched the water off and reached for a towel. If Morgan was her new boss, it would be the first time ever that she'd worked for a handsome young man instead of a grizzled old one. Most ranchers she'd met had skin that the wind and sun had dried like leather, and all but one had been over sixty. She giggled a bit as she wrapped the towel around her and padded back to the bedroom.

It would be a nice change.

Maybe that's why I never married, Heather thought in amusement. *I spend all my time with horses and men old enough to be my grandfather.*

She knelt down and pulled a few personal items out of her knapsack, and the laughter faded on her lips. She lifted a framed photo and stared at it. It had been taken at her graduation, and her beaming mother and brothers flanked her as she grinned at the camera.

Fifteen years ago.

This is the only family photo I have, she realized in a moment of stricken clarity. *I must be the only thirty-year-old woman on earth without a photo of a man on her nightstand.*

My photo would be of a horse.

She sputtered with laughter, then sobered; and on mature reflection, sighed a bit as she placed the picture on the floor.

Chapter 8

The little bell over the outer door tinkled, and Heather looked up from her computer in pleased expectation. She hadn't had any patients for the first few days of her new job, and she was hoping for something to do.

She wiped the last crumb of her bologna sandwich off her mouth, wiped her hands on the back of her jeans, and stood up.

A deep, rumbling male voice called from the lobby. "Hello?"

"Coming." Heather slid her bare feet into a pair of leather loafers and walked out to go see who'd paid her a call.

As she walked into the lobby, a tall black shadow blocked the light in the main doorway. The shadow had a cowboy hat on, and it reached up to swipe it off as she crossed her arms and leaned against the wall.

"You must be Heather Weston," the deep voice added, and the shadow took a step inside and resolved into the shape of a tall, broad-shouldered man.

One end of Heather's mouth curled up as his face came into focus. She'd been right: it was the man that she'd seen in the jeep that day, and he was even better-looking close up than he'd been at a distance. He had a full head of wavy, ink-black hair that lapped against his shoulders, bushy black eyebrows, keen eyes, a proud nose, and a fierce black cowboy moustache over a strong chin.

He was tall and lean and wearing a long black leather jacket that wasn't quite a duster, and a pair of beat-up jeans over black leather boots.

He looked like he'd stepped out of a gunslinger western.

Heather pushed off the wall and extended her hand. "You must be Morgan Spade."

The tall man took her hand, and his fingers were rough and warm as they curled around hers; but he dropped her hand quickly and stepped back again.

"Yes, ma'am. Pleased to meet you." Morgan looked down and rubbed his nose. "I'm sorry I wasn't here to welcome you when you arrived," he mumbled in a low voice. "I was out of town."

"Oh, I understand, " Heather assured him with a smile. "And everybody here made me feel so welcome." She nodded toward a chair. "Please, sit down. Would you like something to drink? I made some coffee."

The man looked down and shook his head. "Thank you, but I can't stay long. I just wanted to come by to say hello." He looked up again, and the keen glint in his eye was a startling contrast to his sleepy voice. "I guess Arthur showed you where things are?"

"Yes, Arthur was wonderful." Heather gave Morgan a short, straight look and suddenly decided to take the bull by the horns. "I was very touched by his faith in my expertise. Most ranchers take one look at me and assume I could never handle the tough jobs."

Morgan rubbed the back of his neck with one long brown hand; but he addressed her challenge frankly. "Well, I'll admit straight out that I wasn't expecting a woman vet," he told her. "But Arthur knows his stuff all right," he muttered, and looked down at her. "You'll get plenty of chances to show that you know yours."

Heather raised her chin. "That's all I ask."

She got another glimpse of those keen eyes. "Fair enough. Well, here's how we do. I come by here about once a week to get a report on the animals getting tended, and how they're coming along, what they need. If there's some special problem, or if I have a question, I might come by more often, but that's the usual."

Heather tilted her head. "That sounds about right."

"You have any questions I can answer?"

Heather considered. "Yes. I'd like to have a chat with you over lunch sometime soon. I like to get to know the people I work with."

Morgan seemed taken aback by her invitation, and he coughed, "Well, I don't have the time today, but we'll do that sometime."

"Good."

Morgan straightened up, replaced his hat, and touched the brim. "Well, it was good to meet you, Heather. If you have any questions, or something comes up, you can just call my cell. Welcome to the Seven, and I'll talk to you soon."

"Thank you," Heather replied faintly, and watched quizzically as her long, tall visitor nodded to her, turned, and walked out.

Well that was strange, she thought to herself, and drifted to the doorway. She stood watching as he climbed back into the green jeep parked outside her office, cranked the engine, and drove away.

Heather crossed her arms and stared down the drive after him. Arthur had praised her for having a healing touch. For having a sense for wounded things.

There was something about her tall, dark visitor that felt a bit off to her doctor's heart. She couldn't put her finger on just what: the way Morgan met her eyes only briefly, his seeming reluctance to talk to her, his reluctance to stay long.

He didn't behave like a happy, relaxed man; and she felt a flick of compassion for Morgan Spade, followed by a spark of ambition to find out more about him.

Chapter 9

Morgan frowned at the road in front of him and tightened his grip on the steering wheel. He'd been dreading his meeting with the new vet, and it had been even more awkward than he'd thought.

He'd come back from Oklahoma to be told a dozen times, by a dozen different people, that their new vet was a woman. He'd been expecting a seasoned old man, not a fresh-faced blonde beauty. It had been a shock to find out that Arthur had thrown him a curve ball. Arthur was usually a sensible, down to earth man.

He sighed and muttered under his breath. Heather Weston was a slip of a girl who looked like a good stiff wind would blow her away. She had long, wavy blonde hair and big blue eyes, and she looked ridiculously young in her big, blousy cotton shirt and jeans. She looked like the sort of girl you'd see on a college lawn strumming a guitar.

There was no way she was gonna work out as their vet. She was too skinny and small to work with big, fractious animals, and she was gonna cause all kinds of trouble with their hands. As soon as the single ones saw her, they were gonna start making up excuses to go hang around the vet's office.

He couldn't say that he'd blame 'em, either. Heather Weston was as pretty as a birthday cake in a bakery window, all blue and pink and gold. Those big, innocent-looking eyes of hers would bring down just about any man; and he expected his hands to start acting like young men always did when a beautiful woman arrived.

Distracted.

Goofy.

Maybe even dumb.

It wasn't her fault that she was pretty, and he was sure she had every intention of doing a good job. But a young, lovely vet on a cattle ranch just wasn't gonna work out.

Morgan frowned. He owed it to her and to Arthur to give her every chance, and he would; but he gave it only a month or two before he'd have to find somebody else to do that job.

One more thing on his plate.

He pulled his car into the big barn yard and killed the motor. His top hand, Hank Thompson, saw him and came ambling over with his hands in his pockets. Hank bent down to talk to him as he rolled down his window.

"Well, Morgan," he grinned, "did you meet the new lady vet?"

He scowled at him. "I did. I wish somebody had told me earlier what Arthur was planning to do. I would've put a stop to it then, but now we're gonna have to play along until she sees she's not right for us. I want you all to kinda help her out."

Hank's freckled face split into laughter. "Ol' Arthur must be getting sentimental," he joked. "Never figured him to do such a crazy thing!"

"Well, that just goes to show that you can always be surprised," Morgan grumbled, as he climbed out of the car. "How we doing?"

Hank bowed his head and kept pace with him as he walked toward the barn. "Those two mares are about to foal."

Morgan glanced at him. "How soon?"

"Any day now."

Morgan frowned as he entered the barn yard and turned toward the huge entryway. "Let Heather look at 'em. It'll be a good test."

Hank objected, "One of the mares is a first timer. Might be a little harder."

Morgan slowly stopped to turn to look at him, and was silent for a long moment as he considered. "Let her tend the mares, but stay close in case she gets stuck."

"I will."

Morgan entered the ranch's huge main barn, the barn used to house and feed the working stock. The familiar scent of dried hay, wood shavings, and old leather greeted him like a hand on his shoulder, and he took a deep, calming breath.

"Any other issues?"

Hank shook his head. "Not with the horses. We have a couple of dead cows up on the north side, but that's because they got bit on the muzzle by a rattlesnake. Big one, too. We killed it, and it's got to be at least fifteen feet."

Morgan grunted. "There's probably a nest of 'em up there. We need to go clean it out."

He walked down the wide, airy corridor between the horse stalls on the way to the one that housed his own horse, Cochise. Cochise was a gleaming black stallion, and he always kept him as brushed and groomed as a show entry; but Cochise was a working horse, the best one he'd ever had. He was smart and responsive, quick and strong.

As he neared, Cochise stuck his head out of his stall, flicked his ears toward him, and bobbed his head. Morgan grinned at him and reached in his pocket for a few pieces of carrot.

"You miss me, eh?" he murmured, and extended an open hand. The stallion took the carrots off his palm, and nuzzled against his chest. Morgan stroked the horse's gleaming neck in pleasure and felt his cares lifting off his shoulders.

Hank watched him with his hands planted on his hips, and Morgan turned to smile at him. "The old boy's in a good mood today," he rumbled. "Guess because he's about to be a father again. Ain't it, huh, boy?" He smoothed Cochise's shining black mane.

"It ain't his foal by the first time mare, is it Hank?" he asked suddenly, and was relieved when Hank shook his head.

"You sound worried," he teased. "But you know all Cochise's foals have been strong and born pretty easy. And *both* the foals are his."

Morgan scratched his ear and consulted his memory. "The young mare is Ladybug, right?"

"That's right."

Morgan frowned as he stroked Cochise's neck. "Let Heather tend Ladybug," he said at last. "I promised her a chance to prove herself."

Hank shook his head in doubt but replied, "You're the boss." He slapped Morgan on the back and walked off, and Morgan glanced after him.

Yeah, I'm the boss, he thought ruefully. *But sometimes I wish you and I could switch places. I'd like to be just a plain old ranch hand for a change.*

But the manager of the Seven Ranch didn't have that luxury. It was his responsibility to see that everything ran smooth; and so Morgan pulled his phone out of his back pocket.

It was time for him to have a long, heart to heart talk with their old vet.

Chapter 10

Arthur looked up from his restaurant table with a broad smile. "Well hello, Morgan! I was glad to hear from you. How are things over at the Ponderosa?" The older man's affable face was lit by the flickering candle on the dining table, and he smiled as he lifted a cup of coffee to his lips.

Morgan shook his hand and pulled up a chair. "Well, never a dull moment with us, Arthur. You know that." He glanced up at the waiter who appeared like magic at his elbow.

"What can I get for you this evening, Mr. Spade?'

Morgan set his hat down on a nearby chair. "I'd like a cup of black coffee and, ah—the grilled tenderloin with the baked potato."

"Yes, sir."

Morgan laced his long fingers together on the table and regarded his old friend fondly. "How are you liking retirement so far, Arthur? You're in that new resort community out near the lake, isn't that right?"

Arthur nodded and set his cup down. "That's right. I love it there. Dorathea, not so much. She says I get in her way now that I'm around the house all day."

Morgan chuckled and shook his head. "You and Dora need to come out and have lunch with us at the ranch. We haven't seen your missus in a while."

Arthur tilted his head in acknowledgement. "We'll swing by one day. I promised Dora that we'd go on a vacation, and she's pushing me to make good now that we're all moved in."

"Oh? Where you off to?"

"She wants to go to Alaska," Arthur replied, and wrinkled his nose. "She likes the cold weather. I expect to freeze."

Morgan laughed and leaned back as the waiter arrived with his coffee and a steaming pot.

"Here you go, Mr. Spade. Your entree is on the way."

They both watched as the waiter bustled away, and when Morgan turned back to the table, he saw that Arthur's shrewd blue eyes were weighing him.

"How's Heather working out?" Arthur asked softly, and his eyes searched Morgan's face.

Morgan met his eye. "Well, Arthur, since you mention it, I did have some questions about that," he rumbled. "I got to admit, I wasn't expecting you to choose a woman for that job."

His friend put out a hand in appeal. "Now, I know what you're going to say, Morgan," he said earnestly, "but I've worked with Heather before, and she knows her stuff."

Morgan shifted his weight in his chair. "I'm sure she does, Arthur, but—"

The older man shook his head. "I know she looks like she's a college kid, and sometimes she acts like one; but she's about your age, Morgan, and she's got a real gift for veterinary medicine. Just give her a few months."

Morgan nodded slowly. "I intend to," he replied softly. "I'm going to give her every chance. But I can't lie now, I don't see her working with a bull, or even a big horse. She's tiny, Arthur," he declared. "I worry about her getting hurt around our horses, to tell you the plain truth. If she got kicked by an upset mare, it'd mostly kill her!"

"Wouldn't do you any good, either," Arthur replied dryly, and Morgan looked away in exasperation.

"Look, Morgan. I've worked with her, and I can honestly tell you she's the best I've ever seen, especially with horses," Arthur argued. "She knows how to read horses and gentle 'em down, if you're worried about her getting kicked. I worked with her one summer up in Wyoming, when you sent me up to that enrichment conference at Jackson Hole. She's a skilled surgeon, she has a broad knowledge of ranch stock, and she's a—really, an extraordinary diagnostician," he murmured, and shook his head.

"I'll give you that, Arthur," Morgan replied. "All of that. I just don't want to be responsible for her getting hurt. You know as well as I do that grown men, big linebacker-type hands have got their heads stove in working with Longhorns and fractious horses. Well, those men were big enough to take it. But she's not!"

The waiter arrived with a fragrant, steaming platter, and he leaned over to set it carefully down in front of Morgan.

"Enjoy."

"Thanks," Morgan grumbled; but his appetite had waned. He unrolled his napkin, grabbed his fork, and used it to point at Arthur's chagrined face.

"What am I going to do if she gets hooked by one of our Longhorns, Arthur? Or stomped by a horse?"

His friend gave him a quizzical look. "She's a vet. She accepts the risk, Morgan. And her risk wouldn't be any different than mine, these last few years," he shrugged. "I was an old man in that job. At least she's young, and has quicker reflexes."

"It's not a joke, Arthur," Morgan replied quietly. "I'm worried about her."

Arthur sputtered and leaned back in his chair. "Now Morgan, tell me the truth. We've worked together for years. Do you honestly think that I'd recommend anyone that couldn't do that job?"

Morgan looked away and sighed. "No," he grumbled.

The elderly man leaned into the table and stared into his eyes earnestly. "Trust me, Morgan. You always have. I'm not wrong about this. She's going to turn out to be the best vet you ever had."

At that, Morgan raised his eyes to his friend's face. "I sure hope you're right, Arthur," he replied, and addressed himself to his steak.

"You'll see," his friend promised with a wink and a smile; and Morgan pulled his mouth to one side.

I better, he thought glumly. *Cause I've got enough on my plate right now to drive any man crazy.*

The last thing I need is more problems with a woman.

The reminder of his ex-wife was like heartburn in Morgan's chest; and he did his best to drown her memory with black coffee and good steak.

Chapter 11

Heather closed the trunk of her blue sedan with a *thunk* and climbed into the driver's seat. She glanced into the rear view mirror and was relieved that she could still see the orange storage unit where most of her possessions were still waiting to be claimed.

There was about a quarter-inch clearance over the pile of junk for her to see the road behind her. Every square inch of available space in her beat-up car was crammed with luggage, small pieces of furniture, and trash bags full of clothes and linens. The top of the pile was sprinkled with random flip flops, hats, framed art, and a rubber chicken that was somehow still with her from her days at Texas A&M.

Heather glanced at it in satisfaction and pulled the car out of the storage lot and into Sandy Creek's main street. Sandy Creek was like most other rural Texas towns that she knew: it had one big main drag lined with old brick storefronts that were out of an old Western. A block or two further out, there were fast food restaurants and used car lots, and beyond that, small industrial warehouses and big feed stores.

She'd been to plenty of towns like it, and she knew that the best eating it offered would be in some little hole-in-the-wall place that would be run by somebody's grandma; but since she didn't yet know where that was in Sandy Creek, she settled for the next-best eating, which was always in some storefront cafe on the town square.

Heather cruised toward the courthouse square and turned to stare at a fenced-off lot on the right. The only thing it contained was a pile of blackened bricks in a big, ragged square. It looked like something had burned to the ground.

But she was looking for a cafe and so she passed it by, glancing back and forth at the store signs around the courthouse. Sandy Creek had a few touristy gift shops, but mostly its stores catered to the locals and were devoted to farm insurance, hardware, feed and tack, and—what she was looking for. A small shop on the right read *Big Mamma's Cafe.*

Heather pulled up into one of the tiny parking lots just beyond the sidewalk and cut the motor. She glanced in the mirror, gave her hair a quick finger comb, and climbed out of the car. After a morning of lugging her stuff out of the storage unit, she was ready for a hearty lunch.

She wiped her dusty hands on her jeans, tugged her tee shirt straighter, and opened the glass door. A little bell tinkled as she entered the little cafe. There were a few metal tables scattered around in front of a tiny counter, and an elderly woman stood behind it with a cigarette in her mouth and curlers in her hair.

Heather brightened and stepped up to the counter. She put on her friendliest smile for the gray-haired clerk, but the woman stared at her without flicking an eyelash.

Heather glanced up at the menu board. It was everything she had hoped for.

Dry rub ribs with potato salad and apple pie.

Country fried steak with pepper gravy, green beans, and sweet potato casserole.

Fried chicken with buttered biscuits, corn on the cob, and blackberry cobbler.

Heather curled her fingers around the counter and leaned against it with her eyes still on the board. "I'll have the country fried steak, please," she murmured, "with a sweet tea and an extra side of Brunswick stew and crackers."

The old woman spoke no word to her, but turned to face the kitchen counter and yelled to an unseen companion in the back.

"The fried steak," she yelled, with surprising volume for a woman her age; then she shuffled over to the big silver tea canister to draw a glass of tea.

Heather practically bounced in anticipation as she dug her card out of her pocket. She was so famished that her stomach was threatening to rumble.

The old woman slid the glass over the counter like a movie bartender and mumbled, "Seven-fifty."

Heather handed her the card and grabbed the glass. She lifted it to her lips and took an experimental sip. She'd grown up in Texas, and she was something of a connoisseur of tea; but this tea had been made by someone who knew how. Heather rolled it in her mouth. It was ice cold, crisp and not too sweet. It had a tiny bit of bite just at the end.

It was perfect, and it raised her hopes for the rest of the meal. She took the card back, and since the old woman showed no sign of wanting to talk to her, she moved off to a table near the front window to people-watch and wait for her lunch.

Heather settled in with a sigh, laced her fingers together on the table, and stared out the window. There were plenty of people in town that afternoon: Stetson-wearing cowboys from the local ranches coming in for tack or feed, young women with babies doing their grocery shopping, and a smattering of what might be stock buyers, drawn to the area by the big ranches just outside town.

A gravelly male voice called from the mysterious depths behind the kitchen counter. "Fried steak," he announced, and Heather perked up and rose.

The scent of country-fried steak and sweet potato casserole extended vaporous arms to embrace her as she walked to the counter. The old woman slapped a tray down on the counter and slid a plate and a bowl onto it.

Heather leaned over it, closed her eyes, and inhaled the aroma of what promised to be a great meal. She took the tray, walked back to her window seat, and settled back in.

She dug in eagerly, and the first bite of cream-smothered steak told her that she didn't have to look any further for the hole-in-the wall place that was the best eating in town. The steak was tender and crispy, the sauce velvety and smooth with just the right kick of pepper. She bent over her plate and was so deep into her meal that she didn't notice anything else until the little bell over the door jangled again.

Heather looked up with her cheeks as full as a chipmunk's. She happened to make eye contact with the glamorous blonde woman who'd just stepped through the door. The newcomer's long lashes swept her with disdain before she turned to her glance at the rest of the room.

Heather caught a muttered profanity and a whisper of Chanel as the blonde woman flicked a sprig of perfectly-coiffed hair back from her brow with a manicured nail. The newcomer had the figure of a model and was wearing a sleek linen dress in a dull orange. Gold glittered on her neck and wrists as she clasped her hands and stared at the old woman behind the counter.

"I suppose I have no choice," the blonde woman grumbled under her breath, then sailed to the counter with the confidence of a landlord. "Do you have a sandwich or something?"she demanded, and for an answer the old woman merely pointed at the menu board.

The blonde woman sighed and glanced up at it. "Just give me a cup of coffee and a Danish," she muttered, and raised a designer handbag to the counter.

Heather polished off the last of the steak and licked her fingers in preparation to dig into the sweet potato casserole. In between bites she glanced at the blonde woman and thought:

That one sure isn't a local. No one in this town wears Gucci pumps.

Heather tilted her head and considered the woman. She was beautiful, she was svelte, she was exquisitely groomed; but she reminded her of an angry mare with its ears laid back.

"What do you mean you don't have a Danish? You do know what a Danish is, don't you?"

Heather shook her head and addressed her food; but she could feel the woman's frustration and anger from across the room.

It's a shame I can't give her a shot, Heather thought dryly as she took a bite of the casserole. She watched in silent awe as the woman turned without waiting for an answer and blew out of the cafe.

The old woman behind the counter spoke at last. She spat the cigarette out of her mouth and pointed a crooked finger after her angry customer.

"I'm glad she's gone," she declared, "I'm glad that fellow put her in the road! There's not a meaner heifer in the world, than that one."

Heather sputtered over her tea, but the smile faded off her face when the old woman lit another cigarette and waved it at the door. "I remember her name now. That's Cece Spade! She used to be married to one of them Spade brothers." She turned toward the kitchen.

"Which one of them was it, Homer?"

A male voice called from the back. "Morgan, I think."

The old woman snapped her bony fingers and turned back to glare after her visitor."That's right. Morgan, the poor devil! And now she's here again. *Ffft!* I hope he has better sense than to take her back."

Heather turned to stare after the blonde woman through the cafe window. She saw her stomp across the street, slide into a Mercedes convertible, and pop on a pair of sunglasses before pulling the gleaming car into the street. The woman looked like a Hollywood starlet as she roared down the street in a cloud of dust; and a worried frown knitted Heather's brows as she watched her go.

She was seeing, not the retreating Mercedes, but the drawn look on Morgan Spade's face when they'd met.

The little throbbing vein in his temple.

Chapter 12

Heather unlocked the front door of the condo, kicked off her shoes, set a suitcase on the floor and dumped the garbage bags next to it. A strenuous morning and a heavy lunch after had made her sleepy.

But she couldn't afford to be lazy. She had a whole car to unpack and a house to furnish, so she grabbed the stair rail and pulled herself up to the second floor.

A nice cold splash of water would wake her up; and if she followed it with a cup of double-jolt coffee, she'd be good for the rest of the day.

She mounted the stairs and crossed the upstairs hall to the bathroom. She'd just flicked on the water in the sink and cupped her hands when a loud *thunk* made her turn her head. It had come from outside.

She turned off the water, walked over to the big oriole window and swung it outward. When she leaned out of the opening, she saw that a little brown sparrow had flown into the window and was lying on the porch roof like a dead thing, with its eyes closed and its feet curled up.

Heather pulled her mouth down in sympathy, then grabbed the sides of the window and hoisted herself up into the opening. She was small enough to shimmy out if she squeezed through one leg at a time, and she slowly wriggled out of the open window to lower herself on the roof.

Heather touched the roof with one foot, then the other, then knelt down and crawled to the bird. She could see its heart beating, and she bent over it to scoop it gently into her hands. She stared down at its closed eyes in pity and barely stroked its head with the tip of one forefinger.

"Poor little fellow," she crooned. "I'm going to fix you right up."

She glanced up at the window. It was thrown open, but she couldn't climb back through it with a bird in her hands, and she couldn't jump down to the ground, because she was ten feet above the back lawn.

As she was considering how best to get back inside, she heard the sound of a car pulling into her front driveway. She couldn't see who it was, but she heard the crunch of heavy boots on the gravel walkway, and then a knock at her front door.

She hunched down over the roof and called, "I'm in the back! Come around the house!"

There was a long, pregnant pause, then the sound of a slow stride around the side of the house to the back porch. The heavy footsteps paused on the porch just under her, and a deep, puzzled voice called, "Heather?"

"Up here. I'm on the roof."

Heather braced one hand against the roof and leaned out to see who it was. Slowly a black cowboy hat appeared, followed by a frowning face with a bushy moustache and a pair of broad shoulders in a black tee shirt.

Morgan Spade tilted his head to look up at her. "I dropped by the office, but you weren't there, so I came here. We got a couple of mares about to foal, and I thought you might want to have a look at 'em."

Heather brightened instantly. "I'll be glad to," she replied. "Just let me get this little fellow squared away."

"What're you doing up on the roof?" he demanded, and stuck his hands on his hips. "Here, come on down, before you fall!"

Heather glanced down at him through her hair. "A bird flew into the window," she told him, and held up her cupped hands. A stunned sparrow sat there with its eyes squeezed shut and its heart thrumming.

Morgan's dark brows rushed together as he stared at it. "Well the bird's already cracked its head," he drawled. "You don't wanna crack yours. Hold on now," he added sharply, and put up a hand as she crawled down the slanting roof toward the ledge. "Throw it down, and I'll catch it."

She paused an instant to stare at him in indignation. "Throw it *down*? Are you joking?"

"You can't climb down from there with that bird in your hands." He stared up at her earnestly and reached up.

"Well—you are pretty tall," she admitted. His outstretched hands were only a foot or so below the ledge. "Okay, I'm just going to lean down and—"

"No, don't lean down!" he insisted. "Just drop the bird, and I'll catch it."

Heather ignored him and shifted her weight to her foremost leg as she crouched on the lip of the gutter with the bird cupped in her hands. She bent down as far as she dared holding the bird.

"Now be care—"

The bird suddenly decided to end the argument by jumping into the air. Heather grabbed for it, felt herself sliding off balance, and heard Morgan yell once before she rolled right off the roof.

She struck him like a lightning bolt, and he staggered back, swayed, and caught her before she slid off his chest. He grunted and hauled her up into his arms, where she swayed in a tangle of elbows and knees.

Heather looked up through her hair. The sparrow cocked its head at her from the lip of the gutter and flew off.

She rolled her eyes up to Morgan's face. Two dark, frowning eyes were staring back at her.

"Are you all right?"

She tried to adjust her position in his arms, failed, and pushed up toward him just as he was bending down. Their lips bumped together in an accidental kiss, and in spite of its awkwardness, that touch electrified her; but the next thing she knew, Morgan had released her and she slid abruptly off his chest. Her feet slapped against the ground, and she swayed and grabbed at him to steady herself. Her fingers brushed against his chest for an instant, registered the muscles beneath the fabric of his shirt, and just for an instant, she could feel his heartbeat.

His heart was pounding.

He took her by the shoulders and she pulled her hair back from her face. She looked up at him sheepishly.

"Sorry."

His gruff voice growled, "You sure you're alright?"

Heather brushed off her sleeve and tried to recover her tattered dignity. "Oh sure. I'm fine."

His fingers uncurled from her shoulders and he stepped back to stare at her in frowning doubt.

"Wanna come in for a cup of coffee or something?" she blurted.

Morgan rubbed the back of his neck. "No thanks. I was gonna drive you over to the barn to look at those mares, but maybe we'd better do that some other time."

"Oh no, I can do it now," she assured him. "I'd like to look at them. Just give me a minute to get my bag. Come on in."

"Well…"

She left him no choice but to follow her as she struck off to the back porch door, opened it, and looked back over her shoulder to smile, "Just give me a minute to get my bag. Make yourself at home."

He drifted in after her, and his big boots rumbled like thunder as they crossed her mostly-empty kitchen and front room.

She turned to smile at him as she turned to go up the stairs. "Don't pay any attention to the trash bags on the floor. I'm just moving in," she explained, and turned to sprint up the stairs to get her exam bag.

Chapter 13

Morgan watched Heather's slender back disappear up the stairs, then his gaze drifted down. She had only just begun to unpack. The floor was bare, and the walls were, too, except for a cross plaque and a framed photo of the Grand Teton Mountains.

His glance drifted down to the pile of plastic trash bags on the floor. One was open and filled mostly with clothes, but there were a few other things crammed into the top.

He leaned down, pulled out a rubber chicken, and stared at it in frowning bemusement before tossing it back. The object just beside it caught his eye, and he lifted it to take a closer look.

It was a framed diploma from Texas A&M School of Veterinary Medicine, *summa cum laude*, for Heather Weston. His dark brows twitched in surprise, and he replaced it quickly as the sound of Heather's pattering feet announced her approach.

"Now I'm ready," she announced, and slung a black cloth bag over one shoulder as she descended the stairs.

"I'll drive you over," he told her, and led the way out the front door and across the lawn to his Jeep. He unlocked the door for her, let her climb in, and closed it after her before walking around to the driver's side.

He glanced at Heather as he climbed in. She'd taken a pretty hard fall, but she'd shrugged it off like it was no big deal. He glanced at her again, wondering if she really was okay; but her long brown legs showed no marks.

Maybe she was tougher than she looked.

He cranked the motor and put the jeep in reverse, thinking to himself that the more he saw of Heather Weston, the less she acted like the delicate flower of his imagination. She was wearing a baggy white tee shirt, a pair of cutoff jeans and a pair of sneakers, and she hadn't checked her makeup once in the passenger mirror. In fact, she didn't look like she was wearing makeup at all.

After years of marriage to Cece, he noticed things like that.

"I saw your diploma," he told her as he backed out. "So you're an Aggie."

Her face split into a white grin. "That's right. Once an Aggie, always an Aggie!"

Morgan smiled a little in spite of himself. "Yeah, I spent some time there in my salad days," he rumbled. "It's a fun school." He turned to glance at her. "Are you from Texas?"

She bobbed her head. "I grew up in San Antonio and went to A&M. After I graduated, I got a job out in Wyoming for a ranch almost as big as this one. It was a horse ranch. Great family."

"Huh," Morgan grunted in surprise. He glanced at his companion again and decided to reserve judgement about her skills. No vet got a job with a really big horse outfit unless they knew their stuff.

Maybe he'd been a little too quick to judge Heather Weston; but he was about to find out if she had what it took, one way or another.

He pulled the jeep up to the side of the road outside the main barn and climbed out. He hadn't taken two steps before Heather was out of the car and halfway to the big barn doors with her bag slung around her shoulder. She beat him there and disappeared inside, and he had to pick up the pace to keep up.

By the time he got inside the barn Heather had already found one of the pregnant mares. She was standing at the stall door, stroking the mare's twitching neck. She turned to smile at him as he walked up.

"What's her name?"

Morgan rubbed his moustache and drawled, "Her name is Ladybug. She's a maiden mare, and she looks like she's getting close."

Heather stared into the mare's soft, patient brown eyes. "She's a pretty girl." She turned back to him. "Has she been restless?"

"She's been pretty laid back so far," Morgan replied.

"I'll check."

Heather opened the wooden door slowly, and moved softly into the stall. The chestnut mare tossed her head, but Heather held out her hand and soothed it with a gentle hand.

"*Ssshh,* Momma," she murmured, and bent down to glance at the horse's belly. "Yeah, her udder is pretty full, and she's beginning to wax a little," she murmured. She passed a hand over the mare's flanks. "She feels a little sweaty, too. Her ligaments are totally relaxed. So she's gonna foal any time now." She glanced at him over her shoulder. "You say there's another pregnant mare?"

Morgan nodded and rubbed his moustache. "Over here. I'll show you."

He led the way to another stall. "This is Maribelle. This is her third foal, so she's an old hand now."

Heather slipped past him to check on the other mare, a striking brown and white Appaloosa. She was so big she looked ready to pop, and when Heather checked her, all the signs of an imminent birth were there. She straightened up and sighed.

"It looks like they're both due any time," she announced ruefully, and turned to question Morgan with her eyes. "I'd like to stay here tonight to watch them, and I recommend moving Ladybug to the foaling stall. She looks like she could start within hours."

"I'll get you a sleeping bag and a pillow," Morgan replied, and disappeared. Heather patted the mare's flanks and followed Morgan as he walked to Ladybug's stall and let the mare down the long aisle to a roomy foaling stall with fresh straw on the floor.

Morgan left her there, then reappeared a few minutes later with a sleeping bag in his arms. "I found a cot," he mumbled. "Where do you want to set up?"

"Just leave it outside of the stall door, thanks," Heather murmured; and as they watched, the young mare sank down onto her knees, and then rolled over onto the straw.

"Yep," Heather murmured, and leaned down to pat the mare's neck. "There she goes. I'll go ahead and wrap her tail and wash her."

Morgan rubbed his nose. "Well, I'll be going now. I'll have Hank check back on you every few hours. If you need him sooner, or run into trouble, he'll be in his office. That door across the way." He pointed to a door at the end of the opposite row of stalls.

She glanced up at him, and the sky-blue from those big eyes hit him harder than he liked to admit. "Thanks, Morgan," she smiled.

"Yep." Morgan nodded to her and turned away; but he wasn't easy in his mind. He was about to find out if Heather Weston could clear the first hurdle of her new job. It was pretty easy. A pregnant mare did most of the work in a foaling, as long as there weren't complications.

He hoped there wouldn't be any complications.

Morgan glanced back over his shoulder. Heather was sitting cross-legged on the cot, like a child. She was hardly bigger than one, and he frowned and shook his head as he walked out.

Chapter 14

Heather sat down on the cot just outside the foaling stall and opened her vet bag. Ladybug had struggled to her feet again and was now pacing back and forth in restless discomfort.

Heather glanced up at Ladybug as she walked to and fro. The way the mare was acting, she was willing to bet that she'd foal before sunup.

But that was hours away. It looked like it might be a long night.

Heather reclined on the cot, laced her hands together, and closed her eyes. She had plenty of time to wait, and it was best to let nature take its course anyway unless there were complications with the delivery.

Morgan had given her no reason to expect any; but she closed her eyes and followed her usual custom when facing a birth or a surgery. She breathed a quick prayer: *Lord, please give us a healthy delivery.*

She sighed and opened one eye to sneak a peek at the mare. Ladybug was kneeling down to lie on her side again. The young mare laid down on the straw and lowered her head to stare at the wall.

Heather watched her in sympathy, but it was early yet; and so she closed her eyes. She slowly slipped off into a light doze. She could dimly hear the mare breathing, moving around, and occasionally struggling to her feet. She drifted in that twilight state for she didn't know how long, then roused up with a guilty start and checked her watch.

It was two hours later than when she'd fallen asleep.

Heather frowned, sat up, and then rose to check on the mare. She was lying on the straw and raised her head as Heather entered.

Heather walked in slowly, extended a hand to the mare and murmured, "It's all right, Momma. Let's see about you."

She moved around the mare and checked her. Ladybug's water had broken, and she was moving into labor. Heather stepped back a few paces and waited. The baby would be coming quickly now.

The mare grunted and tossed her head, and her flanks heaved. Heather crouched down on her heels and watched as the contractions began.

Ladybug surged up and struggled to her feet, switching her tail. She paced back and forth, panting, then sank down to her knees and onto the straw again.

Heather frowned as the mare writhed under a new contraction. She could see the foal's feet sticking out, and the end of its nose between them. She patted the mare's flanks.

"Come on, Momma," she murmured.

Ladybug closed her eyes in mute exertion as she was shaken by another contraction. The foal's head and front feet peeked out a little more, and then its shoulders.

Heather rose slowly, walked out to grab her bag off the cot, and returned. She paused in the doorway as Ladybug struggled to her feet, paced back and forth a few times, and then sank down onto the straw again.

Heather moved around the mare and settled in behind her. When she checked, the foal was halfway out, and she waited as Ladybug's head sank to the floor in exhaustion.

"Just a few more minutes, Ladybug," she murmured. "Your baby's almost here."

Ladybug writhed with a final contraction, and the foal's hindquarters and feet came rolling out. Heather smiled as the new foal raised its head from the broken amniotic sac.

"Welcome to the world, little baby," she whispered, but was careful not to interfere. Ladybug turned her head to look at the baby and nickered softly. She raised herself slowly to her feet, then turned to lick her foal clean.

The baby was ink-black with a white blaze on its forehead, and when Heather tilted her head to check, it was a little colt. The foal tried to pull itself up on its wobbly legs and failed as Ladybug licked it dry.

A rustling at the stall door made Heather look up. To her surprise, it wasn't Hank standing there, but Morgan. She slipped around the mare and foal to join him.

His eyes were on the colt, and a quiet pleasure glowed in them. "Well, well," he murmured. "He's a little beauty. He's gonna look like his daddy. My horse, Cochise."

He turned to her with a smile. "Everything go alright?"

Heather tilted her head. "Like clockwork. She came through like a champ. I'm going to clean them up and watch them until morning, and then you can call me if anything comes up. I'll be back tomorrow to take care of the routine things."

Morgan's eyes on her were full of warmth. "You did great, Heather," he murmured, and to her surprise, he reached out and touched her arm briefly. Heather felt her face going warm with pleasure, both at the praise and the touch. Morgan looked so handsome as he stood there, his face deeply shadowed in the dim light. It was the wee hours of the morning, and the stable lights were burning low. They glanced off the planes of his face: the high cheekbones, the proud nose, the strong chin.

The full, defined lips under that bushy moustache.

Heather's eyes lingered on them, then moved up to his eyes. They gazed at one another for an instant, but a restless nicker from a few stalls down made Heather's eyes move away from Morgan's face, and the moment passed.

It's just as well, she told herself. *This man is my boss. I need to keep my mind on business.*

Still, those dark, beautiful, sapphire blue eyes drew her own like a magnet, and it took the *bang* of a mare kicking the side of her stall to make Heather smile apologetically.

"I better go and check on that," she murmured. "It sounds like the other mare might be going into labor."

Morgan turned to watch her as she slipped past him. "You're going to be pulling an all-nighter here, then," he observed. "You sure you don't want somebody else to sit up with her?"

"I'm sure. This isn't my first rodeo," she smiled, with a glance back at him. She could tell that Morgan was a bit boggled by the idea of a lady vet.

But that was all right. He'd come around.

"Well," he mumbled, "if you're sure. This'll be Maribelle's fourth foal, but her first by Cochise."

Heather turned to glance at him over her shoulder as she paused in the stall doorway. "Is Cochise your stud?"

"Not our main one," he replied, as he slowly followed her. "But Cochise is the best ranch horse I've ever had. There'll never be another one like him. I want foals by him for sentimental reasons."

Heather shot him a teasing glance. "Are you sentimental?" she smiled.

To her surprise, Morgan smiled back a little; and she couldn't help noticing that he had beautiful, even white teeth under that moustache.

"A little, I guess."

"I'll tell you a secret," she murmured. "So am I."

She turned to check on the second mare, the striking Appaloosa. She was moving back and forth in the stall and switching her tail.

Morgan stood at her shoulder, gazing down at the mare. "Well, I'll let you take care of it," he murmured, and she thought she caught a tinge of reluctance in his voice. She wasn't sure if that was because he still wasn't sure that she was up to the job, or if he just didn't want to go.

She was hoping he didn't want to go; and then caught herself dreaming and pushed that hope out of her mind.

"I'll talk to you tomorrow, Morgan," she told him. "Don't worry. You'll probably have two beautiful new foals by breakfast."

"Thanks, Heather. I appreciate it."

"Sure."

He nodded to her, backed away, and then turned to stride down the corridor and out of the barn. Heather watched him wistfully, and then was impatient with herself for doing it.

What is it about that tall, dark drink of water that messes with my head? she wondered wryly. *I've seen gorgeous guys before.*

She didn't know the answer; but she did notice one thing.

It took a full thirty minutes before Morgan Spade's keen, sapphire-blue eyes faded from her memory, and she was able to concentrate on the mare again.

Chapter 15

Morgan walked into the barn the next morning just as dawn painted the eastern sky pink. A rooster crowed from somewhere out in the fields as he opened the big door.

The stalls were still dimly lit, but he could see Heather walking out of Maribelle's stall. He knew she hadn't had a wink of sleep, and sympathy bloomed in his heart. He quickened his pace and called to her softly.

"How you feeling, doc?"

She looked up and smiled at him, and to his dismay, that sweet smile went through him like an arrow.

"I'm all right," she yawned, and stretched a bit. "You wanna come and see?"

She motioned toward the stall door, and he walked up beside her. The Appaloosa mare was nursing a strong, beautiful white foal spattered with black leopard spots.

"What a beauty," he breathed, and turned to smile at Heather in amazement. "Filly or colt?"

"This one's a filly," she told him. "Strong, too. She was on her feet the first try."

Heather slung her bag over her arm, and the weary slump of her shoulders went to Morgan's heart. He knew how it felt to be bone tired after a long day tending horses.

A voice in his head warned him to keep his distance, but he heard himself mumble, "You had a tough shift out there. Why don't you stay here tonight and go home tomorrow?"

Heather rolled her eyes toward him and gave him a crooked smile. "Thanks," she sighed weakly. "I can't lie, I'm about to fall down."

That flick of compassion in Morgan's heart bloomed into a little flame. He took Heather's slender arm. "I'll show you up to the guest room. You can wash up and have a nice long sleep. You've earned it."

The look of gratitude in her eyes warmed his heart, and he walked with her up to the second floor, then on down the corridor a few doors down from his own apartment. He opened the guest suite door and flicked on the lights. The glass wall still showed a gray sky just beginning to bloom with dawn, but the soft lights in the room revealed a palatial suite with marble floors and modern art on the walls.

Heather threw her bag onto a chair, scanned the room and nodded, "Nice place. Where's the bathroom?"

Morgan gestured toward the far wall. "Through that door."

She turned to give him a weary smile. "Thanks Morgan. You saved my life. I'm going to wash up and fall face down in bed."

Morgan smiled a bit under his moustache and looked down at the floor. "Well. I'll see you tomorrow, then."

"See you."

He walked out, and Heather closed the door softly and slowly behind him. He turned to glance at it for an instant before turning for his own door down the hall.

Now that he wasn't looking at a beautiful woman, he noticed that his muscles were sore and weary, too.

The next morning Morgan took Kit down to breakfast, but Heather wasn't around. When he poked his head into the dining room, the table was empty, and he wasn't surprised. Nobody in their family used it. Nobody ate where they were supposed to. They scattered out all over the house, plates in hand: in front of the t.v. in the entertainment room, out by the pool in warm weather, or in front of one of a dozen fireplaces.

Morgan led Kit over to the big fireplace in the atrium, partly because it was cold that morning and there was a big fire going in it, and partly because he wanted to see if Heather left the house. She'd have to walk past them to go.

But after they'd finished their breakfast, and he still hadn't seen any sign of her, Morgan broke down and snagged Miss Ada as she bustled past on an errand of her own.

He cleared his throat and rumbled, "Miss Ada, I had a guest spend the night. Have you seen her this morning?"

Their severe, ramrod-straight housekeeper gave him a look of frowning disapproval. "No, I have not. Nobody but the family's been down to breakfast."

Morgan's frown lifted. "Thank you, Miss Ada."

Miss Ada gave him a frosty nod and walked off, and he was left to conclude that Heather had been so wiped out that she'd slept late. He couldn't say that he was surprised. She'd spent a sleepless night in a horse stall.

She deserved to sleep as late as she wanted.

He and Kit went back up to their apartment, and he found all kinds of reasons to stick close all that afternoon; but there was no sign of Heather until late in the afternoon. Lunch had long passed, and dinnertime was passing, when there came a soft knock at his door.

He got up and went to answer it, and Heather was standing there in the hall with a sheepish look on her face.

"I guess I overslept," she admitted. "I'm going to be heading back home now. I just wanted to come by and say thanks for letting me crash here."

His eyes flicked over her. Her hair was shampooed squeaky clean and gleamed a dull gold, with some brighter threads glittering like highlights around her face. Her face was scrubbed pink, and her skin smelled faintly of honeysuckle soap.

He came back to himself and pulled the door open. "Have you had anything to eat?"

She tucked a sprig of hair behind one ear and a faintly embarrassed look flitted across her expressive eyes. "Well…"

Morgan suffered a flick of guilt. "Why don't you come in and have a bite before you go," he suggested. "Kit and I are just having dinner. I can make you a plate."

A faint blush bloomed across her face. "I wouldn't want to put you out," she murmured, but he shook his head. "No trouble. Come on in."

She smiled and shrugged. "Well, okay. Thanks. I am a little bit hungry."

He pushed the door wide open, stood back to let her in, and got another whiff of honeysuckles as she passed.

He led her to his big sunken living room. A nice fire was cracking in the big stone fireplace, and he bent down to scoop the remote off a table.

He flicked a switch, and a wall panel rose to reveal a big screen t.v. He handed her the remote.

"You make yourself at home. I'll have dinner out in a minute."

Kit came padding into the room as he spoke, and Heather brightened at the sight of him. He gestured toward his son.

"Heather, this is my boy Kit."

Wonder dawned across Heather's face, and Morgan was struck by the look she gave his son. As if Kit was a brand new foal, and the prettiest one in the pen.

"Howdy, Kit. I'm Heather," she told him softly, and extended her hand. Kit shook it weakly, but Morgan noticed that he seemed okay with their evening guest.

"Hi Heather."

"Why don't you show Heather how to use the t.v. while I go get us some dinner," Morgan told him, and turned for the kitchen; but he paused in the doorway and glanced back.

Heather and Kit were already on the couch with their heads together over the remote. He chuckled and shook his head, then went to fetch supper.

He came out again about twenty minutes later, carrying plates on his arm like a waiter. The scent of ribs and potato salad made Heather look up and beam at him.

"That *really* smells good," she told him, and passed a plate to Kit; and Morgan noticed, with some amusement, that Heather didn't even wait for a fork to dive in. She picked a rib up with her fingers, popped it into her mouth, and frowned appreciatively.

"*Mmm-mm!*" she moaned. "I've said it before, nobody makes ribs like a rancher. This is great stuff!"

"I'm glad you like it," he sputtered. "I'll be back in a minute with drinks. You like coffee or tea?"

"Tea for me, thanks."

When he came back later, drinks in hand, the t.v. was blaring. When he bent down to pass out the glasses, Morgan noticed that Kit and Heather were watching a football game.

"What's this?" he asked, as he sat down on the couch next to Heather.

She turned to him with a smile. "The Aggies are playing tonight," she told him with an apologetic look. "I wanted to see the score."

Morgan settled in with his plate on his knees. "Let's see the Aggies, then." He took a bite of potato salad, then glanced over at Heather's plate. To his amazement, it was so clean it looked almost washed. All that was left of the ribs was a litter of bones.

I've only been gone a few minutes, he thought in awe. *She must really have been hungry.*

The announcer declared, "The Aggies and the Fighting Tigers of LSU are in a real brawl tonight, folks. Aggies 7, Tigers 7 in the third quarter!"

Kit leaned out and asked, "Dad, can I be excused?"

Morgan turned to glance at his plate. "You didn't finish your ribs," he objected, but Kit shrugged.

"I had all I wanted."

"Okay then," Morgan conceded. "Say goodnight to Heather."

Kit rubbed one eye with a knuckle. "Night."

"Night, Kit," she replied instantly. "It was nice meeting you."

Kit smiled a bit and shuffled off sleepily. Morgan watched him go, then asked, "If you'll pass me his plate, I'll take it back to the kitchen."

Heather turned to stare at him as if he'd suggested tossing the plate into the fire. "You're not going to throw away those ribs, are you?" she objected. "He left half of them."

Morgan felt his mouth dropping open and stammered, "Well, I—"

Heather took the plate in her hands. "It would be a shame to waste them," she went on, and Morgan replied in surprise:

"Well, you're welcome to them, if you have room."

"Thanks!" Heather smiled, and began enjoying the ribs immediately. Morgan stared at her in awe.

To be such a skinny little thing, she sure does have an appetite, he marveled. *She eats like a trail hand on a cattle drive.*

"*Mmm,*" she mumbled, and licked barbecue sauce off her slender fingers.

Morgan settled in to finish his meal. He and Heather watched the game in comfortable silence as the teams battled through the third quarter, and then into the fourth. The score was still tied in spite of a thrilling contest.

"The Aggies kick off in the fourth," the announcer declared, and Morgan and Heather watched as the Aggie kicker sent the football down the field to the arms of a Tiger quarterback.

The two teams battled back and forth without scoring right down to the last minutes of the fourth quarter. The announcer cried breathlessly, "There are only two minutes left in the game, with the Tigers holding the ball. It looks like they're going to run out the clock!"

Morgan watched in rising suspense as the Tiger quarterback pretended to throw the ball, then tried to fall on the ball. But to his amazement, an Aggie linebacker flung the Tiger defenders aside, hit the quarterback, and knocked the ball up into the air. He caught it, almost dropped it, dodged to evade a line of Tiger linebackers, and took off running.

Morgan half-rose from his seat as the Aggie linebacker dodged, spun, and skirted all obstacles to make it to the clear. He sprinted like a mad thing as his teammates formed a running ring around him, and Morgan watched in disbelief as the Aggie linebacker ran the length of the football field to score the winning touchdown.

The announcer's voice jumped to a joyous shriek. "What a play! Aggies score, Aggies win, 14 to 7!"

Morgan surged to his feet, just like he was a 20 year old in a football stadium, and Heather jumped up and down and screamed.

He'd barely turned toward her, when the next thing he knew, his hands were clamped around her shoulders, and he bent to honor a sacred and time-honored school tradition.

To kiss your date when the Aggies scored.

The screaming in the television crashed on, but for him, it quickly faded into the background. His lips closed over Heather's lips, and her arms curved around his neck, and suddenly they were the only two people in the world.

All the pent-up hunger inside him poured into that kiss, and Heather rose to meet his hunger, twined it around her like a trailing flag, danced with it as that kiss extended into their arms and shoulders, wandered onto her neck, under his ear.

The announcer's frantic voice screamed: "The Aggies are going crazy! It's pandemonium!"

The sound slapped Morgan back to himself. *What am I doing,* he wondered with a sudden jolt of electricity. *I don't need to get tangled up with another woman.*

His fingers slowly uncurled from Heather's shoulders, and he looked down and cleared his throat.

"Um…I'm sorry, Heather," he mumbled, and to his embarrassment, he felt himself going red.

"It's all right," she replied softly, and turned her big blue eyes on him. There was a warm smile in them. "Everybody knows that you have to mug down when the Aggies score."

He rolled his eyes to the ceiling and cleared his throat again. "Huh huh huh," he half-laughed, and Heather giggled and reached up to touch his sleeve briefly.

Morgan frowned, stepped back from her suddenly, and stared down at the floor. He controlled his voice with a stern effort.

"Um, I think I should call it a night," he mumbled. "I've enjoyed it, Heather, but I need to check on Kit. He's waiting for me."

Those sky-blue eyes searched his face, and Heather's tone sounded just a bit confused when she whispered, "Okay, Morgan."

But she stood up on tiptoe to plant a quick parting kiss on his cheek, and his heart jumped as eagerly as a teenager's. He wanted to kiss her back, but he forced himself not to respond.

Heather's eyes looked worried, but she smiled up at him and pressed a finger on his nose.

"Good night, Morgan."

"Night, Heather."

Morgan kept his eyes on the floor as long as she was facing him, but as soon as she turned, he raised his eyes to follow her. He watched as she picked up her bag on the way out, slung it over her shoulder, and then turned to glance at him from the doorway. Those lovely blue eyes were as full of sadness as he was; and he frowned and looked down again.

When he looked up again, Heather was gone.

Morgan reached up and touched his lips in wonder. They were still tingling, and when he put a hand on his chest, he could feel his heart jumping through his shirt.

It was the first time a woman had done that to him since the divorce. No, more than just that: Heather made him feel like he was starting fresh.

Every nerve ending in his body was alight. He felt like a teenager who'd just kissed his first girl and was still standing on her doorstep, staring at the closed door in shock.

The announcer's jubilant voice snapped him back to reality. "Let's watch that last play again, Jim," the sportscaster burbled, and Morgan reached for the remote and flicked the television off. He stood staring at the dark screen in frowning silence.

He still couldn't believe that he'd kissed Heather Weston. He'd kissed her on impulse, in a moment of elation, but he'd kissed her and now their professional relationship was never going to be the same. It was going to be awkward now, even if they never kissed again.

That kiss was always going to be there, lurking in the back of their minds.

Morgan frowned and ran his hand through his dark hair in frustration. *This is exactly what got me in trouble the first time,* he told himself. *I let myself get carried away, and before I knew it, I was all tangled up with Cece. Roped and tied up tight.*

I'm not free of her even now, and the worst part is that my son had to pay for my foolishness. He's still paying.

I can't take that chance. I can't let that happen again.

It would be wrong.

Heather's sky-blue eyes and soft smile glimmered for an instant in his mind, but faded away as he banished them. Morgan drifted to the doorway, flicked off the light, and walked out of the room to check on his son.

Kit was waiting to be tucked in.

I don't want to be involved with anybody anyway, he mused. *I just want some peace, and there ain't no peace with a woman, I don't care who it is.*

Or maybe it's just that I only see what I want to see. Either way, the bottom line is, no more women in my life, or in Kit's.

He cracked Kit's bedroom door silently and peeked in. The bedroom walls were painted to look like a west Texas desert, and a string of mounted cowboys were forever frozen as they herded hundreds of Longhorns across a silver stream.

Kit's dark, tousled head was just visible above his covers. A soft smile dawned across Morgan's face, and he walked in quietly.

He sank down onto the edge of Kit's bed and watched as Kit rubbed his eyes and smiled up at him.

"Hey Daddy," Kit mumbled.

"Hey buddy," Morgan whispered, and rubbed his little boy's head with a big hand. "I think I'm a little late tucking you in tonight. You done gone to sleep without me."

Kit raised up one elbow. "No I didn't," he murmured, but leaned back again as Morgan pulled the covers up around his ears and bent down to give him a peck on the brow.

"You say your night prayers?"

Kit nodded and yawned, and Morgan stared down at him tenderly. "All right then. Where's your stuffed bear?"

Kit's eyes opened a slit, and he objected, "I'm too big now to sleep with a bear, Daddy."

Something like pain jabbed Morgan's heart, and he reached out to caress his son's smooth brown cheek.

"Well, I'll put him next to you, in case you change your mind," he murmured, and tucked the toy into the crook of Kit's elbow. Kit's smooth eyelids were already closed, and his mouth had fallen slightly open.

Morgan leaned down to press one last kiss to his son's cheek. "Night night buddy," he whispered, and rose from the bed. He stood staring down at his son's innocent sleeping face and prayed:

Lord, if something bad happens, let it be to me, and not to him.

He lingered there for a moment, then turned, walked out of the room softly, and pulled the door shut behind him.

Chapter 16

Heather opened the door of the condo, walked in, and locked it behind her. The front room was still bare, and moonlight slanted across its gleaming wooden floors.

The long road to her condo had been dark and empty and deserted except for a startled rabbit who'd jumped across the road ahead of her. But she hadn't really seen it, anyway. Her mind had been projecting Morgan Spade onto that lonely road all the way home.

Heather looked down at her car keys, and she played with them idly as she drifted up the stairs to her bedroom.

It was the wee hours of the morning, the time of true confessions, but she didn't know what to confess. On the one hand, she'd just kissed her boss. She'd never done that before; never even considered doing it. Getting involved with a boss was bad policy. It was dumb because it could end not just in a broken heart, but a lost job.

On the other hand, she'd enjoyed Morgan's kiss so much that she didn't care if it was stupid. There was something about that tall, gruff drink of water that made her want to kiss him.

Morgan Spade was a lonely man. He needed connection. He needed healing.

She'd suspected that from the first time she met him, but it had been confirmed for her as soon as his lips touched hers. Morgan was hurting. He was as wary and remote as a wounded mustang, but he was starving for love.

For comfort, really.

Heather drifted into her moonlit bedroom, collapsed on the bed, and turned to stare up at the ceiling. No one would know from the way he acted that Morgan Spade was all torn up inside. He was silent and stoic. He didn't wear his feelings on his sleeve.

He didn't look like a man with a broken heart, either. He was tall and ripped and drop-dead gorgeous.

For the sake of their professional relationship she'd been trying to ignore his looks, but it was hard to ignore them when you were being kissed. What was a girl supposed to do?

Heather conjured him again in her mind. Morgan had that old-time cowboy thing going on, he was six feet tall, his hair was long and shiny as black silk, and his face was finely chiseled and proud. His eyes were so dark that they looked brown, but up close, they were a deep sapphire with smaller flecks of pool blue, and they were ringed by thick, soft lashes.

And that moustache of his…

Heather giggled a little. She'd almost broken up laughing when Morgan kissed her, because his bristly moustache had just about tickled her to death. But she liked a big, full moustache on a man, so she could learn to live with that.

And his voice…oh, his voice. Heather closed her eyes and heard that deep, raspy baritone again, and even the memory made her feel like a dozen caterpillars were running up her spine.

It always made her a little bit goofy, to be honest.

Morgan was that tall, dark shadow on the edge of a tingly dream, whose voice could both soothe her to sleep, and pull her up from the deepest slumber.

And at two o'clock in the morning, the hour of truth, Heather admitted that she was tempted to throw all her professional norms over her shoulder. She was tempted to risk losing the best gig she'd ever had.

She wanted to see the sadness in Morgan's eyes blow away like mist on a sunny morning. She wanted to see him smile from his heart, wanted to hear him laugh from his belly, and she was willing to take a risk to see it happen.

Was that because she felt compassion for a hurting man, or because Morgan had kissed her and she liked the way he did it?

She still wasn't sure. But one thing she did know: her desire to see him whole again was an ache in her chest.

Heather sighed and turned to gaze out the window and felt a flick of guilt. It was all well and good to moon over a handsome man, but she wasn't even sure he was free. She'd gleaned from what she heard at the cafe in town that Morgan had suffered a painful breakup with his wife. Maybe that was what had hurt him. That would be reason enough.

And it raised another question. The woman at the cafe had said she hoped Morgan didn't *take his ex back.*

Maybe his ex-wife had come back to town to make up with him. Maybe they were working out some kind of reconciliation.

Maybe that was why Morgan had pulled back from her the instant they'd really kissed, when they'd stopped being impulsive and started getting deliberate.

Heather turned over, slipped a hand under her pillow, and gazed out of her bedroom window. A big, golden harvest moon was hanging in the night sky like a ripe pumpkin.

She didn't know anything about Morgan's breakup with his ex, or how recent it had been; but maybe she shouldn't let herself dream about a man who might be reconciling with his wife.

Morgan had built a family already. If he and his wife were getting back together, she had no right to get in between them. Morgan had a beautiful little boy who would be better off if his parents reconciled.

Morgan's personal life was none of her business in any case.

But as she lay there gazing at the moon, Heather was sure of one thing: she wanted to find out more about it.

Chapter 17

Buck swiveled around in his leather chair to extend his arms to Kate as she came walking into his office. She perched on his lap and twined her white arms around his neck.

Buck kissed her cheek and hugged her close. "How're they doing?"

"They're happy as little clams," Kate told him, "Kit and Molly get along like peanut butter and jelly. They're out there in the living room watching cartoons."

"Thanks for helping me look after him," Buck murmured. "Morgan needs a break."

"I know," Kate replied softly. "I'm about to get some lunch ready. What would you like?"

"Whatever it is, it'll be great. Surprise me." Buck pressed a kiss into her glossy auburn hair and murmured, "Call me when it's ready."

His bride slipped out of his arms with a reluctant backward glance. Buck watched her go with a bright expression; but as soon as she was gone, he swiveled around and his smile faded. He crossed his arms and frowned at his computer, mulling over the return of Morgan's ex.

Buck grumbled under his breath. Cece had made Morgan's life hell for years, but she'd finally flounced out of his life when he won custody of Kit. He'd been lucky in at least that way, and the whole Spade family had hoped that Cece was gone for good.

But it looked like their luck had just run out; or rather, that Cece's money had run out, and she was back to bleed Morgan again.

Buck scowled at his computer screen. Cece was *not* coming back to make trouble for the family, he was going to see to that. He wasn't as clear about how he was going to stop her, but he'd figure it out.

Buck scratched his nose. Maybe he should call Eugene on the quiet and tell him the story, just between the two of them. No reason Morgan had to know.

It would probably be smart to get out ahead of this new trouble, because he knew all about Morgan's ex. Cece was capable of just about anything.

Buck sighed and rubbed his eyes. He could write a book about Cece's antics. There had been plenty of them. She'd borrowed money from everybody in the family, and when they'd gotten tired of loaning it, she'd snitched money from their wallets. She'd been so bold and shameless that he'd wondered if she was on drugs. Her favorite trick had been to embarrass Morgan by strutting through the house as nearly naked as she could, especially during family celebrations.

Buck snorted in disgust as he remembered the time Cece had propositioned him on Morgan's birthday. She'd invited herself right into his living room while Morgan's party was going on downstairs. She'd been wearing nothing but a tiny bikini and a smile.

Buck frowned and closed his eyes. He could see her yet, see the smug little smirk on her face as she purred:

How about it, Buck? We've got a few minutes. Morgan's busy at the party. Aren't you a little bit curious about me? I know I am about you.

He'd been thunderstruck by her nerve, but when the shock faded enough for him to talk, he growled:

Get out of my place and don't you ever come back. If I didn't care about my brother I'd march you downstairs right now and tell him and everybody else what a piece of work he married.

Buck sputtered a bit and shook his head. Him and Cece hadn't got along so good after that, and if he'd had his way, he would've kicked her all the way from the front door to the interstate.

Well, that hadn't happened as fast as he'd wanted, but Morgan was better off now.

Way better off; or at least, he had been until now.

Buck frowned and rubbed his brow. He'd pay Cece to go away if she'd only stay gone, but he'd rather pay Eugene to make her do it.

When Eugene solved a problem, it stayed solved; and so he reached for the phone, punched a few buttons, and swiveled around to stare at the wall. A few seconds later Eugene's harried voice barked, "Hello, Buck. How's things up at the Seven?"

Buck got up, leaned over, and pushed his office door closed before replying quietly, "I wish I could say everything was good, Eugene.

"This is just between me and you, now. We got trouble with Morgan. He doesn't know I'm talking to you, and if you tell him I called, I'll say you're the biggest liar in the world."

Eugene's dry laughter crackled through the line. "I understand. How can I help you, Buck?"

"Cece's back," Buck drawled in a sour tone.

"Of course," Eugene sighed. "What does she want this time?"

"Well, money," Buck retorted, "but she hasn't showed up to ask for it yet. Morgan's all twisted up because she told him that he's not Kit's father. He's worried she's gonna start another custody fight." He paused, then added, "what odds do you give her?"

Eugene's sigh deepened. "Well, for her personally, not good. She's already lost custody of Kit. But if another man can establish in court that he's Kit's biological father, then he might get visitation rights.

"Of course, if Morgan proves in court that he's Kit's biological father, that ploy falls apart. I'm assuming you think this is a trick to extort money from Morgan."

"You've met his ex," Buck retorted. "And I don't think it's extortion, I know. Is there some way we can keep Cece from getting at Kit? Morgan's worried sick that she's gonna show up and tell Kit he's not really a Spade."

There was a long silence on the other end of the phone. "If you had proof that she was deliberately using that threat to extort money from Morgan, a judge might revoke her visitation rights," Eugene replied slowly. "But even then, it's not a sure bet. Most judges are very reluctant to deny a mother visitation rights to her child. They usually only do it if it can be proven she poses a physical threat to the child. Drugs, alcohol, abuse. That sort of thing."

"Yeah," Buck grumbled. "I wish we had that kind of proof on Cece. I wouldn't put any of that past her."

"Well, short of that, you're not going to be able to deny her access to her son," Eugene informed him. "You can structure her visits. Limit them to certain days and places. Outside the ranch, if you don't want her coming there."

"That's not the issue," Buck growled, and swiveled slowly in his chair. "It's that she might torture Kit with her lies to get at Morgan. There's more than one kind of abuse, Eugene."

"Yes," he muttered, in a softer tone. "But if you're going to make that argument in a court, you'll have to prove it, I'm afraid."

"Yeah," Buck echoed regretfully. "Well, I'd be obliged if you'd mull it over, Eugene. We could sure use some good ideas right now."

"I'll go back over my notes from the custody suit," Eugene promised. "If I see something there I think would help, I'll call you."

"Thanks, Eugene."

Buck hung up the phone. Since he'd presented the legal problem to Eugene, the next best way he could protect Kit was to keep his mother from making a surprise visit. Force her to schedule her visits through Morgan, instead of just showing up at their door.

He turned back to his computer, opened the app to the ranch security gates, and checked one box out of a list of options.

He switched to a camera view of the main ranch entrance, and watched in satisfaction as the big iron gates slowly swung shut.

Now Cece wouldn't be able to crash in on them unannounced. It wasn't much; but it was the best he could do immediately.

Buck sighed and went back to his work, staring intently at a column of numbers on his computer screen. He was just about to scroll down when a soft chime alerted him that someone was at the front gate.

He tapped an icon, and his screen instantly expanded to a camera view of the ranch's ponderous front gates. A Mercedes convertible was parked outside them, and Buck stiffened to see his former sister in law frowning at the camera. She looked as flossy and as bad-tempered as ever in her designer sunglasses and jewelry, and her voice was sharp with irritation as she faced the camera.

"Let me in!" she demanded. "I know somebody up there can see me sitting here!"

Well, I closed those gates not a moment too soon, Buck thought in surprise. He leaned back in his chair and played with a pencil as Cece sat fuming outside the gates. "Open this gate!" she cried. "I'm Kit's mother and I have a right to see him. You can't keep me out!"

Buck grinned at the screen and crossed his arms in enjoyment as Cece gripped the steering wheel in fury. "I'll get a court order if I have to," she sputtered. "You can't keep me out!"

I can today, Buck thought, and watched in grim satisfaction as Cece jammed the convertible in reverse, turned around, and went roaring down the road in a cloud of exhaust.

His smile finally faded into a sigh, and he flicked the camera view off. Cece was back like the bad penny she was; and he hated to admit it, but she was going to get her way about one thing.

As much as he wanted to, he didn't have the legal right to deny her access to Kit.

But that locked gate had at least done some good. It had kept Cece from hitting Morgan with another nasty surprise when he was still shook up from the first one.

Buck shook his head. Compared to Morgan, he'd been lucky. The worst thing that had ever happened to him was when his first wife had died; but at least they'd been close.

And when he found love with Kate, he'd felt almost guilty for having been blessed twice, when poor, straight-arrow Morgan hadn't done anything wrong, but had been so snakebit anyway.

Buck glanced briefly toward the ceiling, thinking, *Thank you, Lord, for letting me find two good women.*

Watching his brother go through a bitter divorce, and then two custody fights just to keep his son, had shown just how wrong things could go when a man got mixed up with a bad woman.

Sadness curled across Buck's heart when he thought about it. Morgan's misadventure with Cece had ruined his life. He was a different man now. He'd always been quiet, but his trouble had made him withdraw deep into himself and his work. Morgan was pretty much living for Kit now, and not much else.

And now Cece was threatening to take Kit away from him, too; but just as a way of shaking him down again.

Buck's eyes narrowed as he stared at his computer screen. He knew he wasn't supposed to hate anybody, but Cece made that harder for him than anybody he'd ever met.

Buster Hogan had tried to steal their water and put them out of business; but even Buster didn't stick in his craw like Cece. Buster might be a snake and a thief, but he'd never tried to use a kid to twist money out of them.

Even Buster wouldn't dream of turning his own kid into a pawn.

The faint sound of childish laughter from the outer room pulled Buck up out of his chair. He walked out of his office and out into the main room of his apartment.

Kit was lying on the floor in front of the t.v. with his chin in his hands. He giggled as a cartoon cat and mouse chased back and forth, and Buck stared at him in pity.

"You hungry, pard?"

Kit shrugged one shoulder. "A little, Uncle Buck."

"Well, we can't have that," he replied. "How does a patty melt sound?"

Kit tilted his head to one side and squinted up at him. "What's a patty melt?"

Buck made a big surprised face, and Kit giggled. "What's a patty melt?" he echoed. "I'll show you. Come on out to the patio, and we'll fire up the grill."

Kit scrambled up from the floor and scampered across the room ahead of him, and Buck watched his nephew with compassion.

Kit turned a laughing face to him as he tugged at the glass patio door. "I like to cook out," he announced. "Larry used to cook hamburgers for us."

Buck stared at him in dismay. He didn't know exactly who *Larry* was, but odds were that he was one of the long line of men that Cece had brought home when she still had joint custody of Kit.

It was one of the reasons she'd lost custody.

"A patty melt is better than a hamburger," Buck told him, to steer the conversation away from Cece's boyfriends. "I'll prove it to you."

Kit plopped down into a lounge chair next to the pool, and a thoughtful look flitted over his face. "I liked Larry better than the other ones," he murmured in a quieter voice. "At least he made me hamburgers. The others just ignored me. Or were mean."

Buck had been leaning over the grill, but his hand froze in the act of reaching for a spatula. He turned an anxious look on his nephew and weighed his next question.

"Mean?"

Kit kicked his feet. "Yeah. One of them locked me in my room all day. I had to beat on the door and yell to get them to open it."

Shock jumped up in Buck's heart, but he turned away and bit his lip. He told himself that it was over now, that it didn't help Kit to dwell on painful memories; but he slapped the spatula against the grill with a *clang*.

"You want tomato on your burger, buddy?"

"Yes, sir."

Buck wiped his hands on his jeans. "I'll go get the meat and the fixings. You just relax, I'll be back in two shakes."

He blew through the open door so fast that he raised a breeze behind him. He was still fuming when his cell phone buzzed, and he raised it to his ear with a frown.

"Yeah?"

Eugene's dry voice jumped out of the phone. "Hello, Buck. I just thought I'd touch base with you. Has Cece come by the house yet?"

Buck glanced over his shoulder. Kit was sitting in his lounge chair by the pool, kicking his brown heels back and forth.

"She came by the other day," Buck replied quietly, "but the gates were closed and she didn't get in. She claimed she was coming to see Kit. She threatened to slap us with a court order."

Eugene grunted. "My advice would be for Morgan to meet with her and set up a visitation schedule. He's not going to be able to keep her away from her son."

Buck frowned. "There must be some way. Kit just told me that one of Cece's boyfriends shut him up in his room all day, and he had to beat on the door to get out!" he retorted. "Can we get that on tape and use it as evidence of abuse?"

There was a long silence. "You might," he replied at last, "but it probably wouldn't be enough to get the result you want." The attorney sighed and admitted, "I think the best thing you can tell Morgan now is to accept that Cece has a right to see her son. He might want to have a heart-to-heart with Kit beforehand, to prepare him for what his mother might say."

Buck's heart sank as he imagined that scene. "You haven't found *anything* that might help us?" he pressed.

"Nothing so far," Eugene answered. "Nothing so damning that it would tempt a judge to revoke Cece's visitation rights."

Buck pulled a hand over his face. "All right, Eugene. Thanks for calling."

"I'll keep you posted," the attorney answered, and the line went dead.

Buck went to replace his phone in his jeans pocket; but on second thought, it was probably time to come clean with Morgan, to tell him what Eugene had said.

And so Buck tapped Morgan's number onto the screen, braced himself to be called a meddling pain, and waited.

Chapter 18

Morgan scowled into his phone and barked: "You did *what?*"

Buck's voice on the phone replied instantly. "I called Eugene about your problem with Cece," he insisted.

Morgan scowled at the paneled wall of his living room. "I never asked you to do that, Buck," he grumbled. "As mad as I am at Cece, this is between her and me. It ain't any of your business!"

"I called a lawyer because I know that Cece isn't going anywhere," his brother explained. "Eugene's the only one who can make her go away."

"No one can make Cece go away," Morgan grumbled. "That's the truth, no matter what Eugene told you."

Buck's voice held grudging acknowledgment. "That may be true. Eugene said that it would take a miracle to get a judge to deny her visitation. He said you need to settle down to it, Morgan. Maybe have a talk with Kit beforehand. Kinda brace him."

Morgan closed his eyes and fumed silently, but Buck was right. There was no way he could keep Cece away forever.

Buck's voice rattled on. "Eugene recommended you bite the bullet and set up a visitation schedule." He paused before adding: "The rest of us would appreciate it if you could make it somewhere away from the main house."

"I'm hanging up now, Buck."

Morgan jammed a thumb on the phone's screen and tossed it away, fuming. Buck meant well, but he had a habit of taking too much on himself.

He was going to solve his problem in his own way.

He hated the thought of taking a paternity test. It was humiliating, and Kit might misunderstand why he'd taken it. Kit might think that the test results mattered to him, and they didn't.

But if the test results proved his paternity, it would put a screeching stop to Cece's latest nonsense. It would take away the threat she was holding over his head. It would take away her incentive to traumatize Kit.

It might send her away for good; but even if it didn't, at least it would send her away for a while. He was willing to do far more than just endure humiliation to keep his son.

But one thing held him back.

The thing that had kept him from taking the test so far, was the nagging fear in the back of his mind.

What if a paternity test shows that I'm not Kit's father?

Morgan sighed and pulled his hands over his face. As much as he hated to admit that possibility, it was real. The Lord only knew how many men Cece had slept with during their marriage. She'd cheated on him like she was trying to win a contest.

He knew that Kit looked like him and acted like him, and he believed Kit was his son: but he had to admit, even if only to himself, that it might be wishful thinking.

If Cece could prove another man was Kit's biological father, she might take Kit away, and then use him as a pawn. She could make him pay for access to his son, make him pay for years.

If it was only about the money, he could bear it, but if Cece succeeded, he might lose Kit altogether. Kit would be spending more time with his biological father.

Kit might even forget about him. It would be easy.

They'd only had five years together.

That possibility was so terrible that he couldn't bring himself to face it. Or at least, he didn't want to put himself through that kind of suspense unless it was necessary.

He was 99 percent sure that Cece was going to challenge his paternity. But until she did, there was still a tiny sliver of hope that she might go away, and he was clinging to it.

His phone buzzed again, and Morgan closed his eyes and ignored it. It was probably Buck calling back. Buck wanted him to talk to Eugene, but he wasn't going to, not now.

He knew what the first thing out of Eugene's mouth was going to be: *You need to prove that you're Kit's father.*

The phone kept ringing, and at last Morgan grumbled and reached for it: but to his shock, the number wasn't Buck's. He pressed the green button with a puzzled frown.

"Hello?"

Cece's demanding voice was like a slap across the jaw. "Morgan, I want to talk to you about Kit."

A thunderous frown pushed his brows into his eyes. "How did you get my number?" he demanded.

As usual, Cece didn't answer his question. She just plowed ahead. "Now I know my rights, Morgan. You can't keep me from seeing my son. Are you going to let me see him, or am I going to have to come back with my attorney?"

Morgan closed his eyes, imagining Kit's confusion to have his mother just suddenly reappear after ignoring him for months.

"Morgan, are you there?"

He took a deep breath and a tight grip on his patience. "All right, Cece. I'll meet you tomorrow at the park in town," he rumbled. "At noon, in that little brick gazebo. We can talk about it there."

There was a wary silence, but she finally replied, "Agreed, then. I'll see you there. Don't be late."

The line went dead, and Morgan closed his eyes and bit back the words that jumped to his lips. He turned off the phone and drifted over to the big glass wall on one end of his living room. Big white clouds sailed in an endless blue autumn sky; but he saw nothing but thunderclouds.

Help me Lord, he prayed.

Here we go.

Chapter 19

Morgan pulled the jeep into the parking space in the little park and killed the motor. It was a cool, overcast fall day, and the trees in the park were burnt orange and gold. As he watched, a breeze sent a shower of leaves fluttering down across the grass.

It was a pretty view, but he was in no mood for it. He'd arranged to meet Cece at the little brick gazebo in the far corner of the park. He'd chosen it because it was remote and usually empty, and he wanted privacy.

He strode down the little sidewalk, climbed the gazebo steps, and walked in. There was no one inside it and no one around, and he leaned back against one wall and settled in to wait.

Morgan leaned against the brick wall with his arms crossed and his eyes narrowed. He watched in frowning disapproval as a Mercedes convertible pulled up, and he stiffened to see his ex-wife and a strange man sitting in it. He scowled as they threw the doors open and climbed out.

He hadn't seen Cece for awhile, and she hadn't changed one iota. There wasn't one blonde hair out of place on her perfectly-coiffed head; she was wearing a designer pantsuit of pale yellow linen; and she was wearing a diamond tennis bracelet and earrings.

Morgan grumbled. He could barely stand the sight of a fashion model anymore, because of her.

Cece slammed the car door shut and charged him with a staccato drumming of her high heels. Her eyes were obscured by oversized sunglasses, but her chin was jerked high and her mouth was pulled tight. Morgan straightened up to his full height and caught himself tensing up as she approached.

"Well it's about time you answered my calls!" she snapped. "I've been trying to get in to see my son for weeks now. You needn't think you're going to lock me out again, Morgan! I'll get a court order if I have to!"

Morgan took a deep breath and a fresh grip on his patience. He knew it wouldn't do any good to argue with Cece about visitation rights, because that wasn't what she wanted. Not really. And he didn't see the need to dance around the real issue.

"What do you want, Cece?" he growled. "It's not to see Kit, or you would've shown up long before now. I don't have the time or the patience to play games with you, so let's cut to the chase."

As he spoke, the man came walking up, and Cece turned to gaze at the tall, dark man as he approached.

"How convenient," she quipped. "Here comes the chase right now."

Morgan crossed his arms and frowned as the man straightened the cuffs and jacket of his business suit, then sauntered up to slide an arm around Cece's shoulders. They both turned to face him.

"This is my husband, Roger Tomlinson," she announced. "We've been together for years. Roger and I were having an affair during the last few years of our marriage, Morgan."

Morgan put on his grimmest poker face, because anger flared up in him again, and that was what Cece wanted. She wanted to get him rattled, make him mad. And when he thought about where she was going with this, he did get mad; but he wrestled his anger down.

He needed to keep his head.

Roger was a slick, good-looking man in a linen suit and a silk tie. Roger's eyes flicked over him with the same expression as if he'd noticed a rip in his jacket.

"I'll come right to the point, Mr. Spade," he announced. "Cece and I think that I'm Kit's father, and I'm going to sue for custody of my son."

Morgan straightened up and felt his face going hot. Rage jumped up in him like fire, and it was all he could do not to put his fist into the snake's gleaming white teeth. He looked down at the ground and drew a deep breath before replying:

"Well, you can do whatever you like, Mr. Tomlinson," he drawled. "But the court's given me custody of Kit for a real good reason." His eyes moved to Cece's gloating face, and her smile froze as they made eye contact. "The judge saw that Cece wasn't a fit mother. If you want to be her fool, that's up to you. But you better be prepared to fight in court.

"Because Kit is mine, and I'll sue you as many times as I have to, to keep my son." He stepped up a pace, and the other man straightened up.

"You better have the stomach for a long court fight," Morgan growled. "Because I'll keep going until one of us is broke."

Cece's rapacious eyes flicked up to his, and she put up a hand in a calming gesture.

"Now we didn't come here to be unpleasant," she put in quickly. "Surely we can all work something out, for Kit's sake."

Morgan struggled, made a last-ditch attempt to control his temper, and failed.

"When did you ever care about Kit?" he demanded. "This is the first time you've even come to the ranch since I got custody. I didn't complain about it, because Kit was better off without you. But don't try to pretend you're seen the light now, Cece. I know why you're here."

Cece pulled a tissue out of her bag and dabbed her eyes. "Losing custody of my son was hard," she sniffed. "You think I don't have feelings, Morgan, but I do." She looked up at him in appeal. "Can't you allow that I want to see my son, and that Roger wants to be a part of his life?"

She shot him another glance. "We can all be civilized about this," she went on, and licked her lips. "Maybe we can come to some kind of settlement."

Morgan narrowed his eyes. "All you want is to see some money, you greedy little heifer," he growled. "That's the only thing you care about. The court gave you visitation rights," he grumbled, "I can't do anything about that. But since you want to pretend that you care about your son, here are my terms. If you want to see Kit, it's going to have to be outside the ranch, and no more than two days a week." His eyes moved to the other man's.

"And if I find out that you've brought *Roger*, or any of your other men with you when you're with my son, I'll go to court to have you kicked so far out of his life that he won't remember what you look like!"

"*Oh!*"

Cece gasped and turned on her heel, and Roger shot him an insulted look, before they both stormed off to their car. Roger opened the door of his car and yelled, "I'll see you in court!"

"You come on," Morgan growled, and watched in scowling anger as they pulled out and scratched off down the road.

But after they'd gone, Morgan's shoulders dropped and he slumped against the brick wall. He looked down at his hands.

They were trembling.

Oh Lord, he prayed, *I was afraid of this, and now it's happened. I'm going to have to take a paternity test.*

But what if I'm not Kit's father after all?

Morgan looked up at the sky, then closed his eyes. He couldn't imagine losing Kit. If he did, he'd lose his mind.

He pulled a hand over his mouth and struggled to control his emotions. His anger was melting into something like panic.

Lord, please. I have to be Kit's father. I have to be.

He pushed off the wall and dragged himself back to the Jeep. He was swept by the need to see Kit, to pull him close, to hold him.

He'd do what he had to do later; but that afternoon, he just wanted to spend time with his son.

He drove back home like a zombie, on autopilot; and when he walked into his apartment at last, Kit was there in the living room waiting for him. Kit raised his tousled head from watching cartoons.

"Hey Daddy."

Morgan cracked a smile that probably looked as crooked as it felt. "Hey buddy."

He sank down onto the couch beside Kit and put an arm around his son's shoulders. Buck had said something about talking to Kit. About preparing him.

It was probably a good idea.

He tightened his fingers around Kit's shoulder. "Buddy, I have some news for you," he murmured, and turned off the television with a flick of the remote. Kit turned curious eyes on his face, then frowned.

"What's wrong, Daddy?"

Morgan tried to smile. "Wrong? What makes you think that something's wrong?"

Kit's eyes searched his face. "I don't know. You look sad."

Morgan did his best to project a confidence he wasn't feeling. "Everything's fine, buddy," he murmured. "I just wanted to tell you that—that your Momma's going to be coming by," he added softly.

He scanned Kit's face keenly, and felt his heart contract to see his son's eyes cloud over. Kit was only five, and he'd already learned to doubt any promises about his mother.

"Really?"

Morgan put on a confident look that he hoped was reassuring. "That's right, bud. I talked to her today. She's going to be visiting soon. Won't that be nice?"

Kit's eyes dropped. "I guess."

Morgan saw Kit's downcast eyes, the slight frown on his face. The doubt and reluctance on Kit's childish face was already like a knife in his ribs. He tried to imagine himself saying, *Your Momma might tell you a lie about me.*

She might say that I'm not your Daddy.

He imagined the look in his boy's eyes, and even the thought of it brought tears to his own. Morgan looked away, thinking, *I can't. I can't do it, at least not now.*

I won't do that to my boy unless I have to.

Not until the very last minute.

He rubbed his nose. "So, that's good buddy," he coughed. "You and your Momma will have fun together."

Kit looked up at him. "Are you coming, too, Daddy?"

Morgan looked away and coughed again. It took him a minute to reply, "No, buddy. I won't be coming. It'll be just you and your Momma."

"Oh."

Panic gripped Morgan again like a hand squeezing the blood out of his heart. His fear was showing him a future when he might have to schedule a visit with Kit.

His son, in everything but name.

He reached out to pull Kit close and smiled down into his eyes. "What say you and me get our fishing poles and go down to the creek. We'll catch some big fat trout and cook 'em in a pan."

To his relief, his son's eyes lit up. "Let's go!" he cried, and jumped out of Morgan's arms and off toward his bedroom. Morgan's eyes followed him fondly, and he called out, "Be sure to put on your bathing suit, buddy. We might do a little swimming."

As soon as Kit disappeared through the hall archway, Morgan's smile faded and his shoulders slumped. He knew he should be on the phone to Eugene, should be busy plotting his legal strategy: but he couldn't make himself do it.

Something in his heart told him that he should just spend time with his boy.

Chapter 20

Heather slipped in between two racks of cotton tops and lifted one of the blouses. It was a pretty pink peasant number with a string tie at the neck, and Heather held it up to herself and turned to face a nearby mirror.

She turned this way and that. It had been awhile since she'd bought new clothes, but she was in a new job, and she wanted to look her best.

Even in her off time.

She was browsing in a little dress shop in town on her day off. It was a quaint boutique in a 100-year-old brick storefront, with a high ceiling and a big front window. It was a pretty fall day, crisp and cool and fair, and the town outside was bustling. Heather glanced up through the window, then glanced again.

She put the blouse back on the rack and drifted to the window. The blonde woman she'd seen at the cafe was back in town. She watched as the sleek Mercedes convertible parked on the curb outside.

The woman was apparently Morgan's ex wife, and to Heather's surprise and dismay, Kit was with her.

A pang branched through Heather's heart, because for some reason, she found the sight distressing. Morgan's ex Cece hadn't struck her as patient or kind, and even from across the street, she could tell that Kit was uncomfortable. He was sitting quiet and still in the passenger seat and he was staring straight ahead with his shoulders high and stiff.

It's none of my business, Heather told herself, but she stood there with her hands pressed against the pane in fascination. Her heart went out to Kit; and she couldn't help wondering if his outing with Cece meant that Morgan was reconciling with his ex-wife.

She slipped out of the front door and pretended to window shop on the sidewalk. Heather watched as Kit's elegant mother wriggled out of the car and swung the door shut. Cece tugged her skintight green dress straight, stood there for an instant to catch her breath, then called, "Stay here for a minute while Momma gets her cigarettes."

Cece teetered off to the little pharmacy in her high heels, leaving Kit alone in the car. Heather bit her lip. Kit sat there, motionless and silent, like a bird in the presence of a cat.

A heaviness almost like grief settled down on Heather's heart. *Poor little boy,* she thought. *He doesn't look happy to be with his Mom, but maybe they're just getting reacquainted.*

And so much for Morgan Spade, she thought sadly. *I guess he just kissed me because he got carried away by that football game.*

Looks like he's getting back with his ex, so I can stop daydreaming about him.

Heather sighed and cast one last glance at the convertible. As she watched, Cece emerged from the pharmacy with a pack of cigarettes in her hand. She paused on the sidewalk, lit one, and blew an exasperated puff of smoke straight up into the air before returning to the car.

"All right, Momma's back," Heather heard her say, and she tilted her head to one side to watch as Cece pulled the door open again and almost fell into it on her shaky high heels.

Heather frowned in concern. The scene struck her as odd somehow, almost painful to watch; but then again, that might be because she wasn't exactly an objective observer.

She was a woman who just found out that her crush was unavailable.

She watched as the convertible swept down the road; but Kit's dark eyes met hers for a split-second as they passed, and a flash of recognition lightened his face before the convertible was gone.

Sweet little boy, Heather thought wistfully, as she watched him go. *I hope things work out between him and his Mom.*

The second wish was a bit harder, but it was the Christian way, and so she added:

I hope things work out between his Mom and his Dad. I hope they patch things up and become a family again.

But as she drifted down the sidewalk, Heather couldn't shake the nagging feeling that something was off. She couldn't put her finger on just what: Cece's shrill voice, Kit's stiff body language, maybe his silence.

I hope I'm wrong, Heather thought wistfully. *Maybe I am.*

But her eyes followed the convertible in worry as it slowly shrank into the distance.

Chapter 21

Morgan rubbed his gloved hands together against the morning chill and gazed out across the Seven's rolling northern pastures. As he watched, a knot of hands on horseback herded five hundred Longhorns down from the hills and into a narrow valley.

They were moving their cattle down from the high, windswept summer grazing hills to the lower and more sheltered pastures at the southern end of the ranch. Morgan watched closely as the hands funneled the herd to the south. He wanted to get those cows down into the tree-lined valleys, where they'd be more protected from the autumn chill.

Morgan squinted up at the sky with a frown. It was a cold, cloudy day. The clouds were a heavy, leaden gray, threatening of a downpour to come.

He shifted impatiently in the saddle. The air already smelled of rain, and the breeze was picking up. It played with Cochise's dark mane and ruffled the tops of the distant trees.

Morgan turned up his jacket collar, pulled down his hat, and nudged Cochise into motion. His stallion moved a bit stiffly, as if it was gripped by the cold, and Morgan let his horse take its time.

One of the riders broke from the others and moved up the slope to meet him. It was Hank, and Morgan nodded in greeting as his top hand walked his horse close.

"These are the last ones," Hank announced. "We'll have them down into the south pasture by noon."

Morgan's eyes flicked to the sky. "Get them under cover as soon as you can. It looks like it's about to open up, and I'd rather have them dry, than to have them in the south pasture today."

"We'll take them down to the trees just beyond that hill," Hank replied and pointed to a faint line of green just above the southernmost rise. "They should stay pretty dry there if it comes a soaker."

"Thanks," Morgan told him.

"Yep," Hank replied, and turned his horse's head. "Once we get 'em in, the next thing on the docket is moving the fall calves down to the barn pens. They're getting their first round of vaccines today."

Morgan nodded in approval. Heather had scheduled a half-day to get the usual vaccinations done. He had to admit that she was doing a great job so far, but her size still worried him.

He fretted about her getting gored or trampled by a cow if things went wrong, and the better he got to know her, the more he worried about it.

He still wasn't sure Heather was going to work out as their vet, or if she even should.

Hank's voice broke in on his thoughts. "You need anything else from me?"

Morgan shook his head. "You go on. I'm just looking around this morning."

Hank raised a hand in farewell and sent his horse down the slope. Morgan watched him go, then turned Cochise north, up the slope of the hill.

The wind picked up, and Morgan rode into it, with his head down and his shoulders hunched. The weather matched his mood that day. He just wanted to get away from everything.

To let the rain and the wind wash the trouble out of his heart.

Cochise moved along, one step after another, and the first big raindrops spattered the rocky ground. A fresh blast of wind swept them, followed by a hail of rain. Morgan let it roll over him, let it roll off his hat, off his rain jacket. Water spilled off the edge of his hat as he watched another gray wave come on like a wall.

Morgan hunkered down in the saddle and let it come. There was something about the rain that was cleansing to him, something about being out in the elements that made him feel at home. He'd gotten that from Big Russ, and he intended to pass it down to Kit, once he got old enough.

There was something healing about being under the open sky, and it worked for him no matter what the weather was, or the season. It worked in the pouring rain, and the driving snow, and the baking heat.

Carson always laughed at him for it, and Jesse told him he was a fool. That was because they were horsemen, not cattle men. Being a cowboy meant you had to be out in it; and after awhile, you wanted to be.

The rain poured down, and Morgan lifted his face and let it roll down into his eyes and over his cheeks. The touch of the rain was cool and wild, pure and straight from the sky, and its simplicity helped him think.

He thought about his life, about his home and his son, about what he wanted.

He was tired of fighting, but he meant to go on fighting. He'd defend his son against anything that might jump out of the brush to threaten him; a rattlesnake, or a coyote, or a cougar.

That was easy.

But now Kit was being threatened in a complex way; and he was a plain man.

Morgan urged Cochise over the rocky crest of a high, barren ridge, through rushing rivulets of milky brown water. It was dangerous terrain, but both he and his horse knew it well enough to walk it in the pouring water.

Morgan swayed in the saddle as Cochise picked his slow way through the rocks and down a steep decline. Big Russ had always told him that the best way to solve a problem was to get off alone somewhere. To do your best to clear your mind, and let the answer come to you.

Big Russ had said that it had always worked for him; and it had most always worked in his own life.

But now, as the rain splashed off his shoulders and ran down his face, Morgan wondered if it was going to work for him this time. He was trying to clear his mind, but his mind was a jumble of thoughts and faces.

Kit's trusting face, and Cece's twisted one, and even Heather Weston's, looking at him like he was a lame horse.

Sometimes he felt like one.

But one thing was sure: he was going to do whatever it took to protect his son.

Kit was all he had; and if Cece or her husband wanted him, they were going to have to climb over him.

Chapter 22

"I found him tangled up in a barbed wire fence," Hank mumbled, and rubbed his nose. "Thought I'd bring him by and see if you could doctor him up."

Heather slipped her hands into leather gloves and reached for the small brown owl that Hank was holding. "Careful now," he warned. "He's cranky."

The owl struggled as she took it and opened its mouth to screech in protest; but Heather smiled at its outraged face.

"We'll fix you right up, sweetie," she crooned, and looked up to see Hank grinning at her.

She sputtered and added, "I mean the *owl.*" She lifted it up and scanned its wings. "It looks like one of his wings is broken. I'll take him back to the surgery."

"Thanks, Heather."

"Sure. I'll let you know how he does." Heather moved back to the surgery, opened a big cage, and placed the owl gingerly on a perch. It shook itself out, bent down, and screeched at her.

The bell over the front door tinkled, and Heather stripped off the gloves and walked back to the front, expecting to see Hank leaving.

But what she saw instead was that same tall, dark shadow in the doorway. Heather's heartbeat quickened, and she tucked a sprig of hair back from her brow.

Morgan swiped off his hat as he entered, and his expression looked a bit chagrined. Heather felt her own face going warm, and reflected ruefully that it was a bit awkward to go back to business with Morgan after they'd kissed one another.

"Hello, Heather."

"Hi."

"I just dropped by to hear about what's going on," Morgan mumbled, and stuck his hands in his jeans pockets.

Heather's eyes flicked over the planes of Morgan's face, and for an instant she felt the same tingling his lips had caused as they moved over hers; but another glance at him banished her high school flutters.

There was that same indefinable sadness in his eyes that she'd noticed when they first met. It was heavy on him that day, and she instantly brightened in an effort to banish it.

"Well, you just missed Hank. He brought me an owl that got caught in a fence," she smiled. "I was just putting him up when you came in. I patched up one of the barn cats who lost a fight with another barn cat, I'm tending a couple of calves with colic, and you know about the mares."

Morgan nodded and shot her a serious glance. "Yes, I do. You did a good job, Heather."

Heather went warm with pleasure at the compliment. "Thanks, Morgan."

"Let me take a look at those calves you got."

"Sure."

Heather turned to lead the way through the office and back to the big pen outside the back door. She unlocked the gate, and Morgan walked into the pen and inspected two fat brown calves.

Heather opened a cabinet and pulled out two big plastic bottles. "You want to help me feed them? It's about lunch time."

Morgan reached out and Heather handed him one, and he knelt down in front of the closest and stuck the bottle into its open mouth.

Heather laughed as the calf sucked at the bottle loudly and rolled its brown eyes. She knelt down to offer the bottle to the other calf and patted the calf's smooth head.

"They look good," Morgan observed quietly. "Are they on the mend?"

"I'd say so," Heather told him, and glanced at his calf. "They were a little bit croupy at first, but their lungs are looking better now. The last x-ray looked almost clear. I'd say give them another day or two, and they'll be back to their Mammas."

"Sounds good." Morgan raised his head to look at her. "Is there anything you need, anything you want to ask me?"

Heather glanced at him wistfully, thinking, *Yes. I want to ask why you look so sad. I want to ask if you're back with your ex. I want your life story and all your dreams.*

She shrugged and glanced away. "I think I'm good." Her eyes returned to his and she added, "But I'd still like for us to have lunch. Get to know one another a bit."

To her disappointment, Morgan looked away. "I'll have to see if I can get away sometime," he rumbled, and stood up abruptly. He tossed the empty bottle down and clapped his hand clean. "Everything looks good, then. If you think of anything you need, just let me know."

He walked back into the office, and Heather watched his broad back retreating in helpless regret. Morgan Spade was a tall, rugged cowboy with a gravelly voice and dark, scruffy hair. He was the most exciting man she'd ever met, and he'd kissed her in a way that guaranteed she was going to dream about him.

But he was unavailable; or at least, it sure looked that way.

Heather stood up, patted the calf's head, and locked the pen door behind her. She followed Morgan into the office and out into the lobby.

Morgan turned in the front door, set his hat back on his head, and put a hand on the knob.

"I'll be seeing you, Heather."

Yeah, she thought wistfully, and gave him a weak smile.

"Bye, Morgan," she murmured, and watched as he turned and walked out. She drifted to the door and waved as he looked up from his car; then turned back inside.

Chapter 23

Cece clasped her hands nervously and paced back and forth across the hotel suite. A big picture window overlooked the interstate in the distance, and a luxurious pool area two stories below.

Her elegant companion stood at the window smoking and gazing off into the distance.

"Roger, I'm having second thoughts about this," she told him, and stopped pacing to throw him a pleading look. "Of course I want the money, but even if we establish you're Kit's father, this is going to take a long time. I know Morgan, and he means what he says. He'll fight like a tiger for Kit."

Roger half turned to look at her, cigarette in hand. "Won't you?"

Cece went red to the roots of her hair, and she pinched her lips into a tight, angry line. "I already have, haven't I?" she snapped, and then took a fresh grip on her patience. "But that's not the issue," she insisted. "I'm looking at the risk-reward here. We could be in court for years. And if we win, then it'll be more negotiation, more time, more wrangling with Morgan for money and access to Kit."

Roger turned back to the window. "So?"

Cece's eyes narrowed as they rested on his back. "So I'm not sure I want to do that," she declared. "I've been in court, it's a massive pain and a time suck and—"

She stopped and put a hand to her throbbing brow, and Roger glanced at her, tossed away his cigarette, and walked over to take her by the shoulders.

He stared down into her eyes and lifted her chin. Cece gazed up at him pleadingly, and he smiled at her.

"I know you're tired," he murmured. "You've been through hell, darling. You've had to fight one of the richest and most powerful families in Texas. You're amazing." He leaned in to kiss her gently, and Cece closed her eyes.

"You deserve to see your son," he whispered. "And as Kit's mother, you deserve your share of the Spade money. You've contributed to Kit's well-being."

Cece shot him a worried look, and he smiled again. "You're just rattled, baby," he chuckled. "You're upset, and I don't blame you after the way they treated you. But we've come this far. We can't stop now."

Cece pulled out of his arms and paced to the far wall. "I don't know, Roger," she fretted. "Kit is older now. He remembers things better. I don't want him to—to think poorly of his mother."

Roger walked over to her with a frown. "Hey, hey," he murmured, and turned her to face him. "Kit has no reason to think badly of you," he soothed. "Except for the lies Morgan's been telling him about you. If we get custody, then Kit will believe what *we* tell him."

Cece looked up at him and half-shrugged. "Maybe," she muttered. "But we're looking at a long, drawn out court battle. Don't forget, they have the best lawyer in Texas. *Eugene*," she drawled, and made a disgusted face. "That scruffy little weasel dug up everything I ever did and presented it in court for the world to see. It was humiliating, Roger."

"None of the Spades are saints, either, Cece," Roger soothed, but she turned away impatiently.

"Well, they won custody of Kit, that's all I know," she snapped. "So now I have to beg and scrape and go where I'm not wanted to maintain contact. I hate it, Roger. I'd like to tell them all where to go and how fast to get there."

He burst out laughing and turned away. "I'm sure," he sputtered. "But we have to go where the money is, don't we?"

Cece grumbled and gnawed on a pink, manicured nail. "There must be a faster way, Roger," she muttered. "I'm not up for a five-year slog. Why should I be, if we can think of another way?"

Roger shrugged and threw a hand in the air. "Fine. If you've got a better idea, let's hear it."

Cece shook her head. "I didn't say I had a better idea," she complained. "I'm saying that I don't like this one. I let you talk me into this, Roger, but you're not the one doing all the work. I'm the one having to face Morgan and his brothers. They're all right there in the house with him, and they all hate me!"

"What if they do?" Roger replied softly, and took her by the arms. "You're Kit's mother. They can't change that, and they can't deny it. You may not have custody, but you have visitation rights. You can use that to work on Kit. Get to Morgan through him!"

Cece threw off his arm angrily. "Don't try to manage me!" she snapped. "This is going to be done my way, or not at all, Roger. You're not running the show here. Don't forget that you need me," she warned him.

He frowned at her. "Baby," he murmured, "we're a team, you know that." He reached out for her and she backed away, but he reached for her again.

He put his hands on her shoulders and kissed her cheek. She turned her head impatiently, but allowed him to kiss her again.

"I'm not changing my mind, Roger," she told him softly, then turned her eyes to his. "But I wonder if this way is going to be as good as we think."

He scanned her eyes and seemed to recognize the look in them. "Okay," he agreed slowly. "If you want to change it up, we'll do something different."

"Something faster, anyway," she muttered, and Roger laughed and kissed her.

"Patience never was your strong suit," he sputtered. "But maybe you're right. We don't necessarily have to follow through with the threat of a custody lawsuit. Morgan might fork over money to avoid one, if I turn out to be Kit's father."

"When will you get the test results back?"

Roger drifted back to the window and scanned the northern horizon in the direction of the Spade Ranch. "A week, they said. Maybe ten days, it depends."

Cece tossed her head. "Well, we have a fifty-fifty chance," she muttered. "With any luck, we'll be able to use it. But even if the test's negative, we still have time. I know Morgan. He won't want to take a paternity test."

Roger sputtered scornfully. "Is he that sure he's not the father?" he scoffed.

Cece shot him a green glance. "He'll worry about Kit finding out," she spat. Her glare gradually softened, and she turned away.

"He won't take the test until he has no other choice," she added softly. "So we have a little time to come up with a smarter plan." Her eyes returned to Roger.

"Think of one!"

Chapter 24

Morgan climbed up into the saddle and glanced over Cochise's twitching neck at Kit. He was sitting on his pony, all tricked out with a cowboy hat and boots.

Morgan gazed at Kit fondly. He was wearing a little black Stetson and a black shirt to look like him, and his eyes were shining with excitement.

"Are we all ready to go?" Morgan asked.

"Ready!" Kit cried. He was astride a pony as black as Cochise.

"All right then." Morgan nudged Cochise out of the stable yard and into the road beyond. It was a pretty fall day, cool and crisp and clear, with orange and brown leaves skittering across the drive as their mounts clopped along.

Morgan put on a smiling face for his son, and they were going to have a happy day; but he knew he was indulging himself. He should be at home plotting his next legal move, but he just couldn't get his head on straight.

For some reason, he hadn't been able to call Eugene. All he wanted to do was spend time with Kit.

Buck had been up in his grill about it.

Again.

Morgan, he'd urged, *you're walking around here like a zombie. That's understandable, but you don't have time to wallow around in it, buddy.*

You want me to take care of this, I will.

He'd told Buck to let it go, and they'd almost got into a fight about it. Buck's heart was in the right place, but it was just plain none of his business, and he'd told him so.

Not that telling Buck that ever did any good. He'd already called Eugene once.

Morgan closed his eyes and willed himself to push his worries to the back of his mind. He had a fine, sunny day to spend with Kit, and he wasn't going to let anything spoil it.

He reached down to pat Cochise's gleaming shoulder as they moved. "You sleepy, old man?" he murmured, and the inky stallion tossed its proud head. It seemed to him that Cochise was a bit slow that day, but on the other hand, his horse was thirteen years old. Not exactly a colt anymore.

He pushed it out of his mind and half-turned in the saddle to ask, "Which way you want to go today, Kit—down by the creek, or up into the hills?"

"Hills!" Kit cried, and Morgan turned around and winked at his son.

"Hills it is, then." He turned Cochise to the left, off the road into the grassy meadow beyond the barn.

The oak trees on the edge of the barnyard were a dull red, and a shower of leaves fell all around them as they passed under their shade. The horses in the north pen lifted their heads and pricked their ears to watch them go. A brisk, chilly breeze swirled around them as Morgan led the way up the trail to the hills just beyond the main house.

He set a slow, easy pace for the pony to follow, through the grazing pastures around the massive red barn, under the thick branches of another ridge of ancient oaks, over a narrow creek.

Morgan turned Cochise around on the bank to watch over Kit as he led his pony down the gentle slope of the bank and into the shallow water.

Morgan watched with quiet pleasure as Kit took the crossing like an old hand. He was barely old enough to ride, but he was already confident in the saddle. His little Stetson, plaid shirt, and silver belt buckle made him look like a real cowboy, and he was on his way to riding like one.

He was going to be a great horseman.

Morgan waited for Kit's pony to reach the bank and climb its shallow slope safely; then he turned Cochise around to blaze a trail through a wild meadow filled with stirrup-high grass. It stretched out to the crest of the nearest hill, a football field away, and it rippled and swirled like the ocean under the breath of a cool fall breeze.

"Are we still on our ranch, Daddy?" Kit called, and there was a touch of fear in his voice. Morgan half-turned in the saddle to nod at him.

"We sure are, buddy. We aren't close to the boundary." He pointed to the horizon, far off over a range of low, rolling hills. "You see way out yonder in the distance?"

Kit leaned forward in the saddle and peered intently. "Yeah."

Morgan turned to smile at him. "Even that's still the Seven. Even that's not the boundary line."

"*Wowww,*" Kit breathed in little-boy awe.

"Yeah, this is your home, buddy," Morgan told him softly, as he sent Cochise through the grass. "This is your heritage. Your ancestors have lived on this land for hundreds of years. Some of 'em, longer than that."

He pointed to a low, indistinct lump under a ridge of oak trees. "I'm going to show you what I mean. You see that grassy bump up ahead?"

Kit sat up in the saddle. "Yeah."

Morgan reined Cochise to a halt. "All right. I'll race you to it!"

Kit laughed and urged the pony. "Ha!" he cried, and the pony broke out into as quick a trot as it was able to achieve. Morgan watched Kit shake the reins with a chuckle, then nudged Cochise after him.

"Ha ha, Daddy, I won!" Kit crowed, and turned the pony's head around in front of the grassy bump in the meadow. Morgan bowed his head in apparent defeat and grumbled, "Dang it! You were too fast for old Cochise today, all right. He *is* an old man, come to think of it."

He swung himself out of the saddle, tossed the reins over the stallion's neck, and walked over to help Kit down from his pony. "Come here, buddy. I want to tell you a story."

He lifted Kit from the saddle and carried him over to a log just in front of an old sod dugout. Morgan sank down onto the log, facing the dugout, and settled Kit on his lap.

He pointed a long finger at the sagging wooden door of the sod house. "You know what that is?"

Kit stared at the tumbledown wall of sticks and clumps of mud, and the grassy roof. He shook his head solemnly.

Morgan hugged him close. "This is a sod house," he said softly. "It was built on this land by Big Russ' great-grandfather, Daniel Spade. He came out west on a wagon train to build a life for himself and his family. When they first got here, they had nothing to live in except a covered wagon, and no money. So Daniel took a shovel and dug mud out of the creek we just came over, and he built a sod house for his wife and his babies to spend the winter in. This house."

Kit's dark eyes widened in awe. He extended a small hand to touch the rough wooden door.

"It's small," he murmured, and glanced up. "The roof has grass on it!"

"That's right," Morgan nodded. "It's small, and it ain't pretty. But that dirt roof helped to keep them warm when the cold wind came blowing over that hill, and when the snow started falling down." He turned to scan the lumpy sod walls.

"It helped them survive that first winter. And come spring, Daniel used his mules to plow a field, and he planted a crop. They filled up a root cellar to help them over the next winter.

"Daniel started out with nothing but his hands and the bare dirt. But bit by bit, he kept adding on, adding on. And he built a life for his family, right here on this land. And now, almost 2oo years later, his family's still living on it."

Kit frowned in confusion. "I thought we were Pawnee, Daddy," he objected, and Morgan smiled.

"That's right. Some of our ancestors were Pawnee. They've lived here even longer, for thousands of years. So our roots are deep in this land. This is our home."

Morgan paused and frowned. Pride and pain swirled in his chest as he went on, and his voice roughened with emotion.

"We've got the best of both worlds in us, Kit: red and white. We've got the love of this land in us like the Pawnee, and it's a fierce, deep-down love. We love the sky and the prairie and we live out on it."

He turned to caress Kit's cheek with his knuckle. "But we've got the grit and the heart of the pioneers in us, too. The courage to start out fresh and build a new life with nothing but your bare hands and the bare earth.

"Us Spades are tough, Kit," Morgan whispered, and tears started to his eyes as he stared down into his son's face. "And you're a Spade. Never forget that."

Kit's awed eyes widened. "I won't, Daddy," he breathed, and Morgan seized him and kissed his cheek fiercely, then closed his eyes and buried his face in his son's hair.

"I know it, Kit," he whispered. "You're my boy, you're a Spade, and nothing's *ever* going to change that."

Chapter 25

Heather crossed her arms over the stall door and stared at Ladybug and her new foal in approval. The ink-black colt was romping around his mother, bright-eyed and alert.

Heather raised her head to glance down the barn's central aisle. It was a clear, cool September morning, and the massive barn doors were closed to keep it warm inside. A dozen horses, mostly the eldest and the newborn, were snug in their stalls. The soft nicker of the horses, an occasional mew from the yellow barn cat, and the incoherent mumbling of a radio from the office down the way created a low, pleasant background hum.

Hank came ambling out of his office with a steaming cup of coffee in his hands. He nodded to Heather.

"Morning, Doc."

He walked over and stuck his head around the stall door. He watched as the colt bobbed his head and gamboled around his mother. "He's a fine one, ain't he?"

Heather smiled wistfully. "Beautiful. He's coming along nicely. Nursing well, nice and lively."

Hank sighed. "Well, this one and the Appaloosa are the last foals of the year. Morgan wanted some more by Cochise. He loves that horse."

Heather turned to glance at the stall down the way. Cochise's stall was empty.

"I don't see him," she murmured.

Hank pushed back and crossed his arms. "Morgan took him out this morning. Him and Kit went for a ride up in the hills." He shook his head and took a thoughtful sip of coffee. "Poor devil."

Heather tried to let that last, tantalizing comment die, but she found that she couldn't resist the temptation to cock her head and chirp, "What—what do you mean?"

Hank straightened up, as if he was worried he'd said too much, and Heather added quickly, "It's none of my business. I just wondered."

She rolled hopeful eyes to Hank's troubled face, and to her relief, he shrugged and mumbled, "Well, I guess there's no reason you shouldn't know, it ain't exactly a secret. Morgan's ex has come back, and he's all churned up about it." He shook his head regretfully.

"Oh?" Heather asked, and did her best to sound indifferent. "Are they getting back together or something?"

Hank sputtered. "That'll be the day," he scoffed. "They fought like wildcats over Kit, and Cece was such a—well, she lost custody of her son, and the mother almost never loses custody."

Heather digested the information, and finally ventured, "That is unusual. Did she suffer from—mental illness, or some emotional problem?"

Hank snorted. "She didn't suffer from nothing except being sorry," he retorted. "Now I know that isn't nice to say, but it's the truth."

Heather frowned and fell silent, and he went on, "I'm not guessing about it, either. I saw Cece Spade come sneaking out of this barn loft one morning early with her shoes in her hands. I never saw who she was with, but I know one thing. Morgan was in Amarillo all that week."

Heather's curiosity withered under this news, and she glanced at him in dismay. "Oh."

"That's a big part of why she lost Kit," Hank added, and pressed his mouth into a thin, disapproving line. "She had so many men in and out of her house that Kit might as well have been living in a hotel. The custody trial was the talk of the town!"

Poor Morgan, Heather thought in pity. *What a terrible thing to go through.*

Hank shook his head. "Now if you tell anybody I said that, I'll deny it, but that's why Morgan's distracted these days. Cece's back, and she's nothing but trouble to him."

Heather looked up at him quickly. "Oh, I won't repeat what you said. It's just such a shame," she frowned. "I didn't know things were so…bad."

Hank stepped back and took another sip of coffee. "They won't be for long," he opined. "The Spades are real good about jerking crooked things straight. And when you start talking about Kit, man, Morgan's going to bring it. They all will. You gotta say one thing for that family. They stick together."

Well, I'm glad of that, Heather thought sadly. *At least Morgan and Kit have the support of their family.*

What a terrible shame.

Heather frowned at the floor, thinking of her own interest in Morgan and Cece's relationship. She had almost been rooting for them to stay enemies, or at least broken up, and guilt burned her when she imagined how much Morgan and Kit had suffered.

It wasn't right to hope that about anyone, and she felt heartily ashamed of her selfishness.

"Well, I have to be getting back to the surgery," she told him suddenly. "I'll be back to check on the foals, of course, and if you need me for anything else, just call." She glanced up at Hank's freckled face and smiled faintly.

He looked a little confused at her abrupt exit, but he nodded. "Sure, doc."

Heather turned on her heel and walked out of the barn so briskly that she raised a breeze behind her. Her face was hot, and she was sure it was red.

She'd asked for that story, she'd been dying to know about Morgan and Cece, and now that she did, she wished she didn't.

It was like most gossip. It made her feel sad and sorry she'd asked; and she rubbed her hands as she hurried to her car.

Chapter 26

Buck yawned, lifted his morning cup of coffee to take a fortifying sip, and padded across the great room to his front door. He opened it up to see that just as usual, Miss Ada had paid a postman call.

She'd deposited his morning mail in a neat bundle on a table beside the door, and he grabbed it and turned back inside.

Buck sank into a chair in front of the fireplace, flicked on the gas jets with a remote, and stuck his feet up to the roaring blaze. It wasn't yet eight o'clock and it was still chilly in that big, drafty great room. A cold, cloudy sky stretched out on the other side of the big glass wall, and the rolling hills beneath them were turning a golden brown.

Buck sighed and sifted through the mail piece by piece. *Clothes catalog, shoe catalog, jewelry catalog.* Buck tossed the glossy magazines onto the couch, thinking that the complexion of his mail had changed a lot since he'd got married.

Junk mail, saddle catalog, Cattlemen's Association newsletter, handwritten envelope.

Buck frowned and reached for the envelope. It was addressed to *Buck Spade, Seven Spades Ranch,* in handwriting that he didn't recognize.

He tore the envelope open, thinking that it was probably crank mail. He got a lot of that: crazy business offers, photos from college girls wanting a rich sugar daddy, even occasional death threats. No one had taken a pot shot at him yet, but you could never say never.

Buck unfolded the letter and raised the cup to his lips, but his hand froze halfway to his mouth. His brows rushed together, and he set the cup down with an exclamation.

The letter was written in the same neat, precise hand as the envelope.

Dear Mr. Spade:

My name is Roger Tomlinson. You don't know me, but I am the husband of your former sister in law, Cece.

I am writing to you to deliver formal notice of a legal action I will soon be making that concerns you and your family. I am the biological father of Cece's son Kit, and I am soon going to court to establish my parental rights.

Morgan has shown himself unwilling to pursue an out of court settlement, so I feel I have no other choice.

Fire jumped up in Buck's heart and spattered over him like molten drops against a black caldera. His face twisted and he surged up off the couch with the letter crushed in one hand. He swept across the room, down the side hall, and into his bedroom.

Kate turned over in bed and blinked at him. "I must've overslept," she murmured, and rubbed her eyes. Buck didn't answer her. He scrabbled in his closet.

Kate sat up in bed with her red hair over one eye. She pushed it back and stared at him.

"Buck, what's wrong? You look furious!"

He grabbed a pair of boots out and threw them across the floor. "I'm taking the copter down to Dallas," he barked.

"Dallas? Why?"

"I'm going to see Eugene."

Kate stared at the jeans he'd tossed over a chair. "Well, if you're going to see your attorney, Buck, you should probably wear something nicer than a pair of ranch jeans."

He paused and turned to look at her. Kate's eyes held his, and he grumbled and reached for his suit.

"Can you tell me why you're in such a hurry, and why you look so angry?"

Buck tossed a jacket over the chair. "I'll tell you about it later. Right now I'm too mad."

Kate sat straight in alarm. "Buck, you shouldn't fly if you're beside yourself," she murmured.

"I'll get there in one piece, don't worry," he told her, and kicked the closet door shut. He shouldered out of his robe and pulled on a pair of dress slacks.

Kate watched in confusion as he dressed with short, jerky, angry movements and grabbed for his hat.

"Be careful, Buck."

Buck paused in the doorway, sighed, and looked back over his shoulder. Kate's worried eyes made him walk back to the bed, lean over, and kiss her.

"I'll be back this afternoon."

Chapter 27

Buck set the ranch helicopter down gently on the center of the helipad. He cut the motor, pulled his headset off, and unlocked his seat belt.

One of the helipad workers bent down and crouched under the rotors to offer a hand down from the copter. Buck used his hand to slap the man on the back and climb down onto the tarmac.

He glanced around briefly. Massive skyscrapers surrounded them, stretched out all the way to the horizon like a forest of glass and steel, because they were on the roof of one of the tallest buildings in Dallas.

"Welcome to Dallas, Mr. Spade," the man announced, and put a hand on his arm. "We'll take good care of your bird. Where can I help you go today?"

"The penthouse suite," Buck replied briskly, and unbuttoned his jacket. Kate had talked him into dressing up for the trip, but he hated monkey suits, and as soon as he was clear of the slowly-revolving rotors, he came out of his jacket and slung it over his arm.

The attendant led him across the tarmac to a small stairwell and unlocked the door. Buck walked in and found himself facing an elevator door.

The attendant leaned in to punch in a code, and the doors slid open silently.

"When you get to the penthouse floor, use this key card to open the door," the man told him. "Enjoy your time in Dallas, Mr. Spade."

"Thanks."

The man stepped back and Buck stepped into the gleaming metallic box. The doors slid shut silently, and the elevator sank gently and briefly; then a soft bell chimed and they slid open again.

Buck found himself in a paneled vestibule facing a pair of heavy wooden doors. He slid the key card into an electronic lock, and a loud *clank* announced that the way was clear. He pulled a door open and walked into a long, lushly-carpeted corridor.

He'd made a spur of the moment appointment with Eugene, and it was a tribute to their longstanding relationship that Eugene had cleared his lunch calendar to talk to him.

The handwritten letter, and the other papers that had been neatly folded inside that envelope, rustled faintly inside Buck's jacket as he walked to the end of the hall. He was mad enough to throw something, but he'd forced himself to push his anger down.

With something this important, he couldn't afford to lose his head.

There were a pair of glass doors at the end of the hall with the words *Clemmons, Butler and Shrewsbury* etched in frosted letters, and a secretary was seated at a big desk just beyond. As Buck approached, the secretary stood up and hurried over to open the door for him.

It was the door to Eugene's law firm—the priciest and most exclusive legal sanctum in Dallas.

"Good afternoon, Mr. Spade," she smiled. "Welcome back. Can I get you something to drink? We have a full bar."

Buck glanced at her smiling face. "Just a bottle of water, thank you."

"Mr. Clemmons is waiting for you. I'll show you in."

Buck took a deep breath and followed the young woman across the suite lobby and through a second set of wooden doors. They opened to reveal a conference room with a glass wall and a panoramic view of the Dallas skyline. Just in front of that view, a long, gleaming table stretched the length of the room, and a graying-middle aged man with wire glasses and suspenders was seated at it, waiting.

Buck's eyes zoomed to his lawyer. Eugene's bushy head was tilted to one side and his eyes were sharp and curious. Buck nodded to him as he pulled up a chair.

The secretary turned to a bar cart next to the door and poured out a glass of ice water and placed it on the table in front of Buck's chair. Buck turned his head to glance up at her. "Thank you."

Eugene waited until the secretary had seen herself out and closed the doors before muttering, "Well, Buck, you sounded pretty upset on the phone. What's the news?"

Buck lifted the glass to his lips and took a cooling sip of ice water. "I got an extortion letter from Cece through her new husband. Addressed to me, mind you, not to Morgan. She must've run into a dead end with him."

Buck reached into his jacket and pulled out a sheaf of papers. He picked one out and slid it across the table. Eugene reached out to pick it up. It was a color photo of a handsome, if slick-looking man.

Eugene glanced at it and slid it back. "Who's this?"

Buck rubbed his face with both hands. "It's a man named Roger Tomlinson. He's Cece's new husband. She married him a year ago."

Eugene frowned and settled into his chair. "Well, that's interesting, Buck—but why do we care? After all, your family has done its time with Cece and her men."

Buck glanced at his lawyer indignantly. "I care because Roger Tomlinson is a con man and a criminal. I paid for an internet search on him before I came down here. He almost did three years in Beaumont for scamming Social Security money out of little old ladies. They didn't have enough evidence to nail him, but I looked at the court transcripts, and I think he's as guilty as sin."

Eugene turned away to grumble under his breath, then added, "Cece and this prize winner deserve one another."

Buck reached into his jacket for another paper, and he threw it out over the table. "Eugene, the letter I got claims that Roger has taken a paternity test. They say it shows that he's Kit's biological father."

Eugene's mouth fell open in dismay, and he grabbed for the paper. His eyes scanned it hungrily.

Buck waved an arm in the air. "Of course it's all lies. Kit's the spit and image of Morgan. He's Morgan's son, anyone can see it!"

Eugene gave him a look of pity and let the paper fall down onto the gleaming table. "Have you told Morgan about this?"

Buck stared at him. "Of course not. He'd lose his mind!"

Eugene exhaled in relief. "I think that's wise," he replied slowly. "There's no reason to alarm him with this when it might not be necessary." He sighed and took off his glasses to rub his eyes. "Considering what you told me about Tomlinson's background, this could be fraud. I'm going to examine every aspect of his claim."

Eugene laced his fingers together, leaned across the table, and fixed him with an earnest stare.

"But no matter what this is, the best thing Morgan can do is take a DNA test," he urged. "That's the only thing that's going to settle the issue in the eyes of the law." Eugene sighed and slid his glasses back on. "It's going to be a hard sell, but you're his brother."

Buck shook his head in grief, because it wasn't going to make any difference what he or anybody else did to cushion the blow. Morgan was the most even-tempered, level-headed man in the world, except when it came to his son. If some jailbait con man tried to mess with Kit, Morgan was going to come unglued.

"Of course I'll try to get him to take the DNA test," Buck mumbled. "But I don't know if it'll work. I think Morgan's putting the test off because he's afraid of what it might show. Then too, trying to manage Morgan is like herding cats. He's independent. Stubborn, once he makes up his mind."

Eugene rubbed his eyes. "Well, like I said, this could be fraud, and it's certainly blackmail. There are things we can do to fight this. And I promise you I'll give this case my undivided attention for as long as it's needed," he promised and shuffled through his papers. "It looks like what Tomlinson took is a home test. Home tests aren't as reliable as DNA tests administered in a medical setting. They can be faked, though they're almost always faked in the other direction, by men trying to avoid paying child support."

Eugene lifted another paper from the table and scanned it. "Tomlinson's claiming paternity," he mumbled, "and he says he's going to sue for custody. He won't get that with his background, and he probably knows it. He's most likely aiming for visitation rights as a way to squeeze your family for money."

Buck closed his eyes and rubbed them with one hand. "Morgan's been through so much of this already. And even the thought of somebody else messing with Kit—I hate to think of what this is going to do to him."

"Well, we have Tomlinson's narrow escape from the pen," Eugene drawled. "He barely avoided going in for three years, so I have that. Of course we'll challenge the paternity test. Home tests aren't admissible in court anyway."

Buck frowned. "Then why—"

Eugene looked up over his glasses. "If this is an accurate result, he's likely to be the father on a second DNA test, as well. They're gambling that Morgan is going to be so afraid of that, and so tired of legal battles, that he'll negotiate. Their goal is clearly to keep their hands in your family's wallet." He shook his head.

"Morgan is going to have to take a paternity test, a real DNA test that'll hold up in court, and pray it shows that he's Kit's father."

Buck frowned at the table, and his mouth twisted bitterly. "Every time I think we've seen the last of that little gold digger, she shows up again to give us fits. And *that's* why she came by the house for the first time in a year, why she wanted to get Kit alone," he growled. "She wanted to swab his mouth and get a DNA sample for that test kit!"

"Most likely," Eugene agreed dryly, and gathered up the sheaf of papers across the table. "From what I've seen of Cece, she doesn't seem to be a very attentive mother."

"She's a heartless, blood-sucking leech," Buck grumbled, and picked up the nearest paper. It was Tomlinson's test results, and it read:

Odds of paternity: 99.2 percent.

He sighed deeply and threw the paper down. "All right, Eugene. I'll go back home and talk to Morgan. Thanks for your help, and for keeping the paternity test results quiet. You're right that Morgan doesn't need to get hit with that, not yet.

"Maybe it'll give us some time to test their claims, like you said."

Eugene gave him another sad, sympathetic look. His voice was quiet as he replied, "I'm going to put this test result under a microscope, Buck, I promise you that."

Buck leaned over and stuck out his hand, and Eugene shook it. "I know, Eugene. We sure appreciate it. If there's anything you need from us, just let me know. You can call or come by the house any hour of the day or night."

He turned to leave, then turned back to add: "And you're going to have to go through me. When Morgan hears about this test result, he's not going to be fit to talk to.

"He's gonna be a crazy man when he finds this out."

Chapter 28

Morgan tugged Kit's pale blue pajama top over his head, pulled it down, then answered his phone with one hand.

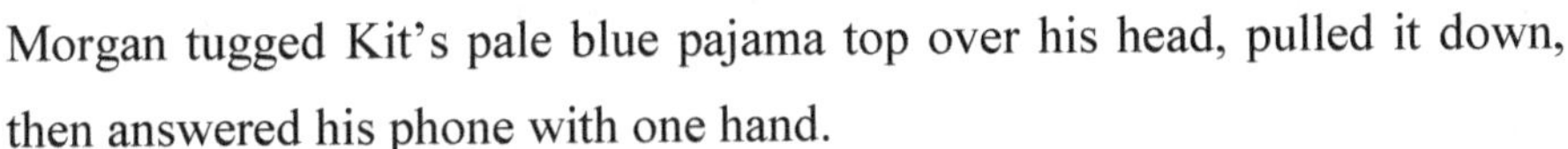

"Go and brush your teeth, buddy," he murmured, and watched fondly as his five-year-old pattered off to the bathroom in his bare feet.

"Hello."

"Hey Morgan," Buck's voice rumbled on the other end. "I know it's late, but can you come up to my place for a few minutes?"

Morgan frowned. He knew every subtle tone in his brother's voice, and he hadn't heard this one since the last family funeral. Something was wrong.

"What is it? Has somebody died?" he frowned.

"No, no, nothing like that," Buck mumbled.

Morgan frowned and glanced toward the hall door. "I'm about to put Kit to bed," he replied. "Can it wait until morning?"

There was a short, pregnant pause, then Buck muttered, "Yeah, you're right, it can wait. Sorry to bother you, bud. Goodnight."

The line went dead, and Morgan frowned at it before tossing it back on a table. He couldn't remember the last time Buck had called him after ten o' clock.

And it must've been twenty years since Buck had called him *bud*.

"Daddy," Kit's high voice called, and Morgan stood up slowly and drifted back to Kit's bedroom in the hall. He arrived just in time to see Kit jump onto his bed and disappear under the covers.

"You making like a mole, buddy?" he sputtered as a Kit-shaped lump rolled to and fro under the blanket.

"I'm hiding," a muffled voice replied, and Morgan smiled and tossed the blanket back. A bright brown face popped up to laugh at him, and Morgan reached out and pulled Kit's tousled head to his. He gave Kit a sound smack on the brow, then pulled the blanket up. Kit snuggled into bed and grabbed his bear, and Morgan pulled the cover up around his chin.

"You decide to take your bear back?" he teased gently.

"Just for tonight," Kit yawned.

"Oh, I see," Morgan murmured. "Well, let's hear your night prayers."

Kit squeezed his eyes shut and gripped the blanket. "God bless Daddy and Uncle Buck and Uncle Carson and Uncle Luke and Uncle Jesse and Uncle Chase."

"Who else?" Morgan prompted softly.

"God bless Aunt Kate and Cousin Molly, and Conchita, and Miss Ada, and my pony, and Cochise.

"Amen."

"Amen," Morgan echoed, and leaned over to kiss Kit again. He put a gentle hand on the blanket and smiled down at his son's sleepy eyes.

"Good night, cowboy. Sleep tight."

He drifted out again, left Kit's bedroom door open just a crack, and walked back into the living room. His eyes moved back to the phone lying on the table. The faint, acrid taste of disaster swirled in his mouth like smoke.

Something *was* wrong.

He stood in the middle of the room, weighing it in his mind; then he walked to his front door and out into the hall.

When he knocked on Buck's door, it opened almost before he'd stopped. Buck was standing there, a big shadow against a square of golden light.

"Come on in, bud," Buck murmured, and threw the door open. "You want a drink?"

Morgan frowned and followed him across the massive great room. It was empty except for them, and the big fireplace was burning low.

"No, Buck," he mumbled, and rubbed his nose. "I just want the truth."

Buck turned to face him with worry in his bright eyes, and what Morgan saw in his face made his frown deepen.

"You talked to Eugene, didn't you?"

Buck paused with his hand on a glass. He looked down and nodded. "Yeah, I did, Morgan. He called me to come down to Dallas, and we talked at his office today."

Fear curled cold fingers around Morgan's heart, and when Buck put a hand on his shoulder and guided him to the sofa, he sank down onto it feeling numb already.

"I told you I was going to handle it myself, Buck," he growled. "You got no call to get Eugene mixed up in this behind my back!"

"I know, I know," Buck admitted. "And I wouldn't, but—Eugene told me it was serious," he added softly, and met his eyes. "Morgan, Cece's got married again. Some guy named Tomlinson."

Morgan's heart sank into his boots. *I knew it*, he thought grimly. *They're not bluffing. They're coming for Kit.*

"Yeah, I know. I met them a few days ago in town," he growled. "They told me they think he's Kit's father."

Buck raised startled eyes to his face. "You know?"

Morgan nodded. "I know. They said they were going to sue me for custody of Kit. I told 'em to come on."

Buck stared at him for an instant in stricken silence, then cleared his throat and adjusted one big shoulder.

"Morgan, Eugene thinks you should get a paternity test," he mumbled, and looked away. "You're going to have to do it sooner or later. It may as well be now."

Morgan frowned at him, but tilted his head in acknowledgment. "So they must've done it. Filed a legal challenge."

"Not yet. Eugene thinks they're bluffing," Buck answered quickly, and with an earnest look from his light eyes. "Trying to scare us. He—he says that a paternity test will put the brakes on it fast. Keep them from bothering you any more."

Morgan glanced at Buck's face, and the look on it tripped another alarm bell in his gut. Buck's eyes were worried. Buck had flown down to Eugene's office in Dallas. Buck had invited him up for this heart-to-heart the same day.

There was way more to the story.

Morgan scanned his brother's worried face. The only question for him was, Did he want to get bad news at midnight, at the end of a long day, or did he want to find out about it later.

He chose later.

He put his hands on his knees and stood up. "I'll think about it, Buck," he rumbled. "Thanks for telling me."

He turned for the door, and he could feel Buck's unspoken objection from across the room. Buck stood up and followed him.

"If you need anything from me, Morgan—anything at all, you just let me know," Buck mumbled, with his hand on the door jamb.

Morgan gave him a frowning look, nodded, and then walked off down the stairs to his own door.

Chapter 29

Morgan huddled into his leather coat against the chill morning mist. It was a gray, cloudy morning, and their red horse barn was floating in a sea of fog. Dew beaded the trees and the grass as his big strides blazed a path through the wet grass.

He always liked to go to the barn when he was troubled. There was something about the soft nickering of horses, and the scent of hay and wood and leather, that calmed him.

Simple things helped him clear his mind: a leather saddle, a cup of hot coffee, a white cloud of steam in the cold air.

He opened the big red barn doors and let the familiar sound of the creaking hinges sink down into his heart. A dozen pairs of curious brown eyes turned to him as he stepped into the barn, and a dozen ears pricked up.

He sauntered down the center aisle, his glance flicking over the rows of horses: Sunny Girl, Apple Annie, Twister, Miss Chiff.

A stall door at the end of the barn opened up, and he saw Heather slip out. He raised his brows in pleasant surprise.

"You're up early."

She looked up at him and smiled, and there was something about her shining hair and glowing face that blended with everything else there, that seemed right and natural. She was wearing a tiny white shirt and tiny jeans and a pair of leather loafers.

She was as pretty as a field full of daisies, and he couldn't deny that. He watched as she came walking up to him, swinging her bag from one hand.

"So are you."

He shrugged and looked away. "Just poking around."

She tilted her head to one side and gave him a keen look. "You know, you've been promising to have lunch with me for a while now. I'm going to hold you to it. Why don't we go and have lunch somewhere. Someplace fun. Get to know each other a little. Talk shop."

He hunched a shoulder, because his head was telling him not to be stupid, but he didn't have an excuse handy.

"Well—"

Her clear blue eyes lit up with a new idea. "I know! Why don't we go up to the fun park in Oak Hill?"

Morgan boggled at her. "That's a kid's place."

Her smile challenged him. "So? It'll be fun."

He half-turned back toward the door. "I left Kit with his aunt," he mumbled. "I can't stay out all day."

"It wouldn't be all day," she countered. "Just a few hours. Come on."

He rubbed the back of his neck. "Well—all right, then."

Her face brightened. "Good! Come on. We'll go in my car. It's parked right outside."

Morgan watched in bemusement as she breezed past him and led the way back out of the barn. *How did that happen*, he wondered.

Heather was already halfway inside her blue sedan as he walked out of the barn. The car was parked on the grass just beside the road, and she leaned over to open the driver's side door for him.

Morgan glanced back toward the house. It was barely visible in the fog.

"Get in."

Morgan grabbed the door, slid in, and adjusted the seat way back to make room for his long legs. Heather cranked the motor and popped a disc into the player.

"Let's have some road trip music," she cried, and rolled the windows down. Morgan watched her in frowning confusion.

"It's kinda cool out for that, ain't it?"

"Naw," she smiled as she pulled out, "you can't go on the interstate without the windows rolled down."

Morgan stuck his elbow on the open window sill and resigned himself as Heather pulled into the road and pushed her foot down. The car took off with a squeal and they went roaring down the long, straight drive as music blasted from the speakers.

Roll down the highway with the speakers pumpin'

Clear your mind baby, don't worry 'bout nothin'

Go ahead go ahead go ahead go ahead

Fly like an eagle child do what I said.

Morgan sat straight up in alarm as Heather gunned the gas and the big main gates came rushing at them. He turned to bark, "Slow down now, those things don't open fast!"

Heather turned to him with a smile. "You worried, grandma?"

He opened his mouth to protest, and she slammed her foot on the brake. To his amazement, the car came to an abrupt stop, but his head didn't slam into the dash like he'd expected.

The automatic eye blinked, there was a loud beep, and the ponderous gates slowly swung open before them.

Morgan turned to her. "You almost—"

The car took off with another roar and swung out into the road, and they blasted off down the interstate in a cloud of exhaust. Morgan scrabbled at the door and shot Heather a goggling glance. She'd popped on a pair of sunglasses and her hair was whipping in the wind pouring through the open window.

He stared at her in amazement. She'd wanted them to get to know one another, and the first thing he'd learned was that she drove like a maniac.

"Slow down, now," he barked in fright. "You want us to get pulled over by the police?" He looked out the window at the trees shooting past. He wouldn't be surprised to see a motorcycle behind one.

Heather pointed at a sign as it flashed and was gone. "The speed limit's 70 here."

Morgan slapped his knees and barked, "Just because it's legal doesn't mean that you should do it!"

She shrugged a slender shoulder. "You said you only had a few hours. I'm just trying to be respectful of your time."

He stared at her and retorted, "I'm not in that big of a hurry!"

Heather laughed and reached down to turn the music up, and a voice wailed:

Jam the pedal and jam the shift,

Yank that wheel baby, drift drift drift!

Heather sang along with the music and reached down to shift gears. Morgan's eyes widened in terror and he slapped at the disc player. "Turn that crazy music off," he barked, "it's getting you too excited!"

"Oh, all right." Heather flicked off the music, then lifted her foot from the gas, and the green blur hurtling past gradually resolved into trees and fields. Morgan closed his eyes and leaned back into the seat in relief; and when he'd revived enough to feel a flick of anger, he turned to object:

"I thought you were a vet, not a Nascar driver!"

Heather draped a hand over the top of the wheel and smiled at him. "I wanted to be one for a while," she grinned.

"I can see that!"

Chapter 30

Thirty minutes later Heather flicked her turning light and slowed to a stop in front of the amusement park gates. The four-story neon sign over the entrance read *Texas Tornado*. A redheaded cowboy rode a bright blue twister with one hand raised in the air.

Morgan watched the flickering sign uneasily as their car passed under the archway. "Now I didn't come here to go on rides like a kid," he warned her. "We came here to have lunch. Talk shop, like you said."

She turned to him with raised brows and an innocent look. "Sure, talk shop. Like we said."

They parked the car in the huge lot just beyond the gate and caught the first trolley cart that came rolling past. Heather hopped up into it and patted the plastic seat beside her.

Morgan climbed in and sank down onto it less enthusiastically, but he couldn't help being a little nostalgic as he looked around. The amusement park was older than he was, and he hadn't been to it since he was eight years old.

The big hill of the wooden roller coaster still soared over the treetops off to the left, a car full of screaming kids splashed to the bottom of the log flume funnel further on, and the race car track looped through the trees.

A tiny smile curled Morgan's lips. The last time he'd been there, him and Buck had fought over who got to be the driver of a little red race car, and for the first time in his short life, he'd won a fight with his older brother.

Heather dug into her bag. "We have to buy tickets to the park to get in," she mumbled. "I'll get them. My treat."

Morgan snapped back to the present. "No, I'll get 'em," he corrected her.

"No, I will."

Heather took off her sunglasses and turned a determined look on him. "It was my idea."

Morgan clamped his mouth shut. He didn't like having a woman pay his way, even if it was her idea. He was old-fashioned that way.

Not everybody was, though; and he could see it'd do more harm than good to argue.

He just decided to pick up the tab for lunch.

The aroma of grilled hot dogs and funnel cakes drifted on the air as they jumped off the trolley and made their way to the main gates. They joined an admission line and shuffled to the kiosk, where Heather paid for their tickets, to Morgan's chagrin.

She turned to hand him a purple cardboard ticket with a smile. "Now we're in," she chirped. "What do you want to do first?"

"Why don't we do what we came to do," he answered. "Talk."

"All right," she answered brightly, and glanced overhead. When he followed her gaze, he saw a sky bucket glide overhead.

"Why don't we talk while we see the park?"

"So my uncle was a Nascar pit mechanic," Heather told him, "and we got into the races free because of a family pass. I spent most of my childhood at rodeos and races."

Morgan glanced over the side of the sky bucket. He didn't like heights, but they were dangling from a cable that was probably as old as he was, thirty feet above the ground. He could see the roofs of the food court buildings and the top of every fair goer's head within a hundred yards.

"I wanted to be a Nascar driver, every kid did, but I wanted to be a rodeo rider more." Heather sputtered and elbowed him in the ribs.

"Here, have one."

Morgan turned to be confronted with a hot funnel cake. He took it gingerly as Heather popped the other one in her mouth.

"So, I shtarted to go to rowdoes," she mumbled, with her mouth full of cake, then interrupted herself to moan, "Mm, this is good. How's yours?"

"I can't remember the last time I had a funnel cake." Morgan took a bite of sugar-dusted, deep-fried pastry as they drifted over the amusement park concourse. The taste brought memories of a long-forgotten summer flooding back.

Heather shot him an amused glance. "You know, if you don't watch out, you might end up having a good time."

Morgan glanced down and thought, *Not while I'm thirty feet in the air.*

When the sky bucket glided down and into the end of the ride, Morgan clambered out as soon as it came to a stop. Heather followed, brushing crumbs off her blouse.

"That funnel cake really whetted my appetite. What's that I smell—fried chicken? Let's sit down somewhere and chat over a plate of chicken and some coffee."

Now you're making sense, Morgan thought to himself, but only said, "I think the cafe's over there," and pointed across the concourse. He gave Heather his elbow and squired her through the crowd to a pale yellow building that looked like the porch of a Kentucky plantation. Faint banjo music played in the background as he walked to the counter.

He looked down at Heather. "What do you want?"

She scanned the menu board. "*Mmm...*I think the fried chicken platter with potato salad and biscuits, plus the buttered corn on the cob on the side, plus banana pudding and a glass of tea."

Morgan turned to the girl at the counter and reached for his wallet. "And a coffee for me."

He looked down at Heather as the cashier rang up the purchase. "You sure you don't want pie with that, or a bowl of ice cream?" he drawled.

Heather looked thoughtful, and glanced back up the menu board. "You know, I might," she murmured. "But I came here to talk, not to eat."

Morgan stared at her, but her face was as sober as a judge's, so he closed his mouth and picked up a tray.

"You said you went to A&M," Heather mumbled, through a mouthful of fried chicken. "What'd you take there?"

Morgan reached across the picnic table to filch a biscuit off her plate and munched it thoughtfully. "Just night courses," he murmured. "Big Russ taught me everything he knew about running a ranch, and that was more than most of my profs knew. There's no substitute for being raised up in it." He shook his head. "I was just at A&M to pick up the newer things, and even that was Big Russ' idea. I didn't think I needed it, and turns out I didn't, except for a few odds and ends."

"What courses did you take?"

He shrugged. "Medical ones. Mostly for cattle, though some were for horses."

Heather leaned back in surprise. "Get out—we went to the same vet school?" she laughed.

"I was only there for a little while," he shrugged. "For about a quarter or two."

"Small world," she marveled. "We might even have met one another!"

I wish we had, Morgan thought suddenly, and glanced down at her bright, pretty face. *I wish I'd met you, instead of going on that vacation to Padre Island and getting tangled up with Cece.*

Heather shoveled a spoonful of pudding into her mouth. "What do you do at the ranch now?" she asked, with a curious look.

He blinked his regrets into the past and sighed, "The Seven's kind of a business, and my brother Buck's the CEO. He takes care of the corporate stuff, the money and the legal issues. I guess you could say that I'm the general manager for the cattle side of the ranch. I tend shop. Most days, I'm horseback and out in the scrub somewhere looking after stock. I run the ranch hands, buy gear, take care of payroll."

She paused for an instant with the spoon halfway to her mouth. "I'd love that kind of job," she confessed. "Outside all day, working with animals. Of course, I do work with them, but—your job sounds really free."

"It is," he murmured, and stared at the concourse outside without seeing it. The Seven's green, open fields, stretching on forever, far from any hint of civilization—they'd kept him sane the last six years. It didn't matter whether it was baking sun or freezing snow out there.

He was always happier in the saddle, out under the sky, than he was in the house with his feet kicked up on the couch.

Talking to Heather reminded him of that feeling.

"You know, I think I might have some chicken after all," he mumbled, and stood up slowly.

"There you go," she smiled in approval, and this time, he smiled back— just a little.

Chapter 31

Cece turned her head on the spa pillow and sighed. The hotel masseuse drizzled warm lavender oil over her bare back and began to knead out the tension in her shoulders.

Her muscles had been as tight as a violin string ever since she'd returned to this Texas backwater town. There was nothing to do in Sandy Creek, no decent bars, restaurants, or clubs. She was staying at the best hotel within fifty miles, and it didn't even have concierge service.

The second-rate hotel was an oasis in the desert, but she felt trapped inside its walls. She'd been on the verge of a scream for the last three, suspenseful days as she and Roger waited for an answer to their letter.

Cece frowned into the pillow. They hadn't heard back from anybody in the Spade family. Roger had been sure they'd come around, had told her that waiting them out was part of the plan.

"We have to make them sweat a little," he'd told her, and his eyes had been bright with confidence. "Make Morgan imagine losing Kit. Let them all marinate in that for a few days."

"You'd better be right about this," she'd warned him, and he'd given her that big, toothy, *trust me* grin that always made her want to slap him.

The soft trill of her cell phone from the nearby counter made Cece's eyes jump open wide.

"Give me that phone," she barked, and the masseuse dried her hands to retrieve the phone.

Cece grabbed it, punched a button, and jammed the phone to her ear. "Hello?"

Buck Spade's voice boomed through the receiver, and she grimaced and pulled her ear away.

"Well, hello Cece," he drawled.

"Buck? How'd you get my number?" she demanded, and motioned to the girl to get out. The masseuse pulled her mouth into a knot but obeyed, and Cece sat up on the table with a towel clutched to her chest.

"I've had your number for a long time, Cece," Buck replied briskly. "I got the letter your husband sent me."

Cece licked her lips and sat up straighter. Her heart was pounding with hope and excitement mingled with suspicion.

"Well?"

She could almost see her big, former brother-in-law. She pictured his face wearing the same expression he'd always shown her—head tilted back, eyes narrowed in distrust, mouth pinched into a hard, straight line.

"I'd never heard of Roger Tomlinson," he muttered, "so I went online and bought one of them background reports. It said he's a con man and a thief. Almost went to jail for ripping off little old ladies."

An unpleasant slap of surprise washed across Cece's face. It was the first time she'd heard *that* news, and she slipped off the table and went pattering across the room for her clothes.

"That's a lie," she snapped. "And you didn't call me to talk about Roger."

"No I didn't," he agreed. "I called to tell you that you're wasting my time and yours to dog this family. If you want to talk about Kit from now on, you'll have to talk to Eugene. He's handling this for us. He's got your letter and the test results you sent. He was real interested in them. Interested in ol' Roger, too."

Ice skittered down Cece's spine. "Eugene?" she echoed in alarm. She reached for her dress and held the phone to her ear with her shoulder.

"That's right," Buck answered softly, and there was grim satisfaction in his voice.

Rage jumped up in her, and her face twisted in fury. "Well, a high-priced lawyer won't do Morgan any good this time, and you can tell him so for me. A DNA test doesn't care how much money you have," she spat. "So even the high and mighty Spades will be out of luck this time!"

"Well, we'll just see about that," he replied softly.

"Yes, we will!" she snapped. "You might bully other people, Buck Spade, but you needn't think that you can do it to me. I'm Kit's mother, and I know my rights!"

The line abruptly went dead, and Cece screamed and threw the phone across the room. It bounced on the polished floor, then went skidding across it to crash against the far wall.

Cece swore savagely and stuck her feet into her high heels, then slapped the dressing cubicle curtain aside and burst out of the spa room.

I'm going back to our suite, she thought furiously, *and Roger better be there and have some answers.*

I don't need him.

He needs me!

Chapter 32

Cece balled her hands into fists and screamed: "He said you were a con man. He said you had a *record!*"

Roger raised both his hands in a calming gesture and inched around the silken hotel bed. "Now darling," he soothed, "are you going to trust the word of a man who hates you, or the word of a man who loves you?" He cocked his head to one side and smiled, but Cece yelled:

"You said you were a *lawyer*. You lied to me!"

Roger shrugged and sputtered. "Darling, you of all people should know what it's like to be falsely accused…"

Cece swore and snatched a vase off the table and brandished it in the air like a weapon.

"Do you have a law degree? Yes or no!"

Roger's wary eyes moved to the vase. "Stop it, now! Calm down, Cece," he murmured, and moved a bit closer.

Cece stared at him in dawning horror. "Oh my—you don't, do you, Roger?" she gasped, and the vase drooped in her hands. "You did lie to me, you're not a lawyer, and now we're up against Eugene Clemmons." Her voice jumped to a shout.

"We're a bad episode in a celebrity court show, Roger!"

The smile faded off her husband's face. He walked up to her, took the vase from her hands, and grabbed her by the shoulders. "What was that you said—who's Eugene Clemmons?"

Cece's head rolled back on her shoulders as she laughed bitterly. "No, *of course* you don't know! Well, you're about to find out, Roger. Notice that I said *you*, not *me*."

She stormed to the chifferobe, threw open the doors, and tossed her suitcase onto the bed. Roger watched her in frowning confusion. "What do you think you're doing?"

"I'm getting out of here while the getting's good," she growled and stomped to the dresser to pull out her clothes. "If you had the brains you think you do, you'd be packing, too."

Roger walked over, grabbed her, and yanked her around roughly. "You can't leave now or the whole thing falls apart!"

"Let go of me!"

Roger's handsome face hardened, and his eyes frowned down at her. "Now you listen to me, Cece," he growled. "You're not going anywhere."

"Let me go, you idiot!"

Cece shrieked as his fingers dug deeper into her shoulders. He suddenly shook her, shook her hard enough to make her shoulders jerk and her hair fall down over her eyes.

"You're staying right here," he told her, with quiet intensity. "I've stuck my neck way out for you. I'm risking jail time, and with my background they'll put me away for life. You're not flaking on me now!"

A soft rap on the door made them both look up sharply. A quiet male voice from the hall outside called, "Mr. and Mrs. Tomlinson, is everything alright? This is management."

Paul clapped a hand over her mouth, closed his eyes, then called back, in an even voice: "Everything's fine, thanks."

There was a long, pregnant pause. "Mrs. Tomlinson?"

Cece rolled her eyes to her husband's. His eyes blazed at her as he slowly pulled his hand away from his mouth.

She held his eye for a moment, then cleared her throat.

"Everything…everything's fine."

There was another pause. The male voice finally murmured, "We had complaints about the noise coming from your suite. I'm going to have to ask you to keep it down."

Roger lowered his head in relief. "We'll keep it down. Sorry."

"Thank you, folks."

Muffled footsteps faded down the hall, and Roger slowly relaxed; but he fixed Cece with a fierce look.

"Morgan may not have reacted the way we hoped," he said slowly and evenly, "but this isn't over, not by a long shot. We're going to hang tough, and stay strong, and we'll come out on top in the end. Now you're going to put your suitcase back in that wardrobe, and you're going to *settle down.* "

Roger exhaled slowly and released her, and Cece rubbed her sore shoulders resentfully.

"Buck Spade was bluffing and you fell for it," Roger scolded her. "Don't be stupid. We need to stay right here and wait. We're going to outlast them."

She shot him a dark look, found her bag, and scrabbled in it for a cigarette. She lit it with shaking hands, then blew an angry puff of smoke into the air.

Roger sank into a stuffed chair near the fireplace, crossed his long legs, and reached for a drink. "And one more thing, Cece: if you try to go anywhere without me, I'll hunt you down."

She looked up sharply and glared at him: but he held her eye and nodded grimly.

"You're going through with this, if I have to twist your arm behind your back every step of the way!"

Chapter 33

Cece turned her head and glanced over at Roger's motionless form. He was lying in bed beside her, a dark, silent lump under the covers. His breathing was deep and regular, punctuated occasionally by faint, raspy snores. She'd been listening to that sound for any hint that he might be faking, that he might be lying there awake; but she was convinced at last.

She raised up just enough to read the bedside clock. Its big red numbers read 4:15 a.m.

Cece moved out of the bed slowly and carefully: she touched the floor with her foot, then swung her leg over the edge of the mattress, then sat up.

She glanced over her shoulder at Roger's face. His eyes were closed, but his mouth was slightly open.

She rose to her feet an inch at a time, then padded across the suite to the bathroom. She'd hidden a change of clothes under the folded towels, and she dressed quickly in the darkness.

Moonlight slanted across the hotel room floor as Cece crossed it wearing jeans and a plain tee shirt. She had her bag slung over one shoulder, and she was carrying her shoes in her hands.

She reached the suite door, pulled back the security latch, and slowly turned the knob. A loud *click* echoed in the silence, and Cece cursed silently as Roger mumbled and turned over in bed. She stood there, frozen, her heart thrumming; but silence gradually fell again, and she opened the door and fled.

She slipped into the hall, then into the first stairwell. She hurried down the concrete steps, expecting any minute to hear Roger shout in the corridor behind her, but the hotel was swaddled in the profound silence of the wee hours.

She reached the first floor of the hotel and walked out into a small corridor whose only contents were a humming ice machine and a rack of travel brochures. There was a glass door at the end of the hall opening onto the pool area, and she made for it.

Cece burst out into the early morning darkness and half-ran across the lawn to the ghostly parking lot. She found her Mercedes, unlocked it by hand to avoid the beep of her key fob, slid in, and locked the door tight. She glanced back at the hotel's top-floor windows, but they were still dark.

She hurriedly cranked the car, yanked it into reverse, then pulled out of the hotel lot. She blew through a red light to turn onto the empty side street on her way to the highway.

She glanced back at the hotel one more time, and as she watched, one window on the top floor blinked to life. As she watched, a man-shaped shadow appeared in the window. She jammed her foot on the gas and the car tires squealed as she careened onto the interstate.

Cece moved into the lane heading south and pressed her foot to the floor. She preferred to travel by air, but she decided that this time, it was safer to travel by road. She was going over the border to Mexico, and a car was harder to track than a plane.

Her cell phone suddenly trilled in her bag, but she sputtered angrily and ignored it. Roger had lied to her, Roger had threatened her, and worst of all, Roger had failed her. That meant only one thing.

Roger had officially entered her past.

She laughed scornfully, remembering her husband's 'tough guy' face. He was a con man and a liar, and he'd faked his threats, too.

Well girl, you sure know how to pick 'em, she thought bitterly.

Her phone suddenly winked to life and replayed the message Roger had just left on her phone. He was sputtering with rage.

You can't turn your back on me, Cece, he cried.

Actually, I can, she thought angrily.

I'll find you, he sputtered.

You can try, she countered silently.

Roger gabbled on, and she finally reached over and flicked the phone off. He would certainly try to come after her, but he was stuck for several hours at least, because she'd taken their car and all his credit cards.

Cece glanced at a road sign as it flashed past: *Mexico, 998 miles.*

She sighed and gripped the wheel tighter. Roger might be too stupid to understand it, but Mexico was the safest place she could be at the moment.

Roger had assured her that he was a lawyer, that he knew how it worked, that Morgan was so worn out and weary that he'd settle with them out of court. That they'd be able to bleed the Spades for years to come.

Instead, Morgan had lawyered up instantly, and not just with any lawyer: with Eugene Clemmons. Again. Cece shuddered.

Eugene really *was* a shark. She was still wearing the marks of his pointy teeth, and she had no desire to jump into the water with him again.

She was going to winter in some nice Mexican resort town, Cancun or Acapulco, and wait there until things calmed down again. If Roger wanted to stay and fight Morgan and his vicious lawyer, he was welcome.

The phone winked on again.

Cece, pick up, Roger's voice commanded.

Cece!

Chapter 34

Morgan slumped against the headrest in Heather's car and watched sleepily as she popped the clutch and shifted gears. He was so weary and sore that he hardly even minded that they'd been a bullet-shaped blur all the way back from the amusement park.

I hope we don't get caught for speeding, he thought sleepily. He glanced at the moonlight on the scrub trees as they flashed by, on the silvered pastures rolling by. It was closing in on midnight.

A ticket's going to make us later than we are, and I've already made Kate and Buck babysit Kit all day.

He sighed and snuggled deeper into the car seat. Somehow Heather had talked him into going on all the rides in that amusement park, and every muscle he had was crying. He opened one eye just enough to shoot her a bemused glance. She was as bright and fresh as if she'd slept all day and had just woken up. The cool night air made her bright hair float around her head like a nimbus, and she was singing softly in tune with the mumbling radio.

I must be getting old, Morgan groaned inwardly and adjusted his aching shoulder. When he closed his eyes he was still on that crazy roller coaster, trembling on the breathless crest of the first big hill. Texas countryside stretched out to the horizon in every direction, and a 10-story drop yawned directly below his dangling feet.

When Heather suddenly popped the gas to zoom through the open ranch gates, he jumped and almost yelled out.

"Admit it now," Heather teased, and turned toward him with a twinkling glance. "You had fun in spite of yourself."

Morgan sputtered. *Fun isn't the word I'd use,* he thought ruefully; but to be fair, if he ignored his groaning body, he'd had a real good time.

He grumbled a grudging acknowledgment, and Heather's laughter trilled out in a peal of delight, followed by a little snorting laugh that almost broke Morgan up in spite of himself.

"You'll thank me tomorrow," Heather informed him. "Everybody needs a break now and then."

I'll be soaking in a tub tomorrow, Morgan thought in resignation; but he just grunted again and settled deeper into the seat.

Heather turned and glanced at him again with a mischievous twinkle in her eye. "You know, there's a harvest festival in town in a few days," she told him. "Sounds like a lot of fun. Corn mazes, hay rides, pumpkin carving. Why don't you and me and Kit go and see it?"

Morgan turned his head just enough to give her the side-eye. "I'm old fashioned," he rumbled, and crossed his arms. "I like to be the one to ask a lady out."

He didn't mean it as a rejection, and he was glad to see that she didn't take it as one. Heather pursed her lips and nodded, as if she was conceding the point.

"Okay. So are you asking me out?"

He sputtered and turned his incredulous laughter into a cough. *She sure ain't shy*, he thought to himself; but he was pretty sure he knew how she'd meant the invitation. Heather was a lady.

Just a very…*confident* one.

He weighed his answer for an instant, and turned to look at her. "Yeah," he mumbled, and rubbed his nose. "I guess I am."

A delighted smile beamed across her face. "Good! I accept. See how easy that was?"

He rolled his eyes to hers and sputtered out a reluctant chuckle as she laughed with him.

They turned into the ranch, the main gates clanged securely shut behind their car, and they cruised up the long, dark main driveway. For most of the fifteen-minute trip the only living things they saw were moths, jackrabbits and hunting cats momentarily caught in the ghostly headlight beams.

The pony and thoroughbred stables slowly crept into sight on the right of the drive, a series of long, low buildings with only a faint interior glow to betray the presence of a dozing stable hand.

A few minutes later the roof of the main house crowned the road ahead, followed by the massive glass wall. The low, golden lights glimmering behind it advertised that those inside were asleep.

But Morgan sat up suddenly. "What's that?" he wondered aloud, because the whole front face of the ranch house was bathed in the garish glow of flashing blue lights.

"It looks like a police car," Heather murmured, with a puzzled frown.

Morgan straightened in the seat and fumbled with his seat belt. "Take me right up to the front," he commanded. The closer they got, the more he got the sinking feeling that those flashing blue lights were for him.

Or worse, for Kit.

Fear squeezed Morgan's heart into a small, cold ball, and he was out of the car as soon as it pulled to a stop in front of the big house. Luke and his girlfriend Trina were standing beside the police cruiser, and as he strode closer, Luke looked up in apparent relief.

"Here he is now, officer," Luke mumbled, and pulled his arm tighter around Trina's shoulder.

Morgan's eyes zoomed to his brother's. "Is Kit all right?" he barked.

"Far as I know," Luke replied with an apologetic shrug. "We just got here, and the police car followed us in."

Morgan turned to the officer with clenched fists and a knotted stomach. "You looking for me, officer?"

The officer was a middle-aged, muscular man with a buzz cut and an unreadable expression. He turned around and replied, "Are you Morgan Spade?"

"That's right."

Morgan was dimly aware that Heather was at his side, and his arm went around her shoulder instinctively.

The officer coughed softly. "I was sent here to give you the news personally, Mr. Spade," he murmured.

Morgan's heart jumped in his chest. "This isn't about my son, is it?"

The officer shook his head, but replied, "No, not directly. But since Cece Tomlinson is your son's biological mother, this is a next of kin notification."

Morgan heard Heather gasp, and he frowned into the officer's face. "I don't understand. What are you trying to tell me?"

The officer widened his stance and clasped his hands in front of him. "I'm sorry to inform you, Mr. Spade, that your son's mother has been in a car accident. Her vehicle went over the guard rail and into a canyon just over the Mexican border.

"Neither the car or her body has been retrieved—the canyon is over 100 feet deep—but she's missing and presumed dead."

Morgan stared at the officer in silent shock. He heard Heather's muffled weeping and felt Luke's startled eyes on his, but at least for the moment, he felt nothing except numb.

"I see," he heard himself mumble. "Well—thanks for coming out to tell us in person. I'm obliged to you, officer."

"I'm sorry to bring bad news. We'll let you know as soon as we find out more," the officer promised, and turned back to the cruiser.

Morgan watched as the blue lights flicked off and the police car slowly turned and moved off down the driveway. He stood there watching the car get smaller, and only Luke's hand on his arm brought him back to reality.

Luke's eyes were full of pity. "Anything I can do, Morg?"

Morgan blinked at him. "No. No, thanks, Luke." He glanced down and rubbed his nose.

Luke squeezed his arm. "If you need anything, just holler out." He stepped back and squired his girlfriend back to her car, and Morgan watched them for a minute, then remembered that his arm was draped around Heather's shoulder.

He felt her eyes on him, full of compassion and pity. He cleared his throat and coughed.

"It's getting late," he mumbled. "You should go on home and get some rest."

All right, she replied, in a whisper almost too soft to hear. She took his hand, squeezed it gently, and to his surprise, she stood on tiptoe and pressed a barely-perceptible kiss to his cheek before she slipped away.

Chapter 35

Morgan slipped into his suite and closed the door softly behind him. His living room was moon-washed but otherwise dark and silent.

Morgan drifted to the big glass window and stared out across the midnight panorama stretching away into darkness. He was seeing, not the gentle swell of the Seven's rolling pastures, or the distant lights of town, but Cece as he'd first seen her on the beach at Padre Island. Her big white hat, her white caftan, her smooth, tanned shoulder, the gold bracelet on her wrist.

She'd been young, sleek, and beautiful. So full of life. She'd flirted with him, she'd flattered him, she'd pretended to look up to him. She'd buttered him up in a thousand subtle ways.

She'd bewitched him as thoroughly as if she'd cast a spell over his eyes. It had taken him years to shake free from the sleepy, seductive magic that had made him see a woman who didn't exist, that had masked the truth of who Cece really was.

Morgan rubbed his jaw with his hand. His marriage to Cece had been a near-total loss to him. But there had been one glittering silver lining to his stormy marriage. Maybe he had loved a phantom woman who didn't exist. Maybe the real Cece had proven to be vain, shallow, and selfish, and she'd sure enough put him through hell.

But Cece had given him Kit; and so whether she'd meant to or not, she'd given him the best gift of his whole life.

He couldn't forget that Cece had been the mother of his child, and he'd loved her for as long as she'd let him.

Morgan lowered his gaze sadly. He was mostly grieving for what their marriage should have been, not for what it had been. And when he searched his own heart, he found no other pain in it, because he had no love left for Cece, nothing that had survived their bitter fights and court battles. He'd suffered the death of that love already, suffered it for years, and it was truly and finally gone.

Morgan exhaled softly. The only pain in his heart now was for Kit. Kit hadn't had much of a relationship with Cece, but she was still his mother.

He was bound to be upset.

Morgan's eyes drifted up to the moonlit sky. *Lord, help me break this to Kit,* he prayed. *Help him to take it. He's only five years old.*

He turned on the words and moved through the darkened living room, and on to the hall beyond, as silently as a ghost. Morgan paused outside Kit's bedroom and pushed the door open slightly.

Moonlight was streaming through the bedroom window. It glanced off the cowboy lamp on the bedside table and the baseball glove hanging from the bed post, and in its silver radiance Morgan could make out a little boy-shaped lump under the bed covers.

He crossed the room silently, then knelt down beside the bed and bowed his head to pray over his son. As soon as he closed his eyes, he was back in the maternity ward of the hospital, peering at his newborn son for the first time. Kit had been small and pink and wriggling, a tiny baby with a button nose and a rosebud mouth. Kit had squinted up at him from under a pale blue cap and a blue blanket.

Tears stung Morgan's eyes. He hadn't known if he was ready to be a father. He'd worried about what kind of father he was going to be; but as soon as he laid eyes on that little squirming baby, something reached up and grabbed his heart and hadn't let go since that day.

A wave of love so strong that it scared him.

Morgan reached out and caressed his sleeping son's cheek. *I wish I could take this for you, son,* he thought sadly. *It's way too early for you to carry this load.*

He stared down at Kit's dreaming face, then withdrew his hand and bowed his head. He stayed there for a long time, frowning, praying silently and earnestly; and after a while Kit stirred, sighed, and raised his head just a bit.

"Daddy?"

Morgan put a hand on his son's arm. "Right here, son."

Kit yawned. "Where were you, Daddy? You were gone all day."

Guilt stabbed Morgan, and he reached out to smooth a curl from Kit's smooth brow. He couldn't bring himself to tell his son that he'd spent the whole day at an amusement park like a kid.

"I'm back now, buddy," Morgan whispered, then frowned and added, "Son, a…a policeman came to the house tonight," he murmured slowly. "He brought us bad news."

Kit struggled up to a sitting position. "Bad news?"

Morgan rubbed Kit's arm. "Yes, son. The policeman said that…that your Momma was in a car accident tonight." He paused again, breathed another quick prayer, and added, "Son, your Momma's…passed away."

There was a long, deep silence. Morgan could feel Kit staring at him in the darkness.

"What does that mean?"

Morgan blinked back tears and reached for his son. He pressed Kit to his chest and mumbled into his hair. "It means your Momma died, buddy," he whispered brokenly.

Kit fell silent again, then his little hands slowly curled into fists against Morgan's chest. He shook his head.

"I know, buddy, I know," Morgan crooned, and rocked a weeping Kit back and forth. He kissed Kit's curling hair and looked down into his son's face.

"It's not fair," Kit mumbled into his shirt. "I never got to see my Momma, and now she's gone!"

Morgan whispered, "Life sometimes isn't fair, buddy. I wish I could tell you that it is, but it isn't." He licked his lips, frowned, and added:

"You just remember that your Momma loved you very much. She just didn't know how to say so."

Morgan stared into the darkness over Kit's shoulder. He needed to comfort Kit with whatever he could. And he prayed that he'd told his son the truth; that in some small, hidden corner of her heart, Cece had loved Kit after all.

Kit raised his face in tearful appeal. "Daddy, can I come and sleep with you tonight?" he whispered.

Morgan hugged him close. "Sure you can, buddy. For as long as you like. Come on."

He stood up and helped Kit climb out of his bed. Kit slipped a small hand into his and pattered after him as he led the way to his own bedroom. He flicked on the light, then turned the bed covers back.

Kit climbed into the big bed, and Morgan tucked him in and sat down on the mattress beside his son. He pulled the coverlet up around Kit's chin.

"It's going to be alright, son," he murmured. "I'm right here."

He reached over to flick off the light, then pulled off his boots, climbed into the bed, and folded Kit in his arms when his son reached for him.

Chapter 36

Buck yawned and padded across his living room on the way to the kitchen for a midnight snack; but a faint, flashing blue light from somewhere outside made him frown and amble over to the massive glass wall.

He glanced down at the cobbled drive below to see a police cruiser parked at their front door. Morgan was talking to an officer, and his face looked as shocked as if he'd been surprised by a two-by-four.

Wonder what that's about, Buck mused with a frown. *Whatever it is, it ain't good.*

He turned on his heel and marched to his own front door. The fear that somebody might be hurt sent him charging out to find out what was going on.

He'd barely taken two steps into the hall outside when he met Luke coming up the stairs to his own apartment. His younger brother had a worried, hangdog look that made Buck demand:

"What's the police doing here?"

Luke brushed his fringe of blonde bangs away and raised big blue eyes. He shrugged one shoulder and gestured toward the door.

"Cece was in a car accident somewhere in Mexico," he mumbled. "She went off a cliff. The officer came to notify Morgan that she's dead."

Shock wiped a blank across Buck's face. "*Dead?* They're sure?"

Luke shrugged again. "They haven't found her body, but it stands to reason. He said the drop was more than a hundred feet."

Buck's eyes drifted down. Rhythmic blue lights flashed across the floor at the foot of the stairs. "Thanks Luke," he murmured, and Luke nodded and turned to his own doorway.

"Night, Buck."

Buck stood there in the semi-darkness, debating whether or not to go downstairs. A faint sound made him glance behind him.

Kate was standing in the doorway in her silken nightgown, and her eyes were on his face. What she saw there made her murmur, "What is it?"

Buck made his decision. He slipped an arm around her shoulder and walked her back inside.

"The police just came by to tell Morgan that Cece's died in a car accident," he replied quietly, and closed the door behind them.

"Oh no, Buck," she gasped. "How awful for Morgan!"

Buck tilted his head. "You know, I don't think it will be," he answered slowly. "Kit might take it hard, but I think the last few years have beat the fool out of Morgan. He'll be alright."

Kate cast a grieved glance toward the window. "We'll have to pay special attention to Kit," she fretted, as they drifted back to the bedroom. "Poor little boy, to lose his mother when he's only five years old!"

Buck pulled his mouth to one side. He couldn't help thinking that Kit was better off, but it was no use to tell Kate that. She was a soft-hearted woman, and she'd never met Cece.

His only answer was to plant a kiss on her smooth cheek and pull her a bit closer to his side as they walked back to their bedroom. He let her climb into bed and get settled, then he walked around to his side and crawled in beside her.

He lifted one arm, and Kate snuggled onto his chest with a frown. "We'll have to remember Morgan and Kit in our prayers," she murmured, and Buck reached for the phone on the nightstand.

"Uh huh," he answered absently, and flicked it on. He had a sneaking feeling that there was going to be a message from Eugene, and sure enough. There was a recorded message marked 'urgent', and when he hit playback Eugene's dry voice crackled over the line.

"Buck, I just found out that Cece was in a car accident in Mexico," he barked. "Her car went off a cliff just over the Mexican border. The official line is that she's dead, but her body hasn't been found. Call me."

Buck glanced down at Kate, then flicked over to the text feature. He slowly punched out a message to Eugene with his thumb.

I guess it's wrong, but I'm just glad we're shut of her, he typed. *Morgan and Kit will have a normal life now. Let me know if her husband still wants to make trouble.*

If he does, I'll just leave him to you.

Buck.

He flicked the phone off and tossed it back on the nightstand. The slight motion disturbed Kate, and she moved restlessly on his chest.

When he glanced down, her eyes were closed and her mouth was moving, slightly and earnestly, in prayer.

He sighed and tightened his arm around her, and closed his own eyes; but the only prayer in him that night was short and to the point.

I'm sorry, Lord.

But I may as well say it as think it.

Chapter 37

Heather dashed a hand across her eyes, but her vision was so blurred that she had to pull the car to a stop on the way back to her condo.

She pressed her brow against the steering wheel, curled her fingers around it, and drew a shaky breath. Her heart was broken for Morgan and Kit.

She closed her eyes and saw the policeman's stolid face as he told Morgan that his ex wife was dead. Morgan's face had looked so stunned and hurt; and she couldn't bring herself to imagine how Kit would take that awful news.

Heather pulled her mouth down unhappily. Morgan had just started to loosen up, to allow himself a little break from his responsibilities. It seemed unfair that even that little reprieve had been yanked away.

Heather drew a shuddering breath and wiped her tear-stained face with one hand. Her long day was beginning to catch up with her, and she needed rest; but she breathed a little prayer for Morgan and Kit as she cranked the car and sent it down the dark drive again.

Heather parked the car in the little drive at last and dragged herself up the porch steps of the condo. She unlocked the door, closed it behind her, and slowly walked up the stairs to her own bed.

She tossed her keys across the floor and fell face down onto her bed. She fell asleep almost as soon as her head hit the pillow, and she slept deeply for hours. But sometime in the wee hours of the night, a small sound and a blast of cold air woke her up again.

She shivered and pulled the covers up around her ears. The house had been warm and comfortable when she'd come back home, but now it was cold. As she lay there huddled in the blanket, a faint pinging on the roof alerted her that a light sleet was falling outside.

Heather frowned. Sleet was unusual in the fall in that neighborhood, so they were probably in for a cold and early winter. Heather chewed her lip as she thought about the animals in her care. The new foals were safely tucked away in the big, warm barn, but it would be a good idea to break out the blankets for the horses out in the pasture.

She turned over restlessly and pulled the blanket more snugly around her. *It never rains but it pours,* she thought unhappily. *One thing after another.*

When she woke again, the sky outside her window was a leaden gray, and the bedroom was still cold. Heather struggled up and flicked a button on her clock radio. A robotic voice announced:

The National Weather Service forecasts a winter storm for southern Oklahoma and north central Texas today and tomorrow. Freezing rain is likely and some secondary roads may be iced over. Use caution if you must drive.

Heather sighed and flopped face-first into her pillow. It was ice cold, it was going to be a miserable day, and she was going to have to go out into it.

Fifteen minutes later her alarm went off with a startling shriek, and Heather groaned and rolled out of bed. She was still wearing her clothes, and she shuffled off to the bathroom to shower and dress.

When she hurried out of the condo and down the porch steps, thirty minutes later, she was pulling on a chunky oatmeal colored cardigan and was holding a blueberry muffin in her teeth. The walkway was pebbled with sleet, but she had her best leather boots pulled on over her jeans. They had tire-tread rubber soles and were equal to almost anything.

She opened the car door, tossed her bag inside, then reached for an ice scraper to clear a circle on the windshield. She managed to clear a window as big as a platter, then slid inside the car and cranked the motor. The car sputtered, almost died, and finally growled to life; and Heather backed it carefully onto the drive and made her way to the barn.

Heather drove with one hand and held the muffin with the other. The sky was dark and threatening even though it was barely eight in the morning, and the drive was pebbly with ice, but the sleet had stopped falling for the moment.

Heather glanced at her bag. Her cell phone was tucked into it, and she was tempted to call Morgan; but something in her heart whispered to give him space. It was a very private time of grief, and Morgan would want to be alone with his son.

She wanted to comfort Morgan, but she didn't want to intrude.

By the time she reached the barn, the sleet had started up again, and she opened the car door and dashed across the barn yard to the big double doors. She burst in with a gasp and bent over to shake ice crystals out of her hair and wipe melting ice off her neck.

Heather straightened up, then paused just inside the door in spite of the cold. A pair of furtive yellow eyes were staring at her from just behind a bale of hay, and she bent down again to inspect them. They belonged to the barn cat, a yellow tom that she'd doctored up before. When he turned his head, she saw that something had given his left ear a perfect piercing: a tiny, perfectly round hole.

They stared at one another, and Heather told him, "Well, you just can't stay out of trouble, can you? Let me have a look at that ear."

She picked up the complaining tom and turned him this way and that in her hands. "The wound doesn't look infected," she thought aloud, and juggled the cat on her hip so she could rub the affected ear. The tom complained again, but in a tone of irritation instead of pain, and Heather laughed and set him down again.

"Stay lucky, Romeo," she told him, and watched in amusement as he scampered off.

Heather looked up. There were horses in every stall—the old, the young, and those Hank decided weren't up to the icy weather outside. Heather walked past a dozen curious pairs of eyes, rubbing one long nose after another as she went.

The sound of faint, jangling music drifted out of Hank's office, and she moved to the doorway and peeked in. The wooden desk held an old computer and was covered with papers, but the old leather chair was empty.

"Hank?"

Heather walked to the back of the cavernous barn. The big back door was open just a crack, and when she opened it, a cold breeze eddied in; but the back pen was empty of both horses and Hank.

Heather closed the door tight and rubbed her arms. The barn was heated, but the sleet made the breeze ice-cold. She walked back to Hank's office, found his coffeemaker on a table, and started a fresh pot.

The sound of the big front doors creaking open announced Hank's return, but Heather was still scooping fragrant coffee into the machine. She heard heavy boots on the groaning barn floor, and welcoming nickers from some of the horses.

Heather finished with the coffee and put the tin back on a shelf before drifting back out of the office. She expected to see Hank standing in the barn aisle, but to her surprise, the tall figure standing at one of the stalls was Morgan.

His long hand was stroking Cochise's black nose as the horse nuzzled his chest. Morgan's dark hair fell over his brow as he murmured a quiet word to his horse.

Lantern light was behind him, and it traced his whole profile with a golden pen, making his black hair gleam like silk. That light glanced off his solemn, heavy-lidded eyes and threw the grim set of his mouth into shadow. The sight of him went through Heather like an arrow.

She was irresistibly drawn to wounded things.

She approached him slowly and softly, one quiet step at a time, as if he was an injured mustang; but when she got close, she stopped.

The lantern light glanced off the strong planes of Morgan's face, and its bright beam caught a tear as it carved a cold path down his cheek.

Heather stopped dead and put a hand up to the wall, but she could tell that Morgan sensed her presence. He didn't turn his head, but he lifted a hand to dash the tear away. His deep voice mumbled: "I thought the place was empty."

Heather moved closer, her eyes riveted to his. She reached up to take his chin and gently turned his face toward her. Her heart twisted with compassion as she searched his eyes.

"Don't try to hide it. You can grieve," she whispered. "You can grieve, Morgan."

His eyes stared down at her steadily, and the pain she saw there made Heather reach up to twine her arms around his back. She stood on tiptoe and raised her face to Morgan's, and he bent down to take her in his arms.

Heather closed her eyes and just held him, and after a silent moment or two, Morgan wept, silently and slowly, as her fingers curled over his shirt. His big shoulders shook with his grief, and Heather's heart melted in sympathy as she wept with him. She could only imagine what Morgan was feeling: grief for Cece's death, grief for their broken marriage, grief for the fighting and upheaval Kit had been forced to witness.

Heather blinked back her own tears. She could see the trouble plain as day: Morgan had never allowed himself any rest. He'd been the strong one for years, he'd had to suck it up for Kit's sake and swallow his frustration and anger. He'd held up the sky to make his son feel safe and loved.

But she could see that the sky had been heavy.

Morgan pulled back from her a bit, rubbed his nose, and looked down with an embarrassed expression that made Heather rush to comfort him.

She could only imagine how hard it was for him to be caught weeping.

"Don't fret about it, Morgan," she whispered earnestly, and looked up into his face. "Sooner or later, even a cowboy has to cry."

His eyes moved to hers, and Heather felt herself slipping into those sapphire depths. Her hands tightened around him, and he bowed his head, and their questing lips met and blended.

Heather closed her eyes and abandoned herself to the touch of Morgan's lips on hers, the tickle of that bristly moustache, the firm, taut feel of his skin against hers, the slightly salty taste of it. His lips on hers were gentle, slow, respectful and sweet; and they made her skin tingle from one end of her body to the other.

Morgan sighed and pulled back a bit. He looked down into her eyes and mumbled, "I don't have any right to get involved with you, Heather."

She frowned. "Why not?"

He looked away, then back. "I'm emptied out," he rumbled. "Numb. I got nothing to give you but sadness. It'd be selfish of me to get tangled up with a pretty young thing like you. So full of life." He brushed a tendril of hair back from her brow.

Heather gazed up into his eyes and smiled. "You look plenty good to me, buster."

Morgan sputtered and shook his head. "You'd regret it," he whispered.

Heather's smile faded, and she held his eyes. "Why don't you let me decide who I want," she murmured, and stood up on tiptoe. She twined her arms around his neck, frowned, and kissed him slowly, deliberately, and hard. His hands slowly moved to her arms, and his long fingers curled around them.

"Stop it," he mumbled, and turned his face away; but Heather moved to his neck, kissed the soft spot just under his ear.

"Stop it, Heather," he mumbled, and pulled out of her arms. "I won't let you make the same mistake I did." He looked down at the floor. "You don't know what it's like to love somebody who's dead wrong for you."

She moved to meet his gaze. "Why would we be wrong for each other?" she pressed. "Don't you like me?"

He shook his head and looked away. "I like you just fine."

"Well then, what's wrong?" She moved close and twined her arms around him again. "When a horse bucks you, and you fall off, you get up and climb on again, don't you? It's the same with love. It hurts to fall out of love, but you don't stay on the ground. You get back in the saddle."

Morgan rolled skeptical eyes to hers, then he sputtered with reluctant laughter. "You like to argue, don't you?"

She faced him down. "When it's important."

To her consternation, Morgan stepped back from her, out of her embrace. He nodded to her as he retreated.

"You'll thank me later," he rumbled, and turned to walk out of the barn.

Heather bit her lip, frowned, and stuck her hands on her hips.

No, cowboy, she thought in determination.

You're going to thank me.

Chapter 38

Buck rubbed his nose and settled into the hard wooden pew. He and Kate and most of his family were sitting in a little funeral home chapel just outside of Sandy Creek.

Morgan had decided to hold a private memorial service for Cece, since as far as they'd been able to find out, no one else was doing it.

Not even her husband, and that was weird; but Morgan had decided to make the gesture for Kit's sake. A beautiful spray of yellow roses dominated the front of the chapel. A framed photo of Cece was displayed on an easel in front of it. Buck stared at it dryly. It was probably the classiest photo that had ever been taken of her, a head shot with her blonde hair perfectly coiffed and two little diamond earrings in her ears.

It looked like a photo of a model.

Buck stifled a sigh and stretched an arm along the pew, behind Kate's back. He felt like the biggest hypocrite in the world sitting there, because the most honest feeling in his gut was that the world generally and the Spades especially were better off without Cece. But Kit needed closure, some clear, formal way to say goodbye to his Momma, and they were all going to see that he got it.

The funeral home chaplain stood up at the front of the room, cleared his throat softly, and walked to the wooden lectern. He gave them all a solemn look.

"Dearly beloved, we are here to pay our last respects to our sister Cece Tomlinson," he intoned gently. "I didn't have the privilege to know Cece well, but it's easy to see that her family loved and cherished her."

Kate stirred beside him and cast a tearful glance toward Kit. He was sitting poker-straight in the front row beside Morgan, and his face was as blank as the wall.

Buck slipped his arm from the pew to Kate's shoulder and pulled her slightly closer. Kit sure enough looked like he was in shock, and Morgan was just…absent. He hadn't said a word to anyone the whole morning, and Buck knew his brother was remembering every miserable day he'd spent with Cece.

The chaplain paused and looked out across the mourners in the little room, past him and Kate, past Carson and Luke and Jesse and Chance. They were all there except Will. Will was in the Air Force, and he hadn't been able to get leave.

"Is there anyone here who would like to say a few words of remembrance?" the chaplain asked softly.

Buck repressed a snort. *You don't wanna hear what I'd say,* he thought tartly, then repressed a sigh, because Morgan slowly unfolded his lanky frame and walked up to the lectern. The chaplain put a hand on his arm and stepped back to give him the floor.

Morgan looked down at his hands, then up at his family, then over at Kit.

Kate dug in her bag and pressed a handkerchief to her mouth as Morgan mumbled, "Cece was a beautiful woman, and I loved her with all my heart." His eyes moved to Kit's face, and a wintry smile crossed his own.

"We weren't a perfect couple. I guess no couple is. But we sure got one thing right. We had the best boy in the world, and we both knew it. His Momma and I both loved Kit. We both knew that our boy was the best thing about us."

Kate shook her head and sobbed quietly into her hanky, and Buck blinked back a tear of his own. The memorial service itself might be a big show put on for Kit's benefit, but he knew that Morgan meant every word he was telling his son.

He glanced at his other brothers. All of them were staring at Morgan in sympathy. Luke wept openly and wiped his eyes, Carson rubbed his nose, and Chase stared at Morgan in frowning compassion. Jesse was stone-faced and had his arms crossed in front of his chest, but even he had to clear his throat.

Morgan shook his head sadly. "Cece and me couldn't make it work, but I'll always remember her like she was the first time I saw her. The only thing in my heart for her now, is the memory of the happy times."

Kate broke down and wept audibly, and Buck pulled her into his chest. She leaned into him with her face in his jacket as Morgan nodded to the chaplain and slowly walked back to his seat. He turned to Kit and stretched a protective arm around his son's shoulders.

The chaplain returned to the podium. "Let us bow our heads in prayer, beloved."

Buck bowed his head as the chaplain prayed, "Dear Lord, please comfort Morgan and Kit and all of Cece's family and friends. May they, as Morgan said, remember the good times. Amen."

"Amen," ten voices echoed, and Buck raised his head and squeezed Kate's arm as she pressed her handkerchief to her eyes.

"The family has requested that we sing a hymn," the chaplain intoned, and Buck reached for a hymnal. His eyes moved back to Morgan and Kit. Kit's little head was bowed, and Morgan was leaning down to whisper something in his son's ear.

Buck's heart was wrung in him, and he rubbed his nose and blinked and comforted himself with the thought: *Well, at least these'll be the last tears that Cece will cause this family.*

He found the hymn on the program and joined his voice to his brothers' as they sang:

"Abide with me: fast falls the eventide

the darkness deepens, Lord, with me abide.

When other helpers fail and comforts flee,

Help of the helpless, O abide with me."

Chapter 39

"You little…"

Roger swore under his breath and gripped the plastic wheel of his rental car as he glared at the dark highway ahead. Cece had robbed him, and it was sheer luck that he'd tucked his driver's license and $200 in the back of his wallet.

Otherwise, he wouldn't even have been able to rent the bucket he was driving.

But what that treacherous little vixen didn't know, was that he hadn't called her up just to scream threats. He had a phone tracking app that only needed her number, and it was showing him a bright red dot moving straight down the interstate to the Mexican border.

Cece was speeding through the darkness about 200 miles ahead of him. Soon he'd catch up with her, and then she'd learn not to play tricks on him again.

He glanced at the speedometer. He was over the limit, but he didn't want to go crazy. Sure and steady would win the race.

Cece was burning gas fast, and she'd have to stop and refuel soon. He was gaining on her, and if he kept steady he'd catch her well before she got to Mexico.

She didn't know he was following her.

He glanced at the rolling eastern horizon. Dawn would soon be blooming across the eastern sky; but it would be dark again by the time he caught up to his wife.

And that suited his purpose just fine.

By nine o'clock Roger pulled into a truck stop cafe for gas and a quick breakfast. It was a dingy hole in the wall, but he'd been running on fumes and he didn't have time to look for a better restaurant.

He parked the clunky blue sedan in front of the cafe and climbed out with a gasp of relief. He'd been folded up in the tiny car for hours, and he was furious and hungry.

He opened the grimy door with distaste, moved to a corner booth, and slid onto the plastic seat. He was facing a glass wall, and he had an excellent view of a row of parked semis.

A tired-looking waitress appeared at his elbow with a pen and a pad. "What'll you have, honey?"

Roger shot her a green glance. "I'd like black coffee." He glanced at the counter and got a glimpse of what looked like a work release con at the griddle.

"What else, honey?"

Roger closed his eyes and rubbed his brow. "Ham and eggs, buttered toast."

The waitress closed her pad with a snap. "Coming up."

Roger glanced up at her. "Make it snappy!"

She raised an eyebrow and moved off, and Roger shook out his napkin. He was just resigning himself to a long wait when his phone beeped in his pocket.

He dug it out quickly and snarled, "So you finally called me!"

There was a long pause on the other end, and a dry voice drawled, "Yes, you may well have been awaiting a call from me, Mr. Tomlinson."

Roger's brows rushed together. "Who is this?"

There was a slight cough on the other end. "My name is Eugene Clemmons, Mr. Tomlinson. I'm the attorney representing the Spade family."

Roger sat bolt upright on the booth. "Oh."

The dry voice went on, "I was given some materials by my clients to review. I understand they were sent by you."

Roger licked his lips. His heart began to beat strangely, and he felt a bit short of breath.

"Are you still there, Mr. Tomlinson?"

"I'm here."

"Well, I won't take up much of your time," the lawyer sighed. "But I'm going to offer you some advice, Mr. Tomlinson, and I suggest you listen, because my advice is usually expensive. Go away, and don't bother my clients again. Trust me when I tell you, I have enough on you right now to send you to Beaumont. I believe you've almost been there once already, isn't that right?"

Roger went red to the roots of his hair, but stifled the expletives that jumped to his lips.

"If you try to claim paternity of Kit Spade, if I find out that you've so much as called my clients again, I'll see you behind bars. I have every little thing I need to put you there.

"Good day, Mr. Tomlinson."

The line went dead, and Roger sat there with the phone to his ear for an instant before he came to himself.

The waitress appeared again with a pot of coffee, and she reached over to pour some into his cup. Roger stared down at it in stunned silence.

"Your food'll be here in a few minutes," she murmured and bustled away.

Roger stared out the window at the big trucks and shook his head. *Cece was right after all*, he marveled. *That stinking shark of theirs just fixed me, all right.*

He pulled his hands over his mouth, thinking furiously. His first plan to get the Spade's money had fizzled out, but he had a backup plan in reserve. The only catch was, he needed Cece even more this time to make it work.

He needed her willing cooperation, and that might not be easy to get back, now that he'd roughed her up a little.

He frowned into space, working out the details in his mind, sorting out the things that might go wrong. He couldn't afford to fail this time. With luck, he could still succeed; but luck was something he'd been short of lately.

Still, he had some things in his favor. He had no doubt that he could smooth Cece down if he tried. If Cece had one weakness in her cold, greedy little heart, it was a man who knew how to make her feel good; and he did.

The waitress appeared again carrying a tray. She set a steaming plate down on the table in front of him and stood back.

"Enjoy."

Roger stared down at the food and reached for his coffee cup. That chilling phone call had robbed him of his appetite; but he was going to drink as much coffee as he could stand.

He needed to keep his wits about him when he caught up with Cece again.

He was going to have to turn in the performance of his life.

Chapter 40

Buck stood in the front doorway of the ranch house and waited as a gleaming silver Bentley slowly pulled to a stop in the drive. It was a cold, clear fall day, with a deep blue sky, but he could see his own breath curling faintly through the air.

Buck sauntered down the front steps as the car door opened and Eugene Clemmons climbed out.

Buck walked up and clapped his lawyer on the back. "Well come on in, Eugene! It's a long drive up from Dallas, and it's cold out here."

Eugene adjusted his suspenders and rolled up the cuffs of his shirt. "It is that, but it's worth it. I have good news, and I wanted to deliver it in person."

Buck ushered him into the house and over to a lounge area to one side of the atrium. A lively blaze crackled in an open fireplace, and a steaming pot of coffee and two cups were waiting on the table next to a leather couch.

"Come on over and warm up," Buck told him, and poured coffee into a thick white mug. He handed it over, and Eugene sipped the brandy appreciatively, then sighed as he sank down onto the couch.

Buck took a mug and sat down beside his guest. "You are coming by for our Christmas party, aren't you Eugene? Kate's going all out this year. No more mariachi singers. She's going to hire some jazz trio from Dallas."

The older man shot him a dry glance. "Thank heaven for Kate's musical taste, then," he drawled, and Buck sputtered with laughter.

"Yeah, I know what you thought about the mariachi band, Eugene, but everybody else liked 'em."

"I always enjoy your Christmas parties, Buck," Eugene told him briskly. "I'll be here with bells on. *Speaking* of which."

"Yeah, what's this good news you're talking about?" Buck asked wryly. "It ain't every day you deliver it in person."

Eugene set the mug down on the table and turned to fix him with a serious look. "Yes, it's good news," he replied. "Roger Tomlinson has dropped his attempt to be declared Kit's biological father."

Buck stared at him warily. "All right. That's good as far as it goes. But he could try again any time, couldn't he?"

"Yes," Eugene agreed dryly, "but it's very, very unlikely. I uncovered some important facts about Mr. Tomlinson, and that probably had something to do with his decision."

"Huh! He knew that you were about to come after him with tongs," Buck muttered into his drink. "Ol' Roger's done a lot of dirt, and all that would come out in court."

"It would indeed," Eugene agreed, and took another sip of black coffee. "And it seems that Tomlinson just keeps *on* doing dirt. You remember that DNA test result he sent us—the one that showed a 92 percent match with Kit's?"

Buck snorted. "How could I forget it?"

Eugene pinched his mouth into a straight, satisfied line. "I had it checked out, and you won't believe what I found. It's a forgery. Ordered online from some fly-by-night company that sells fake DNA results for $25. They're for deadbeat dads who want to skip out on the baby's mother. They're meant to fool the man's partner."

Buck felt his mouth dropping open, then he laughed out loud. "Ol' Cece picked a real winner this time, didn't she?" He shook his head.

"Roger Tomlinson's an amateur. A petty grifter," Eugene replied scornfully. "I called to tell him as much, and I told him that if he dares to bother you again I'll make sure he goes in for a long, long time." He shook his head. "But he was finished even before then. Without Cece's ties to your family he's sunk, and he knows it. That's why he's dropping his legal challenge. This whole thing was an outrageous bluff.

"But," he added briskly, "it's over now. If Tomlinson dares to bother you again, just let me know. I'll tear him into so many pieces in court that each one will have to go to a different jail."

Buck burst into delighted laughter and held out his coffee mug. Eugene touched it with his own in a quiet toast.

"Here's to good news," the attorney murmured, with a faint *clink;* and Buck shook his head as he took a relieved sip of coffee.

"To good news."

The sound of heavy footsteps approaching made them both look up, and Buck broke out into a wide grin as Morgan came walking by.

Buck winked at his attorney, then called: "Come on over here and say hello to Eugene, Morg. He's got something to tell you."

Morgan approached them slowly and with a wary look. *Poor fellow,* Buck thought in sudden sympathy, *he ain't used to getting good news from a lawyer.*

Morgan stuck his hands in his pockets and nodded to Eugene. "Mornin', Eugene," he rumbled. "What brings you up from Dallas so early?"

Eugene pulled his glasses down on his nose and fixed Morgan with a bright, mischievous look over the rims. "I just got some very good news," he announced. "It was so good that I wanted to deliver it myself. Roger Tomlinson's DNA test was a ridiculous fake. It wouldn't be accepted as evidence in any court in America." Eugene opened his eyes wide and leaned forward to shout:

"He's no more Kit's father than I am!"

Morgan's mouth dropped open slightly, and he stared at Eugene as if he couldn't quite believe the news. Buck clapped his brother on the shoulder.

"That's right, Morg! Ol' Roger's picked up his hat and walked out of the ring. If he tries to come back, Eugene says he'll have him dragged off to jail!"

"I can't believe it," Morgan laughed, and they both sputtered to see the joy in his eyes. He ran a hand through his hair, shook his head, and laughed again.

"I can't believe it!"

Eugene smiled grimly. "Believe it. And thank you for thinking of me," he went on. "I can't remember the last time it gave me so much pleasure to send a snake flying back into the bushes."

They both burst out laughing, and Buck slung an arm around Morgan's shoulder. "Come on, Morg," he urged, "this calls for a celebration. Let's take the day off. Go get Kit. Let's take the helicopter up to Thunder Lake and spend the day on the speedboat."

Morgan smiled into his eyes, gripped his arm hard, and shook it. "Give me ten minutes," he replied, and turned to hurry back to the stairs.

Buck watched him go. 'Thank you, Eugene," he muttered, then turned to his friend. "Say, why don't you come with us? It's a beautiful day out. It'll be perfect once it warms up."

"I'd love to, but I can't," Eugene replied. "I have a client deposition at noon, and I'll barely make it."

"At least stay long enough to have something to eat," Buck objected, but the older attorney shook his head.

"Thank you, Buck, but I have to go. I'll take you up on it before long."

Buck sighed and accepted defeat. "Thanks for coming up yourself, Eugene," he said softly. "We appreciate it."

"It was my pleasure." He stuck out his hand, and Buck shook it heartily.

"Come back and stay with us, Eugene."

"I will."

Buck walked his guest outside to the door, then raised his hand in parting as Eugene looked up from his car door. He watched as their unassuming, apex-predator lawyer cranked his car, carefully turned the wheel of the Bentley, and cruised down the driveway.

Kit came pattering up to his side and stopped breathlessly. "Daddy says we're going to the lake, Uncle Buck!"

Buck looked down at his little nephew and raised an arm to drape around his shoulder. "That's right, cowboy. We're going up for a helicopter ride, and then we're going to ride on the speedboat!"

Kit's dark blue eyes lit up. "Kewwll," he breathed, and Buck laughed and rubbed his head.

Morgan walked up with a duffel bag slung over his back. "I'm ready if you are," he mumbled, and Buck grinned from ear to ear.

"Let's   go!"

Chapter 41

"Alley oop!"

It was mid-October, and Heather lifted Kit in her arms and plunked him down atop a stack of hay bales and chrysanthemums. She adjusted her sunglasses, struck a pose, and put a hand behind her hat.

"Take a picture quick, Morgan!"

Morgan fished his cell phone out of his jeans pocket, lifted it up, and centered them in his viewfinder. Kit stuck his hand up behind Heather's head to give her rabbit ears just as the frame froze.

Morgan gave them a thumb's up. He was pretty sure that it'd been a mistake to let Heather wangle him into coming to the festival with her; but he *had* asked her to—kind of—and he didn't go back on his word.

Not that he wasn't having a good time.

"Let's see how it came out," Heather cried, and hurried to his side to inspect the picture. She giggled to see Kit's crazy expression and the rabbit cars behind her own head. "That looks about right," she nodded. "I grew up in a houseful of boys, and we had maybe one or two serious pictures my whole childhood."

Morgan rested his hand lightly on her shoulder as they walked through the festival gates. "You must've had a rough time," he replied, with a gleam of amusement.

Heather eyes laughed at him. "Oh good grief, no! I loved it. I was a tomboy. I ran faster and climbed higher than all of 'em except my oldest brother. Him and I fought all the time. Sometimes I beat him up!"

Morgan laughed in surprise, and Heather laughed with him. Morgan smiled down at her and tightened his hand on her arm just a bit. He was learning that Heather had a real talent for making him relax. He didn't know if she had that effect just on him, or if it was part of her general gift. She was a healer, after all.

It was the first time he'd been off the ranch since the memorial service, and he was surprised by how relieved he felt. Even Kit seemed to be having a good time.

It was a glorious fall afternoon. It was late in the day, but the sky was still a deep, bright blue without a single cloud. It was sunny, but the air had the snap of the first day of fall, and it was fragrant with the aroma of apples and cinnamon and melted caramel and hay.

The festival had been set up in a big field about a mile out of Sandy Creek, and a cluster of tents had sprung up near the entrance. Patrons entered the festival area under an archway of fragrant hay bales, and the main walkway was lined with banks of yellow, orange and rust-colored chrysanthemums. An old wagon was loaded down with orange pumpkins in all shapes and sizes.

Kit skipped along as his side, and Morgan watched him in quiet satisfaction. It did his heart good to see Kit smiling and happy, and it gave him hope that his son's youth and resilience would help him recover from the shock of his mother's death.

Kit's eyes zoomed to a big table covered in pumpkins. A big sign read, "Carve your own pumpkin" in big orange letters.

"Daddy, can I carve a pumpkin?" Kit begged, and turned pleading eyes to his.

Morgan gazed down at his eager face. "Sure, buddy. I'll help you."

Kit scampered into the tent, and Morgan followed at a leisurely pace with his arm around Heather's shoulder. He watched in indulgent amusement as a kindly-looking, white-haired lady faced Kit behind the table. She folded her plump hands and smiled down at him.

"Well, young man, would you like to choose a pumpkin?"

Kit glanced up at him, and Morgan gave him a thumb's up. Kit's quick glance scanned the pile of fat pumpkins. He pointed to a round one with a small brown finger, and Morgan released Heather to walk over and pick Kit up.

"We'll take that one," he told the lady, and she placed the big, round pumpkin down on the table in front of them. Morgan held Kit with one arm and pulled a folding chair up with the other.

He set Kit down snugly in his lap, and reached back into his jeans to pull out his pocket knife. Kit watched in awe as he opened it, gripped the pumpkin, and carved a circle around the top.

Heather pulled up a chair and watched as he finished, then lifted the top of the pumpkin off.

"There you go, sport," he told Kit. "Get your hands down in there and pull all that goop out."

Kit giggled in glee as he stuck both hands down into the pumpkin and began plopping globs of orange gunk onto the plastic tablecloth. As he worked, the older lady showed them a laminated page with dozens of pumpkin faces: smiling faces, scowling faces, scary faces, scarecrow faces.

"We have some patterns here, if you want to follow them," she suggested.

Morgan turned his face into Kit's to murmur, "Which one do you want to carve, buddy?"

Kit glanced at it as he reached deep into the pumpkin. "The scarecrow face!" he demanded, and Morgan nodded.

"The scarecrow it is, then."

He noticed Heather's eyes on his hands as he carved the face on the pumpkin. She was watching intently, as if he was doing a big, important task, and they exchanged a smile as he worked.

"What do you think of that, buddy?" he asked at last, and Kit beamed at him.

"Super cool!" he crowed, and Morgan laughed and pulled him close.

"If you're going to walk the corn maze, I can keep your pumpkin until you want to leave," the older lady told them, and Morgan agreed with relief. He handed her a ten dollar bill, and she tucked it into a little metal box.

"Where to next, chief?" he asked Kit.

"The corn maze!" Kit laughed, and Morgan stood up and swung Kit up with him.

"All right, the corn maze, then. You ready, Heather?" he asked.

Her face was faintly flushed, and her answering smile was soft and warm. The sight of that smile made him stop in his tracks for a second to soak it in.

Somehow she looked seventeen years old, as fresh and pink as a farm girl, and he almost shook his head in amazement. She always looked younger than she was, but that afternoon Heather was lovely, and he'd have to be made out of stone not to notice it.

He felt something in his heart warning him not to get tangled up with another woman, and he meant to be wise. But it was good to enjoy an autumn day with a beautiful woman and a dear little boy, and he couldn't deny it.

So he extended his hand, and Heather took it, and they walked out into the sunshine together.

Chapter 42

The entrance to the corn maze was a canopy of corn husks, and an attendant standing beside it handed Morgan a map. "If you get lost, you can find the way out on the map," he explained, and Morgan tucked it into his shirt pocket.

"Daddy, let me down," Kit asked, and he set his little son down on the ground. Kit's foot had no sooner touched the ground than he went scampering down the corn row directly ahead.

"Don't go too far away!" Morgan called after him, and Kit laughed and zoomed around a corner.

"It'll be all right," Heather soothed him. "He can't get too lost."

Morgan stared after Kit with a worried frown, and Heather squeezed his hand as they walked along together. "It's fun to watch you and Kit together," she told him quietly. "I enjoy it. You're such a good father."

Morgan felt pleasure bloom in his heart, but he shook his head. "Kit's my boy," he replied simply.

The look Heather gave him was like a kiss on his cheek. "Yeah. You know what I like best about you, Morgan? That 'Kit's my boy' is all the reason you need. That you seem to take it for granted that everyone must feel that way."

She shook her head. "I wish everyone did. My own father left us when I was three years old. We made it because my brothers went to work and helped Mom."

He glanced at her in concern. "I'm sorry to hear that."

She shrugged and smiled up at him. "We probably were better off without him," she murmured. "I was too young to remember him, but my brothers told me he was a drunk. Anyway, we made out all right, so all's well that ends well, I guess."

Morgan gave her an answering smile, but he was secretly appalled. He'd lost his parents when he was young, but their grandparents had stepped up instantly. He couldn't imagine growing up without a strong father figure, like Big Russ had been to them.

That Heather had been deprived of that, made her seem smaller, more vulnerable and waif-like than she already did to him, and he stretched a protective arm around her shoulders.

He noticed that she brightened up immediately, and she snuggled in close.

If I didn't know better, he thought wryly, *I'd think that woman likes me.*

Morgan sighed and sobered as they walked along. He still didn't think it was a good idea to get involved with Heather, but now that the threat of losing Kit had been lifted off him, maybe he could relax.

It was a good day to walk in the sunshine with a pretty girl.

Heather glanced up at him. "How's Cochise doing?" she asked. "I seem to remember you being worried about him."

Morgan searched his memory. It seemed to him that he had mentioned something about that to Heather, just in passing. He rubbed the back of his neck.

"He's still a little slow," he rumbled. "I can't see anything wrong with him, though. He's probably just getting older."

"I'll have to take a look at him when we get back," Heather murmured, and casually slipped an arm around his waist.

Morgan glanced down at her in surprise. Things were getting awful friendly between him and Heather. He couldn't pretend he wasn't pleased about that, but on the other hand, it was happening fast. Maybe too fast for a man with a small boy whose mother had just died.

He cleared his throat and pretended not to notice Heather's arm around his waist, but it was hard to ignore. He could feel her hand on him as vividly as if her fingertips had burned through his shirt; but he couldn't think of any tactful way to wiggle free, so he just let her hand stay there.

They meandered through the corn maze, this way and that, and to him, the time seemed to fly. He didn't remember all they said: just Heather's laughing face turned up to his, and the rays of the lowering sun sifting through the brown corn stalks, and Kit's high voice piping from somewhere up ahead. When he looked up, a string of birds flitted over, tiny arrows against a cool blue sky.

It had been a long time since he'd just relaxed and forgot his troubles. And it had been forever since he'd had a smiling woman on his arm, someone who actually seemed to like him.

It felt good.

He caught himself laughing once or twice, felt the tension seeping out of his muscles. And slowly it came to him, a knowing deep down in him, that it wasn't just the sunny day or the lawsuit lifting off him that made him feel so good.

It was Heather being with him. It was the glad way she laughed, the way she always wanted to be close to him, how laid back and unfussy she was. How she didn't expect anything from him except for him to be there with her.

To have a good time together.

He glanced down at her. She was as transparent as a glass full of light. She wasn't hiding anything, and probably couldn't if she tried.

He could see that she genuinely liked him, and he was starting to get the feeling that it might be more than that. He still didn't know how to feel about it, and he sure hadn't decided what to do. He'd have to study on it hard; but for the moment, he was just enjoying her company.

Well—maybe it was a little more than that.

On a sudden impulse, he leaned over and gave Heather a soft, lingering peck on the cheek. She reached up to caress a strand of his hair. They were trembling on the edge of something more when his phone rang, and once again, the moment passed.

Chapter 43

Morgan reached into his jeans pocket to pull his cell phone out. He pressed it to his ear as he walked along.

"Yeah."

Hank's worried voice yelped at him from one end. "Morgan, I'm sorry to bother you on your day off, but I think you should come over here and have a look at Cochise. He's been acting weird all day today, and I can't figure what's wrong with him."

Morgan's dark brows rushed together. "What's the trouble with him?"

He could almost see Hank rub his neck. "Well, he seems weak for some reason. We turned him out into the south pasture down by the creek, and he romped out there all day; but when he came in at feeding time, his legs were shaking a bit, and one of his eyelids is drooping down."

Alarm set Morgan's nerves on alert. "I'll be right down there."

He hung up and slipped the phone back into his pocket. When he raised his eyes, he saw that Heather was staring at him in concern,

"What's wrong?"

Regret billowed across his heart as he saw the look of disappointment on Heather's face. She already knew that he was going to be leaving; and he didn't want to hurt her further by telling her *why* he was leaving.

Because if Cochise was seriously ill, he didn't want anybody but Arthur, his old vet, to put his hands on that horse. He was feeling closer to Heather every day, but he wasn't going to gamble on her.

Not with Cochise.

"I'm sorry, Heather, but something's come up back at the ranch. I'm going to have to go take care of it."

A crestfallen look filled her eyes, and she looked down. "Oh."

He couldn't resist reaching out to touch her arm. "We'll have to do this another time." He turned on the words and went striding down the corn row. "Kit!" he called. "Kit, I need you to come back here now!"

Heather gave him a sympathetic look. "Don't forget Kit's pumpkin," she reminded him.

"We'll get it," he replied, and was relieved to see Kit's curious face appear at the corner of the maze. "We've got to leave, son," he murmured. "I have to go back to the ranch."

Heather looked at him in concern. "Is there something I can do to help?"

Guilt flicked in him, but he shook his head. "That's real nice of you, Heather, but no. Come on, Kit!"

Kit came scampering to his side, and he put his hand on Kit's shoulder and turned him around. "Heather, why don't you and Kit go get his pumpkin, and I'll bring the jeep around."

He strode off toward the parking lot, and his mind was already miles away in that big, drafty barn. Hank's description of Cochise's shaking legs and drooping eyelids sounded serious. Like they might be neurological problems.

If that was right, it was bad. Maybe even life-threatening; and as soon as he was out of earshot of Kit and Heather, he was calling Arthur.

The phone rang for what seemed like forever, and Morgan fretted, *I hope he's not off on that trip to Alaska. He's the only man I'd trust with Cochise.*

Come on, Arthur.

To his relief, someone finally picked up on the other end.

"Arthur?"

There was a smile in Arthur's voice as he replied, "Well, Morgan! It's nice to hear from you."

Morgan walked to his car and fumbled with his keys. "Arthur, I'm calling to ask for your help. Something's wrong with Cochise, and I want you to come look at him. Hank says he's trembling. That one eyelid is drooping."

Arthur's tone darkened with worry. "When did this happen?"

"Today, as far as I can tell." Morgan cranked the jeep and pressed the phone to his ear with his shoulder as he back the car out of the space. "Look, Arthur, I'm not at home, but I can meet you there in thirty minutes. Can you come?"

"Of course," Arthur assured him. There was a small pause, and he added, "Is Heather off someplace else?"

Morgan felt his face going red, but he answered, "No, but I'd appreciate it if you didn't say anything about this to her, Arthur. I don't want to hurt her feelings. I hope I can keep it a secret."

There was a gusty sigh on the other end. "All right, Morgan. I'll be over there as soon as I can drive over."

Morgan relaxed in relief. "Thanks, Arthur, I owe you. I'll be there in a half hour."

"I'll see you there."

Morgan dropped the phone, stuffed it back into his pocket, and pulled the jeep around to the entrance just as Heather and Kit came walking out.

Morgan glanced at Heather's happy face as she opened the door for Kit, then climbed into the passenger seat beside him. Sympathy and guilt swirled in his chest, but he glanced at Kit as he set the pumpkin down on the seat.

"Are we all in?"

When Kit closed the door and nodded, Morgan pulled the jeep away. He prayed that Heather didn't find out about it, but he was sure of his choice.

He loved Cochise like a family member, and Arthur was the only person he could bring himself to trust with him.

Chapter 44

By the time Morgan got back to the ranch, the sun was setting over the western hills. There were long shadows across the lawn as he pulled the jeep up into Heather's driveway.

Heather turned, leaned over quickly, and gave him a quick peck on the cheek. He registered a soft touch and a whisper of honeysuckle, then she pulled back.

"Bye, guys."

Morgan mustered a smile for her. "Bye, Heather."

He bit his lip as he watched her climb out of the car, then turn back to smile at him through the open window.

"I had a great time, Morgan," she beamed.

"We did too, Heather," he told her, and winced at the guilty note in his own voice. He waited for her to climb the porch steps and get safely inside before he pulled the jeep out of the drive.

Morgan sighed and glanced at Kit in the rear view mirror. "Buddy, I'm going to drop you off at the house. I want you to go upstairs and wash up. I'll be back later tonight. You can make yourself a sandwich until dinner."

"What about the pumpkin?" Kit wondered aloud.

"I'll bring it in," Morgan promised. He turned his attention back to the road. The top of the big barn was just appearing over the top of the next rise, and it was hard for him to drive past; but he noticed, with relief, that Arthur's car was already there. He glanced at the barn doors as they passed, but they were closed, and he sighed and drove on.

Kit scrambled out as soon as he pulled the car to a stop, and Morgan yelled after him.

"Slow down, Kit! Don't run in the house!"

The front door slammed behind him, and Morgan sighed and pulled the car around and back down the drive to the barn.

The sound of voices greeted him as he opened the barn doors and walked inside at last. He heard Arthur mumble a question and heard Hank respond, "No, this is the first time I've seen it. He seemed okay yesterday. Maybe a little off his feed."

Morgan strode down the aisle toward Cochise's stall. "How's he doing?" he called, and walked up to the door.

Hank stood back as he pushed in. Arthur was bending down, feeling of Cochise's legs, and he was frowning.

"There's a slight tremor," he mumbled, and Morgan stepped closer. He was shocked to see a faint, rippling tremor in Cochise's legs; and when he put out a gentle hand to turn his horse's head, he saw that one eyelid was drooping lower than the other, just like Hank had said.

Morgan rubbed the stallion's nose, and Cochise turned toward him and nuzzled his chest weakly. Morgan blinked back tears and looked down at the floor.

"Is he in pain?"

Arthur frowned as he ran a hand over Cochise's flanks. "I'll give him something when we get him to the hospital. I'll need to talk to Heather to see what shots or medicines he's had, and we're going to have to do a raft of tests." He stood up abruptly and turned to Morgan.

"We need to get him over to the hospital while he can still stand. At this rate, he's going to be down soon."

Morgan frowned, but nodded. "Hank, bring the trailer around. I'll get the jeep."

He marched out of the barn and dug for his phone as he went. *I should've known better,* he thought to himself as he dialed Heather's number. *Now she's going to be hurt at me. I hope I can live it down.*

The phone picked up, and Heather's cheerful voice chirped on the other end. "Hello?"

Morgan opened the jeep door and slid in. "Heather, this is Morgan. I'm sorry to bother you, but we've got an emergency. Cochise is badly sick, and we're bringing him down to the hospital." He paused again and added, "Arthur's going to need your help."

To his relief, the first words out of her mouth were: "What's wrong with Cochise?"

Morgan turned to glance behind him and backed the jeep up to the barn doors. "Tremors. Eyelid droop."

"Bring Hank with you," she replied briskly. "I'll need to talk to him. And bring me the last few days of samples of Cochise's feed and manure for testing."

"We'll be down in a few minutes," Morgan told her, then added: "Thanks, Heather."

"Sure. I'll see you then."

Morgan tossed the phone down and climbed out of the car in time to see Hank pulling the horse trailer by a hand dolly. He bent down to help him align the trailer with the back of his jeep, then hitched it up tight.

Morgan looked up at Hank. "You'll need to come with us, Hank. Heather wants to talk to you. She needs samples, too."

"Yep."

Morgan hurried back inside the barn, past the other curious horses with their ears pricked high, down to Cochise's stall. Arthur was stroking the stallion's flanks and crooning in his ear.

Morgan put a hand on his shoulder. "We'll get him, Arthur. The jeep's outside." He reached for the bridle on the wall and slipped it gently over Cochise's head. Arthur frowned as the stallion mouthed the bit, but said nothing as Morgan opened the stall door and slowly led Cochise to the barn door.

The other horses watched intently as Cochise walked past, slowly and proudly. A few of them nickered softly, others tossed their heads.

Morgan walked Cochise to the trailer, then helped him move up the ramp and inside. He closed the door, stalked up to the jeep and got in beside Arthur.

Hank slid in behind him a few moments later, and Morgan cranked the jeep and sent it moving down the road as quickly as he dared. His chest ached for a dozen reasons, but the important two were that he might lose a horse that he genuinely loved, and that he'd offended a woman that he…

Morgan shook his head, postponed that decision for the future, and breathed a little prayer as he drove.

It seemed he was always just about to lose something or someone that he loved; and once again, he found himself hoping for a miracle.

Chapter 45

Morgan crossed his arms and paced back and forth in the hospital's big exam room. It was a sterile, unlovely square with cinder block walls, a concrete floor and ugly florescent lights that cast everything in a faintly greenish light.

Arthur and Heather had strapped Cochise up in a sling in case he might fall down, and Morgan stared at him unhappily. The sterile exam room lights washed out Cochise's gleaming black coat and tail, and the stallion stood there in patient misery with his head hanging down.

"I've checked, and it isn't a choke case," Arthur was muttering. "And it doesn't seem to be colic. The x-rays don't show any twisting or blockage of his bowels, and the analgesic I gave him doesn't seem to help."

He looked up at Heather. "What shots has he had?"

"All the recommended," Heather murmured. "Rabies, PHF, botulism, flu/rhino."

"How long ago?"

Morgan turned and walked out of the room and into the dark little hall outside. The murmuring went on inside, and it was looking like they could be there all night. He fished out his phone and called his house.

The phone picked up on the second ring, and Kit's quick voice pipe, "Hello?"

"Hey buddy. It looks like I'm going to be a little late, so you can eat the leftover pizza in the fridge from last night."

"I already did."

Guilt flicked through Morgan's chest. "Oh. Well then, go brush your teeth and get your pajamas on. If I'm not back in a little while, go on to bed."

"Okay, Daddy."

"Love you, buddy."

Morgan hung up with a sigh and rubbed his eyes. He could hear Arthur and Heather puttering around in the exam room behind him, and Heather suddenly came breezing past him with plastic tubes in her hand.

Morgan straightened up and barked, "How's he doing?"

Heather stopped just long enough to explain, "He's about the same. I'm about to test some blood samples."

Morgan watched as she disappeared into another small room, and the soft sound of whirring machinery soon seeped under the door.

Morgan sighed and drifted back into the exam room. He walked up to Cochise and passed a hand over his neck in a gentle caress. Usually Cochise would nuzzle him in return, but Morgan was quick to notice that his horse was now too listless to respond.

Arthur had pulled up a chair and was staring at the horse. Morgan turned to him.

"He's getting worse."

Arthur glanced at him and nodded in silent acknowledgment. "I don't know what it is," he admitted softly. "We can't find any evidence of the usual culprits: colic, blockage, encephalitis, infection." He pulled his hands over his face and looked at Morgan over them.

"Morgan, I think it might be a good idea for you to prepare yourself mentally. Cochise has already lost some ground."

Morgan stared at him in stunned silence. "Are you telling me he's gonna die, Arthur?"

Arthur looked up at him sadly. "I'm telling you he could. I'd say we only have hours to figure this out."

Morgan turned abruptly and stalked out of the room, through the hall, and out of the building. He burst out into the night air and inhaled deeply and painfully.

He stood there for a few moments in silence before he noticed Hank leaning against the front wall of the building, smoking and looking up at the stars.

Morgan clenched his fists and stared down at the ground. Hank glanced at him and tossed the cigarette away.

"Bad news, huh?"

Morgan nodded and looked up at the sky. "Arthur says he could die."

Hank shook his head. "I'm real sorry about that, Morg. It's hard to lose a good horse. Especially one that you've had as long as Cochise."

"He's not just a good horse," Morgan replied quietly, and they both fell silent as the evening deepened into true night.

After another thirty minutes Morgan walked back inside again. He could hear Heather and Arthur talking all the way from the lobby of the building.

"Look at his tongue, Arthur," she was saying. "He's having trouble pulling it back in now. Whatever this is, it does neurological damage, and since we can't find anything else, I think it's got to be some kind of toxin."

"Is there anything in the feed samples to suggest poisoning?"

"N-no. But he could've been exposed to a toxin somewhere else."

"You said you gave him the botulism vaccine, correct?"

"Yes, but it might be something else."

Morgan slowed his pace as he neared the exam room door. When the room crept into view, Heather was standing over Arthur's chair with one hand on Cochise's neck.

"I think we should give him antitoxin plasma."

Arthur shrugged wearily. "Go ahead, if you think it might help. At this stage, it can't hurt."

Heather turned on her heel and rushed past, and Morgan watched her hurry back to the little testing room. He drifted into the doorway and watched as she opened a small freezer to retrieve a plastic pouch.

"Is there something I can do to help?"

She glanced up at him as she turned back to a sink and began to run water.

"You can pray," she replied softly. "We're doing all we can for Cochise, but extra help is always welcome."

She drew a bowl full of warm water, set it on the counter, and set the frozen bag down into it. She looked up at his face, then explained, "This is antitoxin plasma. It has to be thawed slowly. We have about thirty minutes to wait, and then we'll give it to him."

Morgan held her eye. "Does he have thirty minutes?"

Heather paused, then walked across the room to take him by the arm. She looked up into his face.

"We'll just have to wait and see," she whispered gently. "I'm so sorry, Morgan. I know this is hard for you. But if I see that he's not going to make it, I'll call you so you can have a few minutes alone with him. Then we'll all help him pass as comfortably as we can. No pain or stress.

"I promise."

Her eyes glittered with tears. Morgan nodded wordlessly, then walked outside to hide his grief in the darkness.

He walked back and forth in front of the long, low vet office with his hands stuck into his pockets. Hank had long since gone home, so he was alone out under the stars, moving to keep himself warm as the chill of deep night set in.

Time seemed to crawl. The silence of the wee hours blanketed the world, so that the crunch of his boots on the gravel drive sounded loud in the stillness. He could hear every little squeak and hurrying sound in the pasture behind the lot, and even the tiny hum of semi trucks zooming past the ranch gates more than a mile down the road.

He stopped for a minute and glanced at the ghostly light in the exam room window. It was the only light shining in the building.

He turned and stared out to where grassy pastures rolled away in the darkness. He'd raised Cochise from a colt, knew his every strength and weakness, every little quirk of his personality. Him and Cochise had been a team for so long that he almost didn't need the reins. Cochise knew him well enough to do what he wanted without being asked.

That he might lose his old friend, was just…no.

He turned around and began pacing again, when the office door suddenly opened behind him. He turned to see Heather's silhouette in the doorway, and his heart gave a sickly *thu*mp.

"Morgan, come inside," she called.

He rushed to follow her, his throat dry with fear; and he breathed a short, sharp prayer: *Lord, help.*

He hurried into the exam room, and to his amazement, Cochise turned his head to greet him, his ears high and his eyes bright with recognition. He walked up to his horse and put a trembling hand on Cochise's shoulder; and to his joy, his old friend ducked his head to nuzzle his chest.

"We think he's going to be alright," Arthur smiled, and Morgan leaned his brow against his horse's neck in relief.

"Heather was right," Arthur went on, and patted her shoulder. "It is probably some kind of toxin, because the plasma seems to have helped Cochise turn the corner."

Heather stared at her patient with her arms crossed. "Botulism, would be my guess," she murmured. "I'd already vaccinated him against that, and it threw me off; but the vaccine only works against the most common strains. He may have come into contact with one of the other ones."

Morgan cleared his throat, but didn't turn to look at her. "Will he make a full recovery?"

Heather and Arthur exchanged a glance, and Arthur shrugged, "We'll have to wait and see. But I think it's likely that he'll come back most, and maybe all of the way. That vaccine slowed the toxin down, kept it from progressing as fast as it could.

"But even so, if we hadn't caught it when we did, he'd probably have been dead within hours."

Morgan rolled his eyes to the ceiling, turned, and took Heather into his arms without a word. He closed his eyes and pressed his face into her neck and just held her.

Arthur cleared his throat, and the chair creaked as he stood up. "I'll just be outside," he announced to no one in particular, and the door swung shut behind him as he left the room.

"I owe you an apology," Morgan mumbled into Heather's hair. "And a big, fat, thank you."

Heather sputtered a bit, curled her hands around his arms, and pressed him away a pace. She smiled up into his eyes.

"You're welcome," she whispered. "And apology accepted. You're not the first man to doubt me, and you probably won't be the last. But you all come around in the end."

She gave him a peck on the cheek and gestured toward the door. "Go on home, Morgan. You need to be with Kit. I'll stay here with Cochise tonight, and I'll call you in the morning to let you know how he's doing."

He frowned, "Are you going to be all right here?"

She sputtered again. "Of course! This isn't exactly my first rodeo. Go on back to the house. I'll call you."

Morgan exhaled, then nodded in surrender. He turned to give Cochise's twitching neck a lingering caress before reaching out for Heather's arm one last time.

"Go on," she whispered.

Morgan stepped away reluctantly, then opened the door and strode out into the hall. Arthur was waiting there, and Morgan reached out and slapped his back.

"Thanks for coming out, Arthur," he murmured. "I'll be sending you something."

"No you won't," Arthur told him calmly, and turned to accompany him through the dark office. "I'm not your employee any more, Morg.

"I'm your friend."

The older man smiled up at him for a moment, clasped his arm, and walked out of the office. Morgan watched him go in speechless emotion and rubbed his nose.

Lord, I don't know what to say, he prayed.

Except thank you.

He watched as Arthur's car pulled out of the lot and disappeared down the drive; and when he walked out himself, he turned to lock the office up tight before he trudged wearily to his own car.

Chapter 46

"Do you understand what they could do to me if they found out?"

Cece paced back and forth across the floor of the miserable Mexican rental house that she and Roger were hiding in. She shot him a fiery glance. He was lounging on a faded red couch with a shot glass halfway to his mouth. He shrugged.

"It's not a crime to fake your own death," Roger muttered.

Cece stifled the urge to slap him. "And you know this *how,* Mr. Trust me, I'm a lawyer?" she snapped. She hugged herself and fell down into a stuffed chair.

She'd known in her gut that she should've just kept driving when Roger caught up to her on the road. But somehow, he'd sweet-talked her into following him into Mexico.

Maybe it had been because he'd started kissing her; and she had to say one thing for Roger, he had a rare talent for *that.*

She just wished that for once, his brains could match his libido.

They'd holed up in a little *colonia* about fifty miles away from the border. Their rental house was a little adobe cottage with a concrete floor and no air conditioning. Just an anemic box fan stuck in one of the windows. The blades were barely moving. Cece dabbed her brow with a tissue. She was sweltering, she was worried, and she was furious.

She shot her husband a green glance. Roger was so desperate for a big score that he'd gone a little crazy. It made him willing to take big, stupid risks.

That crazy, eager light was still in his eyes.

"Listen to me, Cece," he'd panted. "I know what to do."

He'd licked his lips and whispered, "We're going to push your car off into a ravine. Morgan and his family will think you're dead. It'll make them relax. It'll be a fantastic advantage!"

"You're crazy!" she'd yelled, and tried to get away; but his fingers had dug into her arms.

Anger had washed over his face, but he'd controlled himself with a visible effort. "No, I'm not crazy," he'd told her. "It's perfect, you'll see."

She'd stared at him in disbelief. "This is nuts, Roger. I won't do it!"

His eyes met hers. "We can't prove that I'm Kit's father, Cece," he told her slowly. 'The DNA test fell through. We have to try something else."

She'd stared at him. "You faked the test, didn't you, Roger?" She fell back against the seat cushions, laughing weakly. "You sent a fake test result to the best lawyer in Texas," she moaned. "They can sue us for fraud now!"

"Not if we aren't there, Cece," he countered earnestly. "Listen to me, we'll make them believe that you're dead. We'll lay low for a while in Mexico."

"Oh, my—you really are crazy," she'd moaned, and put her head in her hand. "You need a shrink, Roger."

"I need a score," he'd muttered grimly, and his eyes met hers in the mirror again. "And you're going to help us get a big, fat one."

"How, Roger," she'd replied dully. "You've killed whatever hope we had of winning visitation rights with Kit!"

"I have a better idea, Cece," he'd breathed, and the wild, eager light in his eyes had scared her.

Roger had kept straight on the highway, all the way down to the border crossing. It had almost been dark by the time they'd joined the line of cars and trucks at the checkpoint, and Roger had flashed their driver's licenses to the border guards.

They'd crawled through the bottleneck and over the border, and as soon as he was able, Roger had taken their car off the main roads and had made for a mountain ridge in the distance.

"Where are we going, Roger?" she'd demanded.

His eyes were on the distant bluffs. "This road runs up into those mountains," he'd answered.

An hour later, after a harrowing drive up the hairpin curves of a narrow dirt road, Roger had pulled the car over onto the sloping shoulder of the mountain. He'd turned to glare at her.

"Get out of the car."

She'd stared at him, then obeyed, slowly and warily. She was wearing jeans and sneakers, so she was able to do it, but that was her only comfort as she watched her husband put the Mercedes into neutral, jump out and turn the wheel toward the cliff.

"Roger, stop!" she'd shrieked; but he put his shoulder to the frame and pushed the car until it rolled off the road, through the underbrush, and right off the side of the mountain. She'd watched in disbelief as the rear bumper disappeared into the bushes, and then dived over the cliff.

She'd stared at Roger as he clapped his hands clean and walked back toward her. There was a sudden, shattering crash from far below, followed by a deep *boom*.

Roger had taken her by the elbow. "Let's get out of here before somebody shows up," he'd sighed, and she'd groaned and tottered along after him as they made their way back to town.

Cece reached down and rubbed her ankle. It was still rubbed raw and throbbing from the gruelling hike back to civilization, and even that hadn't been the worst of it. They'd made that long, frightening trek off the mountain mostly in the dark; and it had taken them a long time to find a little house to spend the night in.

She bit her lip angrily. She didn't have her cell phone, because Roger had insisted it go over the cliff with the car. "They can track you with it," he explained, as he'd tossed it into the back seat; so now she couldn't call for a cab.

She didn't even speak Spanish.

She'd had plenty of time to be heartily sorry that she'd married Roger, during the week that they'd spent in that miserable little house. He'd gone mostly silent. He spent most of his time sitting in his chair, staring into space as if he was gaming out the fine points of some ridiculous plot.

He still hadn't told her what his brilliant plan was.

Not that it mattered.

As she fumed over it, Roger rose slowly off the couch, fixed her with weirdly eager eyes, and walked over to take her by the shoulders.

"I have it all figured out, Cece," he whispered, and ducked his head to kiss her neck. She turned her face away in exasperation, and he whispered:

"This way, we don't have to wait to get the money. The Spades will cough it up all at once, not dribble it out to us over years and years. One big, beautiful score, baby!"

She tried to pull away from him, but he turned her face to look at him as he smiled down into her eyes.

"Trust me."

Chapter 47

"Gracias."

Cece pulled the shades down and watched as Roger passed off a sheaf of bills to their smiling landlord. The man tucked the bills into his shirt pocket, waved, and ambled back down the steep dirt drive to the overgrown road below.

She released the blinds and turned back to sink down into her chair. The only entertainment in the whole house was an ancient television, and it got only the local stations. She'd been reduced to watching the Mexican soap operas, even though she didn't understand a word of Spanish.

The biggest thing she'd noticed about them was that there was a lot of slapping, and that *'bruja'* was likely an insult.

That she'd sunk to this was all Roger's fault, and she wished with all her heart that she'd made a clean getaway from the hotel. She could've been in Acapulco by now, sipping a Mimosa on the beach, instead of watching ridiculous daytime television in some Mexican backwater.

The door opened and Roger came walking in, and she turned to him with a narrow look.

"I take it we're going to be here for a while," she drawled. "Goody! I'll have time to learn Spanish from watching Mexican reruns from the seventies."

Roger walked to a little table and poured tequila from a square bottle to a little glass. He took a slow, deliberative sip.

"We have to give the Spades a chance to settle down," he told her. "To get comfortable. To accept that you're gone. Then," he smiled, as he sauntered toward her, "*then* we'll hit them.

"When they don't expect it!"

Cece hunched a petulant shoulder. "You still haven't told me how you want Morgan to drop the ransom money, or get Kit back to Morgan. You surely don't expect me to go sticking back into Texas to drop him off!"

Roger's eyes glittered as he looked down at her. "You really need to have some faith in me, Cece," he replied softly, and took another drink.

"I prefer a logical plan," she retorted, with a green glance. "You promised me one, and that's why I'm still here. I don't have to be, Roger."

Her tall, handsome husband stared at her for a silent moment, set down his drink, and sank into a chair beside her. He put a hand on her leg.

"All right, darling. Here's the plan. When your ex and his family have settled down, say about a month from now—"

"A month!"

Roger sighed gently and gave her a look of mild rebuke. "Think of the money, sweetheart. Eyes on the prize."

Cece heaved a different kind of sigh and looked away. "What then?"

"Then, my angel, we return to that little town when they're busy elsewhere, and Kit is up in his room alone. You know the house. It shouldn't be hard for you to get in and out quickly." He smirked and caressed her cheek. "You and I did it often enough, remember?"

A grudging smile flitted across Cece's lips. "I suppose I could," she grumbled.

"That's right. It should be easy, as long as they aren't expecting it. Now that they think you're dead, even that bulldog, what's his name, should let down his guard."

"*Buck*," Cece barked, in a tone of distaste. "He hates my guts, and the feeling is mutual."

Roger smiled and brushed her hair back from her brow. "Well then, it'll be extra fun to imagine his face when we send the ransom note. *Mmm?*"

"Yes it will," she growled, and closed her eyes. "How will we get Kit back to Morgan, though, once he's paid up? I don't want any harm to come to Kit, Roger," she added seriously. "You know that, don't you?"

Roger frowned at her. "Of course, darling! We'll have a third party drop him off at a prearranged place. Don't worry, I've worked with these people before, they know what they're doing."

Cece exhaled in relief. "Good. I want a safe, smooth transfer."

"Oh, it will be, Cece, never fear," he assured her, and she rolled her head back on the sofa and stared up at the dingy ceiling in longing.

"Oh, Roger, what we couldn't do with a couple of million dollars! Especially in South America, where things aren't so expensive." She sidled closer to him. "Let's go to Costa Rica. Buy a nice condo on the beach and fly down to Rio on the weekends."

"I don't see why not," he murmured with a grin and rubbed her arm. "Every day a party, eh, sugar? You can get all the benefits out of your old man, without all the annoying duties."

Cece's lips curled up. "You can say that again," she grumbled. "He actually made us go to church. Church!"

Roger burst into sputtering laughter. "I can just see you in a church pew," he marveled. "Poor darling! Well, consider this your pay day for the torture he put you through."

Cece closed her eyes. "I can't wait, Roger."

Roger's smile shrank, and he brushed her hair with a gentle hand. "Not long now, Cece.

"Be patient."

Chapter 48

"Angels we have heard on high

Sweetly singing o'er the plains

And the mountains in reply

Echoing their joyous strains

"Gloria

In excelsis Deo

Gloria

In excelsis Deo."

Heather hummed along to the Christmas music floating over the sidewalk. She was window shopping as she strolled along on the courthouse square.

She paused outside a little boutique and stared wistfully at the gowns hanging there; then she walked in as gingerly as if she expected to break something.

She needed a full-length, formal party gown, and *La Belle Mademoiselle* was the fanciest and most expensive shop on the courthouse square.

Heather opened the pale green, antique door of the boutique, glanced around the pretty shop, and sighed. She wasn't the girliest girl in the world, and she felt a bit out of place among the perfectly-coiffed, manicured, and very well-to-do women milling around.

But for the first time in her life, she wanted to knock a man's eyes out with a fabulous Cinderella gown. So far, Morgan had only seen her in faded jeans and everyday clothes and with her hair falling down over her shoulders.

Just once, she wanted to be so drop-dead gorgeous that she'd make Morgan Spade forget his own name.

Heather glanced around the little sales floor of the boutique. The owner had renovated a 100-year-old brick storefront to a dress shop, and it was a pleasant space. Some faint, pleasant floral scent perfumed the air, soft music murmured in the background, and formal gowns of every kind were arrayed on tall racks on the boutique walls.

She drifted from one display to another: tiny formal handbags detailed with seed pearls and beads; scarves and shawls of sheer, candy-colored chiffon. There were glittering jewelry displays: tasteful pearl chokers, exquisite faux diamond necklaces and earrings, striking faux sapphire and ruby bracelets.

Heather adjusted one shoulder uncomfortably. She didn't have a clear idea of what she needed or even wanted. She'd been told once by her mother that she looked best in pastels, but she didn't want to show up at a formal party dressed like a teenager.

"Good afternoon. How may I help you?" a smooth voice purred.

Heather turned to see a plump, smiling, older woman standing beside her. Like the other women there, her hair and nails were perfect, and Heather tucked a sprig of her own hair behind her ear self-consciously.

"Um…I'm looking for an elegant party gown," Heather mumbled.

The woman brightened. "Certainly! Do you have a color or style preference?"

"No," Heather replied, then amended, "I mean, I want it to be flattering. That's about it."

"Of course. We'll find the perfect gown for you."

Heather trailed after the other woman as she struck off across the sales floor. The clerk looked back over her shoulder as she walked to ask, "Would you like something to drink?"

"Um…I guess a mineral water."

The clerk led her through the shop to a large, spacious fitting room behind another antique door. The room was as pretty as a wedding cake, decorated in pink and pale green. Three of its walls were completely mirrored, and a big pink settee was placed at the center of the room.

The woman paused in the doorway. "I'll bring out a few of the most common styles and you can try them on and decide which one you like best. Then you can decide on color."

Heather nodded and sank down on the settee, and the woman disappeared.

Heather sighed and put her bag down on the floor beside her feet. She glanced at her own reflection in the mirror.

I look terrible, she thought in dismay. *My hair is a mess. My face is washed out.*

I must've gained ten pounds!

She was seized by the urge to get up and leave the shop in embarrassment, but it would only be putting off the inevitable. If she was going to become Cinderella at the ball, she had to face the scruffy woman in the mirror now.

After a few minutes the clerk returned with a shining armload of beautiful gowns. She hung them up on a nearby rack, one by one, and Heather followed them with her eyes.

The clerk picked up the first gown. "Now here we have a pink chiffon gown with a high collar, a fitted bodice and a sheath skirt. Very feminine, and it would be perfect for your coloring." She set it aside and picked up the next one. "This gown is very sophisticated and elegant. It's a black spaghetti strap slip dress in watered silk. You're slender enough to wear this, and blondes always look wonderful in black."

She set that gown aside and picked up the last one. "Now this is a more romantic dress, a combination gown with an off the shoulder velvet bodice in midnight blue, and a very full skirt in a blue and green silk plaid." She draped the gown over her arm, and Heather's eyes moved from one to the other in indecision.

"Why don't you try them on and see which style you like best." She walked out on the words, and Heather glanced at the shimmering gowns wistfully.

Well, she thought, *the black one is too slinky and the pink one is too foofy.*

Heather reached for the velvet and silk gown, held it up to her chest, and looked in the mirror. Then she tossed it down over the settee and began to unbutton her shirt.

When the clerk returned, fifteen minutes later, Heather was standing in front of the mirror staring at her own reflection in shock. The older woman set a bottle of mineral water down on a table and broke into a wondering smile.

"Oh, that one for certain," she cried, "it's perfect for you!"

Heather stared at the mirror in disbelief. Her hair was still tumbling over her shoulders in disarray, and she still had ten too many pounds; but the smooth, soft curve of her shoulders glimmered in the lamplight, the rich blue velvet bodice made her eyes look bigger and darker, and the skirt belled out from her waist in a glorious confusion of blue and green silk and rustled with her every breath.

She felt like a princess.

The clerk clasped her hands and beamed at her. "I've worked here for five years," she confided, "and I've seen many customers in beautiful gowns. But I must say, miss, you look better in that one than any woman I've seen in this shop. It might have been made for you."

Heather stared at herself in the mirror, wondering if the woman staring back at her was real; but one thing was clear. She'd found the gown that was going to blow Morgan Spade away.

327

"I'll take it!"

Chapter 49

Morgan walked out of the shower, pulled a towel down from a rack, and slung it around his neck. He could hear his phone ringing dimly from the living room, but he had to get dinner on for Kit, put him to bed, and then dress for the Christmas party that Kate and a small army of caterers were setting up downstairs.

He grumbled as he toweled his long hair. He wasn't a big talker, he didn't like big parties, and he especially didn't like dressing up; but Kate had wanted this year's party to be more formal, and since they all liked her they'd gone along.

But Morgan couldn't help hoping that this fancy stuff would be a one-off thing, and he made a mental note to ask Buck to bring Kate around.

Maybe if he worked on her, they could wear their jeans next year and relax.

Morgan pulled on a housecoat and walked out into the hall, and then turned into the kitchen. There was a pizza in the fridge, and he pushed it into the oven, set the timer, and called out: "Kit?"

A high voice piped from the back hall. "Yes, sir."

"I want you to put on your pajamas and wash up. I'm going to get us some dinner, and then you're going to bed."

Kit's voice was glum, but resigned. "Okay."

The phone trilled again in the living room, and Morgan grumbled under his breath and abandoned the kitchen to go answer it. He picked up the receiver and barked, "Hello?"

To his disgust, a robotic voice on the other end replied, "Your mailbox is full. Please erase replies."

Morgan slapped the receiver back into its cradle and turned away, but then turned back. He was busy, but somebody had just called him and hadn't been able to leave a message. He didn't want to miss another one.

He picked up the phone and began scrolling through his recorded messages to decide which to erase.

His brother Luke's voice murmured on the other end. "Hey Morg, I'm going to be out of town for another week. Don't forget to keep on feeding my dog. I'll be back. Okay, bye."

Morgan shook his head and erased the message.

"Mr. Spade, this is Frank Welling at the First Texas Bank. We just wanted to thank you for helping sponsor our first annual Run for Veterans. We appreciate all our donors and we hope to see you next year."

Morgan erased the message and moved on, and the next voice made him stiffen in anger. It was one of the oldest messages on his machine.

Cece's voice burst out, "I know you're getting my messages, Morgan. You can't shut me out forever. I have a right to see my son, and it doesn't matter how long I've been gone. I've been tired, and you know what? I *get* to be tired.

"I know you're telling everyone that I'm a bad mother, but this whole mess is your fault, not mine. You were the one who wanted a kid, remember? Not me!"

Morgan's hand jumped to kill the recording, and he glanced at the hall doorway in dismay. His heart was thrumming with adrenalin.

He could only hope that Kit hadn't heard it.

He hoped that the last words Kit heard from his mother weren't a confession that she hadn't wanted him.

A slight movement from the door made his head snap up, and to his horror, Kit was standing there, his eyes were two question marks. His voice was small and quavering.

"That was Mommy's voice."

Morgan pulled a hand over his mouth and cast about frantically for something to tell him, anything that would take away the sting of those cruel words.

Kit had heard them, so it would do no good to deny them to his son. Morgan stood up quickly, walked across the room to Kit, and knelt down in front of him.

"Ah...yes, son, that was your mother's voice," he said softly. "That was an old phone message."

Kit's eyes glossed over with the first sheen of tears, and his voice sank to a small, hurt whisper.

"She said she didn't want me."

Morgan reached out and took Kit by his arms. "Son, your Momma...your Momma didn't want children at first, it's true," he murmured. "She wanted to wait a few years. But when you came along, I was the happiest man in the world, and your Momma changed her mind. When you were born, she looked down into your eyes and she fell in love with you, just like I did. At first sight."

Kit's lower lip trembled, and Morgan took him into his arms and whispered into his hair.

"Your Momma and I didn't get along, son, but we both loved you, you have to know that. Even when we broke up, we both wanted you. That's why your Momma and I fought so hard in court. Your Momma wanted you, and I wanted you, but only one of us could take care of you."

Kit's arms closed around him, and Kit leaned his head against his chest. "I'm glad you won, Daddy," he whispered, and tears stung Morgan's eyes. He nodded solemnly.

"So am I, son."

Morgan bit his lip into a thin, angry line. Cece didn't deserve that Kit should remember her fondly, but Kit deserved to be at peace, and so he spun one last fairy tale for his son.

"Kit, your Momma loved you very much. She just didn't know how to show it, that's all," he said gently. "Your Momma didn't know a whole lot about being a mother, and she made some mistakes. But she always loved you. She wouldn't have traded you for anything."

Kit raised his head and looked up into his eyes.

"Really, Daddy?"

Morgan gazed down at his son, put on his most tender, reassuring smile, and brushed a tear from Kit's cheek.

"Really, buddy."

The troubled look faded from Kit's eyes, and his frown slowly lifted. He suddenly looked up and asked:

"I'm hungry, Daddy."

Morgan turned him around and swatted his seat. "I'll make us dinner in a second. Go wash up, like I told you, and I'll be in the kitchen in a minute."

He watched as Kit scampered off into the hall, and after he was gone, Morgan closed his eyes, balled his fists, and swallowed a scream.

The fury that he'd been pushing down for months, for years, began to bubble up in his heart. He didn't have time for it, he had things to do, but it boiled up anyway.

It wasn't for his own sake. He was past being hurt himself, he knew all too well what Cece was. But Cece had found a way to hurt Kit from beyond the grave.

One last twist of the knife.

Morgan sat there with his head bowed, trying to stay calm. It was a bad time for six years' worth of anger to hit him, but the pressure had been building for a long time.

He stood up suddenly, stalked across the length of the apartment, slapped the patio door open, slapped it shut behind him, and glared at the dark countryside below. Faint Christmas music was already wafting out from the atrium below, as the hired band was warming up for the party.

Morgan walked to the rail, leaned out over it, took a deep breath, and screamed into the night. He screamed out all his bottled-up frustration, screamed out all the anger he'd pushed down, all the rage.

He screamed out all his grief at the endless loss and damage that one stupid, impulsive kiss on the beach had cost him.

He stood there, panting, glaring out into the blackness. Cece was gone. He couldn't scream at her, and it wouldn't do any good if he did. She'd been as ignorant of morals as a wildcat.

She did what she did, and he just had to suck it up.

He pulled a trembling hand across his mouth and thought: *Well, it's over now. Over at last, thank God.*

He stood there for a moment more, breathing in the cool, fragrant night, getting the peace of it into his soul. He couldn't afford to come unglued in front of his son, or in front of their party guests. He had to pull himself together.

I can do it, he thought wearily, and slowly straightened up.

He pulled his hair back from his brow, squared his shoulders, and turned back to the house; but his hand was trembling as it reached for the sliding door, and his heart was still jumping angrily in his chest.

Chapter 50

"Come on in the party, doc."

Buck stood inside the glowing doorway of the ranch house and beckoned with his hand. Heather smiled and scurried across the cobbled courtyard in her high heels. It was almost eight and just beginning to snow, and the air was ice-cold.

Buck stood back to let her pass and observed gallantly, "You're as pretty as a basket full of flowers, Heather. Let me take your coat. We've got hot coffee, hot chocolate, or mulled wine if you'd like something a bit stronger."

"Thank you." Heather peeled out of her coat and handed it to her host. "Hot chocolate sounds great right now."

Buck nodded toward an open room on the other side of the atrium. Party guests had gathered in a sunken area paved in gray stone. They lounged on dozens of leather sofa seats built into the stone ring that circled a carousel fireplace. A blazing fire roared in the grate, and the laughing guests were mirrored in the fireplace's copper hood.

Heather glanced beyond the fireplace and saw that a baby grand piano had been set up on the first floor between the sunken room and the main staircase. A smiling young man in a tuxedo began to play softly.

A soft voice murmured, "What would you like, miss?"

Heather turned to see a smartly uniformed waiter at her elbow. He was carrying a silver tray covered with steaming coffee and chocolate in china cups and little plates stacked with delicate cookies.

"Thank you, I don't mind if I do," Heather murmured, and picked up a china cup full of hot chocolate. She took a sip and glanced over the crowd, but she didn't yet see a tall, dark, lanky man dressed in black.

Heather glanced down at herself with a little flush of self-consciousness. She'd done her very best that night to knock Morgan's eyes out. She'd swept her bright hair up on top of her head, leaving two soft corkscrew curls to brush her shoulders. She had on her beautiful Cinderella dress of velvet and silk. She'd even put on a little makeup for the occasion; and a whisper of Chanel followed her as she drifted through the crowd.

"Well, Merry Christmas, Heather!"

Heather turned to see Arthur beaming at her. He was wearing a tux, but he still managed to look slightly rumpled, with his frowsy hair and rosy nose. He gestured toward her flowing skirts with his glass and marveled, "You look like a Christmas angel." He leaned over to give her a peck on the cheek. "It's good to see you outside of that barn. You deserve to get out of the shop now and then."

"Thank you, Arthur." Heather went slightly warm at the compliment. "It is a nice change." Her eyes flicked back to the house beyond his head, and Arthur followed her gaze with his eyes.

"I think I saw Morgan in the room over by the pool," he murmured into his drink, and gave her a twinkling gaze over the rim of his glass.

Heather glanced down at the floor in embarrassment. "Am I that obvious?" she murmured.

"I wouldn't say *obvious*," Arthur replied gently. "But I'm an old man. I've seen that glow in a woman's eyes a few times before."

Heather's lips curled up primly. "Thank you, Arthur."

"Good luck, my dear."

Heather moved through the crowd of laughing, talking guests, and she was waylaid by Kate as she passed. Her redheaded hostess was wearing an elegant, watered satin gown in a dull, ashes-of-roses pink, and it set off her shining auburn hair and creamy complexion to perfection.

"I'm so glad you were able to come to the party," Kate smiled. "I've been wanting to get to know you better. We'll have to have lunch together soon."

"I'd like that," Heather told her.

Kate's shrewd eyes swept her face, and she added: "You know, everyone is here except Morgan. Can you do me a favor, Heather, and find that runaway for me? I think he's out by the pool."

Heather lowered her eyes, but she wasn't able to keep her lips from curving up. "I'd be glad to." She glanced up at her hostess' eyes, and was amused to see an answering smile in them.

"Morgan's a little reserved," Kate murmured softly. "Don't let it throw you."

Heather shot her a look of genuine gratitude. "I won't."

Kate smiled again and stepped aside, and Heather moved through the crowd, past the pianist, who was now playing carols, and on to the big, open room next to a huge pool.

She paused in the doorway. It was another sunken room, with a huge fireplace with a crackling fire on one side, and a glass wall facing out over the pool on the other. The patio was already covered in white, and a dreamy shower of snow fluttered down outside in the light of the gas lamps.

The room was empty except for one man sitting in a leather chair in front of the fire. Morgan was sitting bent forward with his elbows on his knees and his hands clasped, and he was staring into the flames as if he was mesmerized. The leaping fire was the only light in the room, and it cast a golden light on his face and made his eyes glitter.

Heather glanced up. Someone had hung mistletoe over the doorway, and she pulled it down and carried it in her hand as she glided across the room toward him.

"Merry Christmas, Morgan," she murmured softly.

Morgan turned his head to look at her, then slowly rose to his feet. Heather smiled big and bright and held out her hands, and he took them in his.

"How do you like my dress?" she teased, and twirled around for him. Morgan's glittering eyes flicked over her as she made her skirt bloom out in the air like a flower. He shook his head.

"You're beautiful, Heather," he replied in his deep, slow voice. "You're as bright as dawn."

Heather went warm with pleasure, and her eyes moved hopefully to his. He was staring at her intently, and he moved a step closer.

She raised the sprig of mistletoe and twirled it in front of him. "I found this hanging over the door," she smiled. "It'd be a shame to waste it."

She looked up at him hopefully. His eyes were dark and strange, and they bored into hers as he moved close. He took her by the shoulders, ducked his head quickly, and kissed her hard, almost too hard. Heather gasped at the intensity of that kiss, but just as her shoulders began to soften, just as she began to melt into it, Morgan turned her loose and stepped back again, eyes blazing.

His eyes had a hard, almost angry look. He was staring at her as if he was mad.

"Is that what you want, Heather?" he challenged her, and she shook her head in confusion. "Because I'm here to tell you it's not enough. It's easy to get hypnotized by soft music and firelight and a pair of arms around you. But all that stuff is a lie. It doesn't last!"

Heather blinked back tears of hurt as she faced Morgan down. She waved frustrated hands in the air and blurted, "Maybe it was a lie between you and Cece. But it doesn't have to be a lie between us. It can be real." She took a step toward him and fixed him with a pleading gaze. "I *want* it to be real between us, Morgan. I'm ready to make it real, if you are."

Morgan turned away and was walking off, and she hurried after him. She took him by the shoulder, turned him around to face her.

She fought back tears as she stared into his eyes. "I've never met anyone in my life who's as afraid of love as you are, Morgan," she told him. "Why are you holding back? Here we are, alone together in the firelight." She moved toward him, her arms held out.

"Kiss me."

He turned his face away. "That's what got me into a mess the first time. I was a fool then, but I can't afford to be one now. I have to think of my son."

"Why?" she cried, "are you afraid I'll treat Kit as badly as his mother did?" She swallowed the lump of tears in her throat and added in a throbbing whisper, "I would think that the time we've spent together would tell you what kind of person I am. If you still don't trust me, then I don't know what else to say. I've swallowed my pride, I've chased after you like a woman should never chase after any man, because I love you, Morgan. I'm not afraid to say it!"

He shot a frowning glance at her over his shoulder, but said nothing in reply.

Heather drew a long, painful breath and shrugged in defeat. "All right then," she whispered. "I can't force you to love me, if you won't." She stared at him sadly.

"But it hurts me to see you shutting love out, Morgan. You won't be able to live again until you leave your past behind."

She looked down, saw the sprig of mistletoe in her hand, and tossed it down on the marble floor before turning to flee.

Chapter 51

Cece crouched in the bushes a stone's throw from the ranch house. It was snowing and cold and she was stuck in the weeds until she could sneak into the house without being seen. She stared at the big front doors in disgust. She hated everything about that house, but she knew it like the back of her hand; and so Roger had volunteered her to get Kit for them.

He'd finally decided the time was right, and they'd made the long trip back from Mexico to spring the trap at last.

It was early evening, and it was plain that the Spade clan was right in the middle of their annual Christmas party. Every window in the place was blazing with golden light and the faint sound of music and laughter drifted out to her. There was even a faint whiff of grilled steak on the cold evening air.

Cece rubbed her shoulders. She was freezing, and she cursed Roger Tomlinson from the depths of her soul as she glimpsed a roaring fire through the glass wall.

She licked her lips, imagining the warm glow in that room, the clink of bone china, the taste of fine wine and brandy and smoked turkey and glazed ham.

For the first time, Cece suffered a flick of regret that she'd played so fast and loose with Morgan. If she'd played her cards smarter, if she'd been more careful, she'd still be inside that house, still enjoying Morgan's money, instead of crouching in the freezing cold outside his house.

Now, her only hope of regaining her old lifestyle was Roger's crazy plan. She hated it, but Roger was right; his risky gambit was the only shot they had left.

She had no choice but to help him kidnap Kit and get him over the border. Once they were safe in Mexico, they could work out a ransom with Morgan.

One big payday, like Roger had said.

He was waiting for her in the dark just outside. All she had to do was get Kit, throw him into their rental car, and transfer him to Roger's once they were well away. If she knew Morgan, Kit was already in bed sound asleep. Morgan might not check in on him until the next morning.

With any luck, they'd be over the border by that time.

Cece's eyes moved to the second floor of the house. There was one window that was dark and blank… Morgan's apartments.

Cece glanced toward the house, then slowly raised herself up and hurried around the side of the house, keeping well away from the bright lamplight over the front door.

She moved behind the bushes on the side of the house, crossed the pool area on the western side of the house, and moved to the sliding glass doors that accessed the first floor.

Cece scanned the interior of the house. The room immediately inside the glass door was empty and dark, but a brightly-lit hall doorway glowed on the far end, and she could see people moving back and forth in it.

She put her hand on the door handle, and to her satisfaction, the door slid aside easily. She quickly slipped inside, closed it behind her, and moved across the room as silently as smoke.

She paused just inside the doorway and flattened herself against one wall. When she glanced out, she could see Buck and Eugene Clemmons laughing and talking by the fireplace, and she stiffened in anger.

If it weren't for those two, I'd still be here, she thought resentfully. *Buck always hated me, and Eugene's his hired gun.*

Her eyes flitted across the other guests. There was a beautiful redheaded woman talking to two other women she didn't know, and she caught a glimpse of Luke as he walked past them.

There was no sign of Morgan, and Cece was seized by the sudden fear that Morgan had begged off the party. That he was upstairs in his apartment with Kit.

Her eyes moved to the big staircase to the upper levels. She needed to go there, but the whole first floor was working alive with Spades and their party guests.

But there was another way up, and Cece turned away from the doorway and across the room to a small doorway on the northern wall.

It opened onto a little cubbyhole with a tiny service elevator tucked inside. It was the service elevator for the maids and other workers who kept the huge house cleaned and in good repair. Cece smirked a bit as she pressed the button and waited for the doors to open.

She'd used the little elevator more than once in the past to sneak her gentlemen friends in and out; and she'd made some lively memories with its help.

She pressed the '2' button and waited for the doors to slide shut. The elevator opened into a hidden room on the second floor. It opened out onto the main hall, and if she was careful, she could reach Morgan's apartment without being spotted.

The little bell dinged softly, and she slipped out as soon as the doors slid open. She curled her fingers around the knob of the little room and peeked out.

The second floor was dark and empty, but the entire hall was open to the house below; and so she hugged the inside wall as she moved toward the stairs to Morgan's door.

A sudden burst of laughter from below made her jump and freeze; but when it faded back, she moved quickly to Morgan's door and pulled a key card out of her pocket.

She was gambling that Morgan hadn't changed the code since she'd left; and the soft *click* of success made her smirk a bit as she turned the knob and hurried inside.

Cece moved inside the paneled living room. It was dark, but moonlight streamed through the glass wall, and she could see the Texas countryside beyond all the way to the horizon. The luxury of that view, and of the lushly-appointed apartment, brought her another pang of loss and regret; but she didn't have the time to indulge it.

She glided across the darkened room and into the hall beyond. She glanced warily at Morgan's bedroom door and stopped to listen for any sign he was there; and when she heard only silence, she hurried to his bedroom and opened the door a crack. The bedroom was dark and empty.

The coast was clear.

Cece closed the door and rolled triumphant eyes to Kit's door. She curled her fingers around the knob and opened the door softly.

The moonlight painted ghostly blocks of white light on the floor and outlined the little lump in the bed. Cece half-ran to the bedside and sank down onto the edge of the mattress.

She gently peeled the blanket back from Kit's sleeping face, then shook him gently.

"Kit! Kit, wake up!"

Kit didn't respond, and she glanced toward the door, then shook him again.

"Kit, wake up!"

The little boy's eyes fluttered open, then widened in terror.

Cece bent down to hiss, "Don't be scared, sweetie. It's just Mommy!"

Kit watched her in frozen shock. "Are…are you a ghost?"

Cece almost laughed. She sputtered, "No, baby, I'm real. See my hands?"

Kit struggled up in bed and frowned. "But they said you were dead!"

Cece glanced at the door again. "I was in a car accident, but I'm just fine. I didn't die, like they thought I did." Her eyes moved back to Kit's face. "I missed you something terrible, sweetie. Did you miss me?"

Tears started in Kit's eyes. He nodded silently.

"Aw, that's my good boy," she crooned, and brushed his hair back from his brow. "I want you to come with Mommy, now. You're going to come and spend a few days with me."

Kit's frown deepened. "Daddy didn't say anything about me going to stay with you," he mumbled in confusion.

Cece stifled an impatient exclamation, then mustered a smile. "Well, Daddy doesn't know everything," she assured him. "It'll be alright, darling. Don't you want to come and spend a few days with Mommy?"

Kit's eyes searched her face with painful intensity. "Y-yes."

"Good," she told him, and threw the covers back. "Come on. You don't have to change clothes. I have some clothes for you at my place."

She helped Kit as he scooted to the edge of the bed and put his hand in hers.

"That's right, baby," she murmured. "Now, Mommy doesn't want to disturb your Daddy or his party guests, so we're going to be quiet and go out the back way."

She took his hand and pulled him to the bedroom door, then peeked out again. The apartment outside was still dark and empty, but that could change at any moment.

Kit looked up at her. "Mommy, I have to pee," he whispered.

Cece almost spat out an impatient profanity. "Can't you hold it?"

Kit shook his head, and she murmured, "All right, go to the bathroom, I'll wait for you here. Hurry!"

She opened the door and watched as Kit pattered off down the hall; then her eyes moved to the living room. She moved down the corridor toward it and paused on the threshold. She could hear the party crashing on downstairs: someone was playing Christmas songs on a piano and there was a dim, constant hum of people talking and laughing.

Cece glanced over her shoulder toward the bathroom at the other end of the hall. There was a stripe of light under the door, and she could hear the dim sound of running water.

A new sound made her heart jerk and made her head turn sharply toward the living room. It was the sound of heavy footsteps on the stairs outside, coming steadily closer. Cece cursed softly under her breath, because she knew that footstep. She'd listened for it many-a night when Morgan's sudden return would mean she'd be caught with another man.

The hair on the back of her neck prickled as the outer doorknob clicked and turned. At that moment, the bathroom door opened down the hall and Kit came pattering back. Cece turned to him and put a finger to her lips.

"*Sssh,*" she whispered, and grabbed his hand.

Kit straightened slightly. "It's Daddy!"

"*Sssh!*"

Cece watched in terror as the front door opened slightly and dim light flooded into the apartment. She got a glimpse of Morgan's tall silhouette out in the hall.

Kit looked up at her. "Can't we stay and talk to Daddy?"

Cece jerked him to her side. "*Hush!*"

The silhouette in the hall froze suddenly, as if Morgan was listening, and Cece held her breath. There was a long, suspenseful silence in which neither of them moved: then another familiar footstep echoed on the stairs outside.

Buck's voice laughed, "Where you going, Morg? I saw a certain blonde lady downstairs, looking awful lonely."

Cece cocked an eyebrow and thought: *Well, imagine that. He's found a woman.*

Buck's silhouette appeared and reached out for Morgan's. "Come on, Morg. It's too early to turn in."

Cece stood there, waiting, hardly daring to breathe: and to her relief, the door slowly closed, the light faded, and the footsteps slowly moved down the stairs until they melted into the general hum of the party.

Cece closed her eyes and leaned back against the wall for an instant; then she straightened up and pulled Kit after her.

"Come with Momma," she commanded, and charged across the apartment to the outer door. She opened it warily, just a crack: and when she was sure there was no one outside, she opened it and pulled Kit out of the apartment and away from the staircase.

She pulled him to the back of the upper hall, through the small door, and into the service elevator. She dragged him in, punched the 'M' button, and stood in scowling suspense until the doors slid shut.

"I've never been here," Kit murmured. "I didn't know we had an elevator."

Cece glanced at him. "Isn't it fun?" she mumbled, and gripped his hand tighter. "It's an adventure."

The elevator sank gently, and after a moment a chime sounded and the door slid open again. The downstairs room looked as dark and deserted as she'd left it. Cece glanced toward the lighted hall on the other end of it to check that no one was going to walk in on them; but the coast was clear.

"Come on," she hissed and pulled Kit along by his hand. He glanced up at her with a scared expression.

"Where are we going?"

"You'll see."

Chapter 52

"Dashing through the snow in a one-horse open sleigh

O'er the fields we go, laughing all the way

Bells on bob tail ring, making spirits bright

What fun it is to ride and sing a sleighing song tonight!

Jingle bells, jingle bells jingle all the way

Oh, what fun it is to ride in a one-horse open sleigh, hey!

Jingle bells, jingle bells jingle all the way

Oh, what fun it is to ride in a one-horse open sleigh!"

Heather fled through the house, turning her face away from passersby as she searched for a place to vent her feelings in private. She didn't know what had caused Morgan to shut her out, but something had. They'd enjoyed each others' company, their friendship had seemed to her to be ripening into love.

She didn't know what had caused it all to crash and burn, but Morgan had clearly decided not to take a chance on the two of them. Maybe he didn't want to get hurt again. Maybe he was afraid of hurting her. He'd made no secret of his fears for Kit.

But whatever the reason for Morgan's decision, at that moment it felt...*final.*

Heather put a hand to her head, blinked back tears, and turned to flee. She wove through the crowd to a small, dark room on one side of the atrium. There was a little sofa next to the door, and she sank down onto it.

At that moment, all she knew was that she loved Morgan Spade with all her heart, and that he didn't love her back.

She took a deep, shuddering breath and was just about to throw herself on the sofa when a soft chime sounded from the other end of the room, and a little red light appeared near the ceiling. Heather stared at it in confusion, and as she watched a door slid open and two people came walking out.

To her surprise, one of them was Kit: and to her staring amazement, the other one was Morgan's first wife—the woman they'd all been told was dead. Shock slapped the grief right out of her heart, and she sat bolt upright on the couch as she watched the two shadows pass by.

Heather blinked and refocused, wondering if her eyes were playing tricks on her: but though the two shadows moved out of the room quickly, they were real enough. Heather glanced back toward the party, then at the sliding glass door that led out to the pool area. Cece had pushed it back to exit the room, and it was still standing open.

Heather stood up slowly and drifted across the room uncertainly, wondering if she was mistaken.

What's going on?

She walked to the patio door and peered out. To her confusion, it really was Cece, not some figment of her imagination. Morgan's ex was dragging Kit across the big patio by the hand, and as he trotted after her, he murmured, "Where are we going, Mommy?"

His mother barked, "It's a secret. Quickly, now!"

Heather frowned and moved out onto the patio after them. The feeling swelled up in her chest that something was badly wrong: and that feeling accelerated from doubt to certainty in a split-second.

Cece was kidnapping Morgan's son.

Heather lifted her skirts and hurried around the pool at a half-run, dodging recliners and tables as she moved. Cece was already beyond the far end of the patio and crossing the lawn on her way to the front drive.

"Hey!" Heather called out, and broke out into a run. "You there, stop!"

Cece turned to glance at her, then redoubled her pace, dragging Kit roughly over the snowy ground. To Heather's horror, Kit slipped and fell heavily on the slick ground, and she sprinted toward him as his mother yanked him up again and wrangled him to the other side of her body.

"What are you doing here?" Heather demanded. "Where are you taking Morgan's son?"

Cece turned suddenly to confront her, and her face twisted in fury as Heather grabbed Kit's arm.

"Get your hands off him!"

Kit's face clouded in distress. "I want to go back," he whimpered. "It's cold. I want my Daddy!"

He wrenched free of his mother's grip and darted across the patio, through the open door, and back inside the house. Heather turned to follow him with her eyes, but before she could confront Cece something hard and heavy smashed her across the brow. A sky full of stars exploded in her head followed by a wave of pain; and the next thing she knew, she was lying in the snowy grass. A dark curtain fell over her eyes, and she saw nothing more for a long time.

When she came to at last, she could hear the dim sound of the wind rushing past her, and felt faint motion. She opened her eyes.

Heather put a hand to her brow. She was in the back seat of a car, she was cold and wet, and her head was splitting with pain. The scent of cigarette smoke and gardenia cologne hung in the air, and the car heater was blasting.

Her beautiful silk skirts were crumpled and grass-stained, and she'd lost one of her pumps.

Two voices were talking furiously. One seemed familiar, but the other she didn't know. They seemed to be arguing.

A male voice barked, "Why didn't you go after him? He couldn't have got far!"

A female voice answered in agitation. "He was back in the house before I could turn around. All I had left was her, but Morgan might still pay. I overheard him talking to his brother. He likes her."

"Likes her!" the male voice scoffed. "Does he like her enough to pay $10 million for her, like he would for his son? We're ruined!"

"Maybe not," the female voice wheedled. "She's all we've got now. We may as well use her!"

Heather glanced at them warily, then raised herself on one elbow. Dark countryside was flashing past the car window, but there was a sign up ahead. It read, *Mexico, 750 miles.*

Her eyes widened in panic as the last few hours came back to her. Slowly the truth sank in: *Cece was alive.*

Shock and sadness swirled in her heart as she remembered Morgan's tears, Kit's anguish at his mother's 'death,' the memorial service the family had held for Cece.

Cece had put Morgan's whole family through all of that, just to kidnap Kit. Grief swirled in Heather's heart as she remembered the confusion in Kit's eyes, the way they flicked to her face in uncertainty.

Poor little fellow, she thought sadly, *to have his own mother treat him like that!*

Heather's grief slowly hardened into anger, then a grim satisfaction. It was true that Cece had tried to kidnap Kit—but because of *her*, Cece had failed. She could at least be glad that she'd done that much good. Kit was back at the house, safe with his father.

Her relief slowly faded. She was glad Kit was safe, but now, somehow, *she* was in a car with Cece and some man she didn't know.

Heather tried to capture her swirling thoughts, force them to make sense. Slowly a picture formed in her mind, an explanation for where she was.

It looked as if Cece had failed to get Kit, and was trying to cut her losses by doing the next best thing: holding *her* for ransom.

Except that the Spade family had no reason in the world to pay for her release. Heather put a hand to her head in despair. She was nothing to them except an employee who liked Morgan more than she should.

Morgan had made it crystal clear he had no interest in her.

Oh Lord help me, Heather prayed, and sank down on the seat weakly. Her head spun if she moved even slightly, and her stomach was warning her to keep still. A tear trickled down her cheek as she prayed:

Lord, help. I couldn't run away even if I could jump out of this car.

I'm at their mercy!

Chapter 53

"Daddy, daddy, daddy!"

Morgan's ears pricked up at the sound of Kit's crying voice. He turned away from the man he'd been talking to and scanned the room for his son.

His eyes zoomed to Kit's bobbing head as he ran through the crowd of guests, and Morgan straightened in alarm when he saw that Kit's brow was scraped raw, and his expression was terrified.

Morgan set his glass down and hurried through the crowd to meet Kit. He knelt down to receive his son as Kit flung himself into his arms, then stood up to carry him out of the room.

"Hush, hush," he soothed, as Kit buried his face in his shirt. "What's the matter, buddy? You're supposed to be upstairs in bed."

"I was scared, I was scared, Daddy!"

Kit's little body was trembling and cold. Morgan carried him off to the back hall, where it was dark and quiet, and turned his face to kiss Kit's cheek.

"What were you scared of, bud?"

Kit lifted dark eyes to his, and panic was staring out of them. "Mommy came to get me!" he sobbed. "Mommy came to my bedroom and took me away!"

Morgan stiffened, then assured Kit, "No, Buddy, you had a nightmare. Your Momma's not with us any more. She went to…well, she passed away."

Kit shook his head vehemently. "No, Daddy, she came to my room! She said not to make a noise, and she took me downstairs in the little room with the button."

Morgan's heart twisted in pity, and he pulled Kit close. "It's all right, Kit," he crooned, and rocked his son back and forth in his arms. "You had a nightmare, but it's over now. It's all right, buddy."

Kit struggled in his arms. "No, no it isn't all right!" he cried. "Momma took me outside in the snow and I fell down." He showed his palms, and Morgan frowned to see that they were scraped raw.

"How did you get scuffed up, buddy?" he demanded. "Did you fall out of bed?"

Kit shook his head. "No, I fell down on the ground, Daddy! Mommy pulled me hard, and I fell down on the snow. But the other lady chased after us, and then Mommy hit her on the head, and I got away."

Morgan's heart jerked in his chest. "What—what other lady, bud?"

Kit frowned at him. "The horse lady. The lady in the barn. Momma hit her, and she fell down."

Buck walked up behind him and clapped a hand on his shoulder. "Everything all right, Morg?"

Morgan turned to him with a frown. "Kit says that Cece came to take him out of his bed tonight," he replied dully. "He says she tried to kidnap him, and that Heather stopped her." He passed Kit off to his uncle's arms.

"Hold him here for me, Buck. I'm going to go see for myself."

Buck grabbed his arm. "You don't really think that Cece's alive, Morg?" he asked quietly.

Morgan shot him a dark look. "I don't put anything past her," he growled, and stalked off through the crowd.

He pushed through the press of people and into the dark, empty room with the service elevator. The room opened onto the pool area, and he frowned to see that the sliding glass door was standing open. Cold air was swirling in, and a thin layer of snow dusted the floor.

Morgan strode out onto the snowy patio. His heart shrank in dismay to see the print of Kit's bare feet running to and fro, and two separate prints of women's shoes.

Kit hadn't been dreaming at all.

He hurried across the patio, around overturned chairs, and across the snowy lawn in rising fear.

Oh, Lord help me!

Morgan slowed and knelt down on the ground. A blue satin pump was lying on its side, and he picked it up with a frown.

He'd seen it not an hour before, peeking out from underneath Heather's satin skirt. He brushed his hand across the snowy grass, and to his horror, his fingers came back swiped with blood.

Ice skittered down his spine, but he stood up quickly and strode up the grassy lawn toward the front of the house. Another set of prints, the prints of a man's shoes, came down the slope to meet the woman's, then turned back to the courtyard.

He hurried up the hill and burst out onto the cobbled courtyard, searching fearfully for any sign of Heather. The courtyard was empty except for a few cars, and when he rushed over to peer inside, they were empty.

He pulled a hand through his hair, turning around and around in despair as he scanned the lawn bordering the drive. Very little was visible beyond the circle of lamplight.

"Morg?"

Morgan turned and rolled wild eyes to Buck's face as he came striding up the hill and across the courtyard.

"What's going on out here?" Buck growled. His eyes moved to the high heel Morgan was clutching.

Morgan looked down at it. "This is Heather's," he rumbled. "I found it in the grass." He looked up again, and the two of them stared at one another for a pregnant moment; then Morgan stalked to the house.

"I'm calling the police."

Buck grabbed his arm and stopped him. "What are you gonna tell 'em, Morg—that your dead wife kidnapped your—kidnapped Heather?" He frowned into Morgan's eyes. "They'll think you're crazy!"

"I know Cece," Morgan growled, and shook him off. "She tried to kidnap Kit tonight, and thank God she didn't get him! But now she and that thug of hers have taken Heather instead!"

"You don't know that," Buck insisted; but Morgan scowled at him.

"We'll all know it before long," he retorted. "They're gonna call us and demand money, Buck. That's what this is about. That's what it's always been about." He wiped his eyes with one hand.

"I just pray Heather's all right. I found blood on the grass, Buck! I found—"

His voice broke, and Buck reached out to rub his back wordlessly. Morgan shook his head in fury. "If that snake hurts her, I'll break his neck with my bare hands!"

"Come on, Morg," Buck murmured. "We'll call the police. I'll send the guests home. We'll get her back, Morg. Don't worry."

Morgan hurried back into the house, shouldered through the crowd, and grabbed for the first phone he found. He punched 911 and waited for a reply with a pounding heart.

A woman's voice suddenly demanded, "Nine-one-one, what's your emergency?"

Morgan's soul shriveled in fear, and he heard that icy tone in his voice as he barked, "I'm reporting a kidnapping."

Chapter 54

Morgan sat facing the glass wall of his living room, staring out over the darkened sweep of the Seven's rolling pastureland. It was almost four in the morning, and there had been no word.

He tried to pray, but he could only choke out a few words before fear came roaring back to strangle him back into silence.

He couldn't get comfortable. He couldn't sit still, he couldn't lie down, he sure couldn't sleep. His mind was straining toward Heather, where she was, if she was okay.

If she was alive.

Morgan jumped up and stalked across the floor. He ran a hand through his hair in distraction and paced back and forth in helpless frustration.

He couldn't get the picture of her out of his mind, the way she'd looked in the firelight in her beautiful Cinderella gown of velvet and silk. She'd prettied up just for him, he knew it without having to be told; and she'd looked as sweet and bright as an angel.

She'd offered him her love as freely as a child, and he'd sent her away.

Morgan closed his eyes bitterly. Heather might be dead. And maybe the last thing in her mind, had been the memory of him turning his back on her.

Morgan sank into his chair in despair and put his head in his hands. *Oh Lord,* he prayed, *I'm losing my mind. Please watch over Heather. Bring her back alive and safe!*

He rubbed his face with his hands and blinked back tears. He'd thought he was doing the right thing to send Heather away. He thought it was the wise thing, the best thing.

He even thought he was doing what was best for Heather.

But now, the truth was painfully clear. The truth was the aching hole in his chest where his heart had been, the fear that Heather might be dead, that he might never see her again.

His hands clenched as he pulled them down. He might blame Cece for this, and he did. Kit said that she'd knocked Heather down, and maybe hurt her even worse. That trickle of blood on the snow danced in front of him even when he closed his eyes.

But he'd hurt Heather more than Cece ever could. He'd broken her heart, maybe sent her to her death with the memory of his cold words.

Morgan closed his eyes, remembering the hurt look in her eyes, the tears shimmering in them. She'd offered him her heart, that sweet, funny, open heart of hers. It had been a beautiful gift, so freely given, and he hadn't even acknowledged what it had cost her to offer it.

He reached out and picked up the little sprig of mistletoe that she'd dropped on the floor, twirled it slowly.

She'd been right about him. He'd been scared to open his heart, scared to let her in. His past with Cece had poisoned him, curdled him up, pretty much ruined him when it came to love. He'd been so snakebit that he questioned every woman who got close to him anymore.

He'd gotten to believe, over the years, that most women were like Cece. That they couldn't be trusted, especially with a rich man like him. That had been his thinking, whether he'd admitted it to himself or not.

That thinking had colored his whole relationship with Heather. Stunted it, held it back.

Ruined it, now.

She'd been right, he should've known her better. He did know her better. That was what hurt him most, now.

It was too late, even if Heather was found alive and well. He couldn't expect her to come back after he'd rejected her. No woman would.

But at this point, all he wanted was just to hear that she'd been found alive. That she wasn't lying on some cold, dark stretch of road. He was pretty sure Cece wouldn't kill Heather, but Roger was a snake.

He didn't put anything past him.

Morgan drew a deep, painful breath. His only hope was that they'd taken Heather for ransom. That they had a reason to keep her alive. He'd been waiting by the phone all night, waiting, praying; but no call had come.

He was willing to pay whatever they asked to get Heather back safe and sound; but as the hours passed, his hope was beginning to fade.

Surely, if they wanted a ransom, they would've called by now.

A soft knock at his front door made him jump up and stride across the room to yank it open. Buck filled the opening, and his eyes were full of concern.

"Any word?"

He shook his head, and Buck looked down. "Well, the police are looking for her, Morg. We need to hold onto that."

Morgan waved a hand in frustration. "I'd be out there right now, looking for her myself," he cried, "but I don't know where to look. I know Cece, but I don't know her husband. He's the one doing this. I don't know where he'd go. He might take Heather anywhere!"

Buck put a hand on his shoulder, and Morgan turned back inside. "Come on in, Buck. You might as well. I'm not getting any sleep tonight."

Buck drifted inside after him as he walked back over to the big glass wall. He crossed his arms and stared out into the darkness. A faint pattering against the window announced that a light sleet was falling now to cover the snowy landscape with an icy glaze.

Even if they let Heather go, she might freeze to death before help found her.

A tear slipped down his cheek in the darkness, and Buck walked over to put a hand on his shoulder.

Morgan shook his head bitterly. "I said some things to Heather tonight that I wish I hadn't, Buck," he murmured. "I hurt her real bad. And you know how she got even with me?"

He turned to look at his brother's sympathetic eyes. "She saved Kit's life. She kept him from being kidnapped.

"It might've been the last thing she did in this world."

He bowed his head and put a hand over his eyes. Buck sighed and patted his back.

"You know, Morg," he sighed, "There's not much we can do except wait. Now would be a real good time to pray. You mind if I pray for you and Heather?"

Morgan shook his head wordlessly, and Buck bowed his head and murmured: "Lord, we come to you tonight to ask you to watch over Heather. You know where she is, Lord. Please protect her from harm and bring her back safe. We've all come to know Heather, she's a wonderful lady, and she and Morg have come to care for one another. Lord, please comfort Morg and all of us as we wait. Help us to trust hard, and to rest knowing that you love Heather most of all.

"Amen."

Morgan kept his head bowed and said nothing, because he couldn't trust himself to speak. He had his eyes closed, but he could feel Buck's gaze on him for a long, quiet moment.

"You want me to stay with you, Morg?"

At that, Morgan glanced up at his brother's sympathetic face. He reached out to pat his arm. "No, Buck, you go on."

Buck's eyes searched his face in frowning concern. "Let me know if anything happens. Call me, any hour."

"I will."

Morgan sat, watching as the clouds slowly parted to allow wintry moonlight to wash the countryside. Pale, snow-covered pastures rolled away to the horizon.

The door closed softly, and Morgan bowed his head.

I thought I was already the biggest fool in the world, he thought bitterly. *But I was wrong.*

It's worse to walk away from a real woman, than to be fooled by a fake one; and that's what I just did.

He closed his eyes. *Lord help,* he prayed. *Guide the police tonight. Lead them to Heather.*

Bring   her   back   safe!

Chapter 55

The car sped on into the night, and Heather lay silent and still in the back seat and pretended to be unconscious. Her mind was spinning with questions.

Where are they taking me?

If it's Mexico, can I get away when they have to stop at the border? But if I did get away, where would I go, and who could I ask for help?

The faint patter of sleet tapped on the car roof, and a sharp draft of cold air seeped in around the back windows to chill Heather's bare feet. The sound of the sleet soon became louder and more insistent until it became a heavy drumbeat on the car. She heard the soft slapping of windshield wipers.

The man's voice mumbled, "Is she still out back there?"

Heather closed her eyes instantly, and Cece's voice replied, "Yes. I sent her to dreamland."

The man sputtered. "I say we dump her on the side of the road and keep going. They're not going to pay for her."

There was a long silence, and Heather's heart quickened in dread. Cece finally answered, "Well, we've got her now. We may as well try. Morgan's sentimental. He might cough up something for her."

There was another long silence, and the man mumbled: "If they won't pay up, I say we pop a cap in her head and dump her in Mexico. We can't take her with us to South America."

Heather's heart jumped in panic, and Cece objected, "No, Roger, I won't be any party to murder! I'm willing to squeeze Morgan for all I can get, because I figure I've put in my time. But not that. We wouldn't have to kill her. We could just dump her someplace, like you said. Why risk a murder conviction?"

"Because she might *talk*," Roger drawled, as if he was explaining to a small child. "She saw you trying to kidnap the boy. She could testify. If the boy tells, they can blow it off as a crazy kid's story. You're supposed to be dead, after all.

"But if this woman talks, you're done. You wanna go to prison for kidnapping, baby? Because it would be mostly you," he added dryly. "You said you were scared of that big-shot lawyer of the Spades'. Eugene, wasn't it? You said he tore you up in the custody case.

"Imagine what he'd do to you for kidnapping."

There was a long, telling silence, and Heather closed her eyes and bit back the panic that clawed at her throat and threatened to burst out in a scream. She was barefoot, she was wearing a full-length, formal gown, her head was throbbing, and she still felt faintly sick. She couldn't run away in her condition.

Lord please, she prayed. *Make a way!*

Cece lit a cigarette and blew a plume of smoke into the air. "Well, I'd rather go in for kidnapping than for murder," she said at last. "I've gone along with you a long way, Roger. But none of your great ideas have worked out. I tried it your way, and now we don't have Kit and we don't have any money. This girl is all we've got. If we kill her, we can't use her. What's the sense in that?"

Roger made no immediate reply. There was a heavy silence, and Heather lifted her head just enough to see a road sign as it flashed past.

Mexico, 450 miles.

They're taking me to Mexico, she thought desperately. *They'll have to stop at the crossing. Maybe I can jump out and get away. There must be some policemen near the border!*

Heather closed her eyes. She'd just have to take her chances and hope that someone would help her.

Please, Lord!

The sound of the sleet on the roof drummed on, and the sound of the wind hurtling past, and the faint motion of the car. Her captors were quiet for a while; Cece was smoking sullenly, and her husband was driving in brooding silence.

The windshield wipers quickened their tempo as the sound of the sleet intensified. Roger cursed under his breath and complained, "I can barely see the road in this murk. Can you see if there's any gas stations coming up? The tank's almost empty."

A wild hope sprang up in Heather's heart. *Maybe I can make a dash for it at the station,* she thought suddenly. *There might be somebody else there.*

"Be careful, Roger," Cece said suddenly, and sat up straighter in her seat. "The sign says there's a big bridge coming up. You should slow down anyway. The road's a sheet of ice."

The sound of the wind died down a bit, and the feel of motion lessened. Heather saw other vehicles driving past them for the first time since she'd been in the car. As she watched, the signs moving past seemed to slow as they slid by, and she saw the first rails of a huge bridge flash past.

Cece's voice sounded worried. "Do we have enough gas to make it over the bridge, Roger?"

"Of course," he retorted irritably. "Do you think I'd let us run out?"

Cece glanced at him darkly. "I don't know, Roger. You haven't been all that smart so far."

His head snapped around to face her, and his expression twisted. "You shut up or I'll shut that yapping mouth for you!" he warned. "I wasn't the one who lost the kid. If you'd done the job right we wouldn't be in this mess!"

"If you'd been a real lawyer we wouldn't be in this mess," Cece sneered. "But you're nothing but a lying grifter!"

Roger snarled and reached out to slap Cece right across the mouth. He let go of the wheel and flailed at her as she screamed, and the car swerved sharply, then hit a patch of ice and spun in wild circles on the bridge lane. Heather dug her fingers into the seat cushion on as they whirled.

The car suddenly hit the guard rail and smashed to an abrupt stop. In the split-second after, they all collected their wits; then Cece began to curse Roger at the top of her lungs, Roger reached out to slap her again, and Heather scrambled for the car door. She kicked it wide open, and instantly she was blasted by frigid air and sleet. The road below her dangling feet was slick with ice, but she grabbed the door and lowered herself onto it.

"She's getting away!" Roger yelled, and his shout pushed Heather out of the car. The ice burned her bare feet like fire, but she forced herself to slide across the blacktop to the far side of the bridge. She swayed like a frantic toddler, because as she gained the middle of the bridge, she saw a silver finger slowly stretching toward her down the road, warning of worse to come.

It was the lights of a semi truck, barreling toward them through the fog and sleet.

Heather reached the bridge rail and collapsed over it, chilled and wet. She lifted her head to squint at the growing lights as the semi gained the bridge and hurtled toward the crashed car.

It was going too fast to stop.

The blast of the air horn made Heather wince and sink down with her hands over her ears. Cece's scream was the last thing she heard before the massive *bang* and ear-splitting screech of the truck hitting the sedan. Heather clutched the rails as the bridge jumped and jerked with the impact of the collision. Small bits of flying debris rained down on her as she knelt there: little pieces of jagged plastic and pebbles of shattered glass.

A wave of dizziness rolled over her, and Heather felt everything slipping away into darkness: the icy bridge, her burning feet, the sound of tinkling glass, and last of all, the cold.

Chapter 56

It was the dark hour before dawn, and Morgan sat in his chair, staring down into blackness through the plate glass wall. His phone suddenly trilled, and he fumbled for it frantically. He lifted it to his ear and barked:

"Yes?"

An authoritative voice demanded, "Is this the Seven Spades Ranch?"

Morgan sat bolt upright and tried to ignore the electricity that branched up his spine. "Yes, it is."

"This is the Laredo Police Department. I'm Officer Rhodes. I need to talk to Morgan Spade."

Morgan's heart shriveled in fear. He licked his lips and stammered, "This is he."

The officer's voice softened a bit. "Mr. Spade, I'm calling to inform you that there's been a car accident just north of Laredo. Two people are dead, and one is on the way to the hospital, and we have reason to believe that at least one of them is connected to you. We found a map of your ranch in their car and several notes with your name and phone number. Do you know Roger and Cece Tomlinson?"

Morgan closed his eyes. The pounding of his heart filled his chest, filled his mind, and he could hardly bear even to breathe.

"Mr. Spade?"

"Yes, I know them," he croaked. "Who—who else was in the car?"

The officer paused, then replied, "A young woman. We're still trying to identify her."

Morgan's heart stopped. He heard himself asking, "Is she dead?"

"She's on her way to the hospital. I don't know her condition at the moment. Do you know who she is?"

Morgan's slumped against the glass weakly. "I think so," he whispered, then added, in a stronger voice: "Where was she taken?"

"She was taken to Doctor's Hospital in Laredo," the officer informed him. "Can you tell me who she is?

"Mr. Spade?"

Morgan jumped up, stuffed the phone in his jeans, and burst out of his apartment. He skipped down the stairs and blew out of the house and into the inky cold of the courtyard.

He found his jeep and was unlocking it when a voice called, "Morg, did you hear something?"

He looked up to see Buck standing in the doorway. "Heather's in the hospital in Laredo," he yelped. "Look after Kit for me. I'll be gone for a few days."

He slid into the car, slammed the door behind him, and cranked the car. He was already out of the courtyard and moving down the drive before Buck could answer.

He gunned the motor and sped down the long, flat driveway. One ghostly light burned over the big barn doorway as he passed, and a few post lights cast anemic puddles of light over the road as his jeep flashed by. His heart was throbbing in his neck and he felt like he'd been shocked by a live wire: but his wits slowly returned to him.

He picked up the phone and barked, "Doctor's Hospital, Laredo."

He lifted the phone to his ear as it dialed the number, and a smooth voice murmured, "Doctor's Hospital."

"I'd like to check on an ER patient," he barked. "She's been in a car wreck. She would've just been brought into the ER. Young, blonde, wearing an evening gown with a plaid skirt."

"I'll connect you to the ER department," the voice replied, and Morgan bit his lip and tried to quiet his jumping nerves as he waited.

He could see the big ranch gates barring his way up ahead, and he reached up to punch the remote. The ponderous gates slowly creaked apart, and the way was clear as he roared through and turned onto the road with his tires squealing.

"ER," a woman's voice murmured.

"I'd like to check on the status of a woman in your ER," he panted, and pulled a hand over his face. "She was in a car wreck. She's about 35, blonde, in an evening gown."

The woman mused, "We did have an unidentified female arrive about 20 minutes ago," she replied. "She fits your general description."

"How is she?"

The woman sighed, "She's alive and being x-rayed," she murmured. "She suffered a head injury."

Morgan swallowed and croaked: "How bad?"

To his frustration, the nurse replied, "I can't answer that question at this time. You'd have to talk to the attending physician."

Morgan bit back what he wanted to say and replied, "Her name is Heather Weston, and mine is Morgan Spade. I'm on my way down there."

"You can ask the nurse at the front desk, and she'll open the doors for you to come back, Mr. Spade."

"Thank you."

He hung up, and a light sleet began to bounce off the hood of his jeep. The road was already cold and would soon be frozen over.

He had to hurry.

He imagined Heather lying on a hard hospital bed, staring up into a bright light as strangers bent over her. It wrung his heart to think of her there alone, confused, scared, and in pain.

He could only pray that she hadn't been badly hurt, that she hadn't suffered permanent injuries. He shook his head in despair. He couldn't let his imagination go there, or he'd go out of his mind.

His expression twisted, and tears blurred the road ahead.

God, please, he prayed. *If you never answer me again, please give me this. Keep Heather alive. Heal her.*

Comfort her, take away her pain. I can't stand to think of her hurting.

Tell her that I love her, Lord.

And forgive me for not telling her myself!

Chapter 57

Heather's eyes slid open. There was a white ceiling directly over her head, and a light shining in her eyes, but to her grateful relief, she was warm, and somehow, there were socks on her feet.

The next thing that came to her, was that the little white room was moving. A loud wail filled the air, and she closed her eyes again.

When she opened her eyes again, she was still moving, moving faster, moving through a busy hallway. Someone was crying, *stat, stat*, and her bed rattled as it rushed along. There were people moving her bed. She sighed and closed her eyes, and she winked out again.

A voice reached into her slumber like a hand on her shoulder.

Heather.

Heather.

She opened her eyes, but she felt fuzzy and slow and still asleep. There was a face beside her bed, and two dark blue eyes, shining with tears.

They won't let me stay long, a deep voice was saying, and a hand took hers. It felt big and warm and pleasant, and she closed her eyes.

I wanted to tell you that I love you.

I love you, Heather.

"I love you too," she mumbled fuzzily, and turned her head before slipping back into sleep. A gentle squeeze, and that warm hand on hers was the last thing she felt.

When she woke up again, she was lying in a hospital room. Her head ached a bit, but not as badly as before, and her feet were warm at last.

When she glanced over, Morgan was slumped in a chair by her bed. His head was thrown back in sleep, and his mouth was slightly open. He was snoring softly, and she could see all his teeth.

He had beautiful white teeth.

Heather struggled up in bed, then pulled the blanket up self-consciously. Somebody had stripped off her silk gown and slapped an ugly hospital gown on her. She put a hand to her hair in dismay. It was falling down her back, and she was afraid to look in a mirror.

She closed her eyes and sank back onto the pillow. The memory of the previous night was coming back to her, and her brows twitched together in distress. It was so strange and terrible that she was tempted to believe that it was just a bad dream, but here she was, in a hospital room.

Cece and her husband had certainly perished, and Cece's frantic scream echoed pitifully in Heather's memory. She felt sorry for Cece, even though Cece had done her harm.

She'd seemed so unhappy all the time; and yet Cece had possessed everything a woman needed to be happy. Her eyes moved to Morgan's face.

Cece had been richly blessed; and yet she hadn't had the wisdom to see it.

She couldn't imagine anything more sad.

Morgan's eyes opened, and he stretched his long arms into the air and yawned. He noticed her mid-gape, and he closed his mouth and sat up straight.

"How you feeling?" he asked softly.

She gazed at his face. "Better." She picked at her blanket, then murmured, "Thank you for coming. How long have you been here?"

He rubbed his face. "I got here about five in the morning. They called me at four to let me know you'd been found, and it took me an hour to get to the hospital because I had to drive."

She kept her eyes on the blanket. "That was nice of you, Morgan."

He frowned and leaned forward in his chair, clasped his long hands across his knees. "Nice of me? Heather, I don't—I don't blame you for putting me at arm's length after the fool way I acted. I'm sorry." He shook his head, then raised his eyes to hers. "I can't tell you how sorry.

"I hope…you can forgive me."

Heather blinked back the tears that rose to her eyes. She reached out for his hand, and he took hers instantly.

"I'm not mad at you, Morgan," she replied softly. "I love you. I can't switch that off just because I was disappointed, or had a bad night."

"Bad night!" Morgan echoed, then knelt down at her bedside and reached for her. Heather went into his arms instantly, and closed her eyes as he pressed his cheek to hers and curled his fingers around her head.

"I can't believe I didn't chase you down," he murmured fervently. "The first time I laid eyes on you. You're the prettiest, sweetest woman I ever met, and I love you with all my heart."

Morgan turned his head to kiss her, and the touch of his lips was as gentle as a prayer. Heather allowed herself to just receive it, peacefully, like the gift it was.

Joy exploded in Heather's heart like a starburst, like crackling fireworks, and the glow of it lit her from within, warmed her so that she'd never feel cold again.

Morgan kissed her brow. "You sure you're alright?" he whispered.

"Are you sure you are?" she teased with a weak smile. "I wish I would've known that all it took to get you was a bump on the head. I would've walked into a tree that first day."

"Don't joke about it," Morgan replied softly, and brushed her cheek with his fingers. "I've been scared out of my mind.

"But you were right back at the party," he admitted. "I was scared of getting too close to you. Scared of falling in love again. But funny thing," he added ruefully.

"It happened anyway."

Heather laughed delightedly, and he joined her in her soft peal of joy.

A nurse walked in, and Morgan withdrew to let her get to the side of the bed. The woman glanced first at Morgan, and then at her. "Well, I hate to break this up, but it's time for you to have a head scan. We just need to check that everything's okay."

Heather looked wistfully at Morgan and asked, "Can I go home today?"

"If your scan comes back okay, the doctor will probably let you go home, as long as there's someone there to watch you," the nurse replied briskly.

Morgan turned toward her, then to Heather. "There will be," he promised. Heather reached for his hand as the nurse kicked the bed brakes free, and his fingers brushed hers until she was carried away.

Chapter 58

That afternoon, Heather walked uncertainly into the luxurious guest room at the Seven ranch house. Snow was drifting down past the big glass window, and the countryside stretching out below was blanketed in white; but a cheerful fire was crackling in the fireplace near the bed, and there was a pot of hot coffee on the nightstand.

She and Morgan had tussled on the trip back from the hospital. They'd had a brief argument in the car about whether she was going back to her condo or the ranch house, and Morgan had been so adamant that she was staying at the ranch house, that she'd finally given in.

"I don't want to upset Kit," she'd objected softly. "He's been through so much, and now his mother really is gone. You and Kit need some time alone together to process everything that's happened."

"Kit and me are going to have lots of time together," Morgan told her solemnly. "But I want you to be part of it, Heather."

She'd been bundled up to her ears in his jeep, wrapped in a blanket and warm as toast, and they were on their way back to the ranch. She considered his words, then turned to him and pleaded:

"Tell me why, Morgan."

Morgan's hands had tightened on the wheel, and he gave her a quick look. He pulled over to the side of the road, stopped the car, and killed the engine.

She'd stared at him steadily, waiting.

Morgan reached out and took her hand. "Heather, I—I've messed up my life and my son's life. I almost cost you yours."

She opened her mouth to protest, but he put up his hand, and she fell silent. Her eyes flicked over Morgan's face as he sat there, gathering his words.

"I've held back for a long time because I know how bad life can be when a man and woman aren't right for each other. I was worried for Kit. He's already suffered because of my foolishness. I couldn't bear to think of hurting him more."

He sighed and looked down at his hands. "But since I met you, Heather, I've come to see that holding back can be a bigger mistake than jumping in too quick. When I thought I'd lost you, I saw it real plain, but I was afraid it might be too late."

He raised his sapphire-blue eyes to hers. They were clear and filled with so much certainty that they made Heather's fill with tears.

Morgan shook his head. "I said a lot of things to you at the party that I wish I hadn't. I wouldn't blame you if you left here and never looked back.

"But if you did, I'd follow you, no matter how far it was. I'd beg you to let me earn your trust again."

Heather pulled her mouth down like a child and reached out for him, and Morgan pulled her to his chest. She rested her cheek against his chest, and she could feel the vibration of his deep voice as he murmured, "It's not even important anymore whether I'm being smart or foolish. I love you. That's all I know and all that matters."

Heather turned her face into his shirt and wept, and his arms went around her. Morgan rested his cheek on her hair and murmured, "Marry me, Heather. I'll make you as good a husband as I know how."

Heather wept again, then raised her face to his and smiled up into his eyes. "You know the answer," she whispered. "It's *yes* a thousand times, you sweet, old-fashioned man."

They kissed, and Heather closed her eyes, remembering it, as she paused inside the guest room doorway and pulled the blanket around herself.

"I'll go to the condo and get your things," Morgan murmured. "May as well start moving 'em over."

Heather glanced up at him happily, and he kissed her shoulder. "Get some sleep. I expect you're all worn out. I'll be back in a little while."

Heather's eyes followed him as he walked out, then she drifted into the big room and found the big bed. She climbed in, even though it wasn't yet dark, and snuggled under the soft, silken covers. She yawned and stretched luxuriantly.

It was the first time in the whirlwind of the last 24 hours that she'd had the chance to settle down and gather her thoughts. And in that calm, a bright orb of thankfulness rose in her heart and drifted up to Heaven.

Thank you, Lord for my life, she prayed. *You saved it. You saved me last night when no one else could.*

And thank you for an even greater miracle. Thank you for Morgan, and for Kit. I used to think I'd never find love, and now I have not just a fiance, but a son!

I went out empty, and I came back full, in spite of everything bad that happened.

I'm so grateful.

She sighed and yawned again. She was so weary that she sank down into sleep almost at once; but she drifted off with a smile on her face, and with Morgan's gruff voice echoing in her mind.

I love you. That's all I know and all that matters.

Chapter 59

That evening Morgan closed the door of his apartment behind him and walked in softly. He threw his coat down onto the couch and walked toward the fireplace. Kit was lying on the floor on his stomach, watching the leaping flames in silence.

"Hey buddy," Morgan murmured, and bent down to sit beside his son on the floor. Kit raised his face to his father's, glanced at him, and returned his attention to the fire.

"Hey Daddy."

Morgan wasn't able to keep his hand from his little son's hair. He stroked it lightly as they watched the fire.

"I want to talk to you a little bit, son," Morgan ventured, and hoped that he'd find the right words, that his son would be comforted. "A lot of things have happened lately. Tough things."

Kit's small face darkened as he stared into the fire.

"It's normal to be all churned up inside when bad things happen. You can tell me if you feel sad or mad or upset. It'll be just between us men."

Kit's head sank down onto his folded hands. He stared into the fire and was silent for a few moments; then he sighed, "I was sad when you told me Mommy had really passed away," he confessed, then glanced up at him with a confused look.

"But we thought she'd passed away before, and she was alive," he objected. "Could she be alive now?"

Morgan lowered his head and fought back a wave of anger. He'd always known that Cece was shameless; but he'd hoped that somewhere, deep down, she'd had some affection for Kit. Even after years of disappointment, it was a shock to know that she'd cherished no flicker of motherly love toward their son.

His heart twisted with pity for his son's confusion, and he caressed Kit's hair.

"Your Momma really did pass away, buddy," he replied, in his gentlest, most velvet tone. "I'm sorry. It's okay to feel sad, or even mad about that. You can tell me all about it, if you want."

Kit stared into the fire. "I feel sad," he said at last in a small voice. "Mommy always made me feel sad."

Tears blurred Morgan's eyes, and his hand moved to his son's back; but he let Kit talk.

Kit frowned and moved impatiently. "I was sad because Mommy was sad inside. I could see it in her eyes.

"I wish she would've been happy."

Morgan rolled pained eyes to the ceiling and drew a deep breath to reply, "Your Momma was the only one who could make herself happy, buddy. Nobody else could do it for her." He reached out for Kit, picked him up, and took him in his arms.

"But you and me don't have to be like your Mamma," he whispered. "We can be grateful for what we've got. For the Lord, and for his blessings. For each other, and our home here, and for your uncles and all our friends."

Kit hid his face on Morgan's chest, then nodded.

"That's something else I wanted to talk to you about, son," Morgan went on, and breathed a quick prayer. "Heather's become a friend of ours, since she came here," he murmured. "She's nice and she's funny. And she helped protect you last night, because she's our friend. That was real brave of her."

Kit nodded again, solemnly, with his brow against Morgan's chest.

Morgan licked his lips, prayed again, and added, "Son, me and Heather have become…special friends."

Kit stirred in his arms, looked up into his face. "You mean, like she's your girlfriend?"

Morgan tightened his arms. "That's right, son. In fact, we have such special feelings for one another that…I've asked Heather to marry me, and to come live with us.

"How would you feel about that?"

He held his breath as Kit lay still and silent in his arms. At last Kit murmured, "Do you love her more than me, Daddy?"

Morgan's heart twisted, and he pressed a fervent kiss to his son's smooth cheek. "No, buddy. No one will ever love you more than me. Nobody, ever in your life," he quavered. "It's just that…Heather will love you, too.

"How would that be?"

Kit considered, and finally whispered, "I'd like that, Daddy."

Morgan closed his eyes in a wave of relief that left him almost weak. He kissed Kit's cheek again.

"Good, buddy. I'm glad you feel that way, 'cause Heather's looking forward to coming here to live with us. We'll have to make her feel welcome."

Kit nodded, and Morgan kissed him and set him down. He searched his son's face and added, "Is there anything you want to ask me, or talk about?"

Kit's dark blue eyes met his, and he shook his head soberly.

"All right then, pard. You hungry?"

"A little."

Morgan kissed him and stood up. "I'm going to make dinner. How does spaghetti sound?"

Kit's face lit up. "That's my favorite!"

Morgan ruffled his son's hair and gazed down at him in love. "Mine too," he murmured. "We'll have a nice dinner, just the two of us, and watch old cowboy movies."

Kit tilted his head like a bird and peered up at him. "Can it be a John Wayne movie, Daddy?"

"It wouldn't be a western if it wasn't," Morgan murmured. "Go wash your hands now, and get ready for dinner."

He watched as Kit scrambled up and scampered off, then leaned against the wall and closed his eyes in relief.

Chapter 60

Kate stood at the big glass wall of her apartment and gazed down on the countryside, and Buck lowered his horse magazine to stare at her. She was smiling, and she seemed to be following something with her eyes.

"What's so interesting?" he asked mildly, and turned back to his reading.

"Come over here and see," she replied, and turned to give him a mischievous smile. Buck sighed, set the magazine down, and walked over to her side at the window. He slid an arm around her shoulders and looked down at the world below.

"Look there," Kate murmured, and nodded toward three small figures moving from the barn pasture to the open country beyond. It was a trio of riders led by a tall man on a black horse, a fair woman on a bay, and a child on a black pony.

Buck's face softened. "That is a pretty sight," he murmured. "I've never seen Morg so happy, and I'm glad for him. He deserved a good woman a long time ago. I'm glad he's finally got one."

Kate's eyes followed the retreating riders. "I am, too. Heather's as sweet as she can be, and she's so good for Kit. He's really blossomed out this last month. Morgan's an amazing father, but a boy needs a mother, too."

Buck gazed down on the riders in affection. "Yes he does. I'm glad Kit's going to be okay," he sighed, and then looked up and added briskly, "You're going to have to get on the stick, Kate, if you're going to throw their wedding shindig. It's only a few weeks away."

Kate shot him a rueful look. "You don't need to remind me," she sighed. "I have a thousand things to do. Heather's such an easy bride, she doesn't want anything big or flashy, but I want the wedding to be as beautiful as we can make it. She and Morgan deserve that."

Buck gave her a smack on the cheek and turned back to his chair. "I won't argue with you there."

Kate sputtered, "She wanted for her and Morgan to be married on horseback, and it took me forever to talk her out of it. To persuade her it would be warmer inside." She smiled and shook her head. "So all of you can thank me that she and Morgan are going to be married in this house, instead of in the barn."

Buck lowered his magazine and stared at her over it. "Thank you, ma'am," he murmured. "On behalf of all the guests who'd have to sit there for an hour in the draft."

Kate moved away from the window and came to perch on the arm of his chair. "Yes, that was my little victory, but we compromised. Heather and Morgan are going to drive away in a horse-drawn buggy."

Buck goggled at her. "You're taking care of that part, are you?" he teased, and his wife sputtered.

"No, I am not! I'm leaving that to Hank. But that reminds me," she fretted, "I have to call the photographer and set up a photo shoot for that. And call to make an appointment with the bridal shop for Heather's fitting. And the florist, and the minister, and…" She put a hand to her head, and Buck laughed and kissed her.

Chapter 61

A few weeks later Kate stepped back from Heather with a look of smiling delight. "Come over here," she murmured, and took her by the shoulders.

"Look."

Heather stared into a floor-length mirror. The woman who smiled back at her in the glass was as beautiful and happy as an angel. Her bright hair tumbled over her shoulders in wild golden curls, and her eyes and cheeks glowed.

She was a winter vision in her glorious bridal gown. It was a sugary confection whose white velvet bodice and sleeves were trimmed with faux fur. Its blooming skirts of white chiffon were sprinkled with crumbs of icy white crystal that glittered with her every move.

Kate's smiling face appeared in the mirror behind her shoulder. "You're a snow princess, Heather. Let's put on your veil. Hold still, now."

Heather closed her eyes and stood still as her future sister-in-law carefully set a pearl tiara on her head. She stood there, eyes closed, as Kate gently arranged her veil around her shoulders.

"Now open your eyes."

Heather opened her eyes and caught her breath. The tiara circled her brow in a delicate wreath, and the flowing tulle veil, spangled with crystal, enclosed her like a snow cloud. She didn't recognize herself.

She was transformed, body and soul, and she put a hand to her mouth.

"There now, don't cry," Kate soothed, and turned her around.

Heather shook her head. "I can't help it," she wept. "I've never been so happy. It's like a dream."

Kate hugged her as tight as she dared. "I'm happy for you," she smiled, "and for Morgan. You both deserve this day."

Kate clasped her arm and went on, "Now let's get your bouquet." She lifted a bouquet of pink roses and daisies from a box on the bed and passed it over carefully.

Heather took it in her hands and glanced in the mirror. *I do look beautiful,* she thought in awe. *Maybe it's the dress.*

No, she thought again as she stared. *It isn't the dress. It's because I'm so happy. I don't even look like myself.*

Kate smoothed out the skirt of her own dusty pink chiffon dress and smiled up at Heather.

"Are you ready, Mrs. Spade?"

Heather brushed a tear from her eye and burst out laughing. "I've been ready!" she giggled.

Kate bent down to straighten out the voluminous folds of her train, then smiled and planted a kiss on her cheek. "You're going to knock Morgan's eyes out," she whispered. "Let's go."

She opened the bedroom door, and Heather took a deep breath, gathered herself, and walked into the upstairs hall. She ventured out to the top of the stairs, and as she did, seven handsome faces at the foot turned up to look at her. She saw Buck standing at Morgan's side with his hands clasped in front of him and a look of solemn loyalty in his bright blue eyes; and Carson at his shoulder, looking as cool as iced coffee with his dark, slicked back hair, tailored dress suit and silk shirt. Luke, the only blonde brother, grinned up at her with the easy charm of a born cowboy, and even grumpy Jesse looked dapper with his elegant suit and the distinguished silver stripe through his thick black hair. Will stood military-trim, starched and tan in his immaculate dress suit, and Chase's white smile against his tanned face was movie-star perfect; but Heather's gaze skimmed them all.

Only one Spade man wasn't smiling up at her. Morgan was staring at her like he'd been struck, and Heather beamed at him in pure joy. He was more handsome than she'd ever seen him. He was standing there, ramrod-straight in a severe black suit with a high white collar and a string tie. His long black hair was sleek and lapped his shoulders, his fierce moustache was almost tamed, and he was holding a black Stetson under one arm.

He was her tall, silent, old-fashioned cowboy, and she loved everything about him: his sense of responsibility. His integrity. His love for his son, his unselfishness.

The way he'd slowly opened up to her, allowed her into his heart.

The pianist began playing the Wedding March, and Kate leaned forward to whisper, "One step at a time. I've got your train."

Heather glanced at her gratefully, then began her slow descent down the stairs. She kept her eyes on Morgan's face as she moved, memorizing the look in his eyes, the way his mouth dropped slightly open when he saw her, the way one hand clenched and unclenched as he stood there, waiting for her.

Kit was standing at his side in a little dress suit and string tie, and he was holding a diamond ring on a little velvet pillow.

Gratitude welled up in Heather's heart as she moved to join the two men in her life. *Thank you, Lord,* she prayed, as she stepped down the stairs. *I couldn't love any man more than I love Morgan. He's perfect for me, and I'm going to do my best to be perfect for him.*

She reached the bottom step and turned toward Morgan. She was dimly aware of other smiling faces, but she saw only his. His eyes were somber and touched with awe.

She knew that glimmer in Morgan's eyes. It was the look of total commitment. It was saying that he'd break his heart and his hands and his back for her, that he'd keep the vows he spoke to her, that he meant his word to be nothing less than forever.

Tears filled her eyes, but she smiled through them like sunshine through rain and took the hand he held out to her. The touch of his fingers on hers went through her body like a thunderbolt, and she trembled as she looked up into his eyes.

Snow began to fall softly from the sky. It drifted down like white feathers on the other side of the big glass wall as they turned to face the preacher.

The elderly cleric cleared his throat, adjusted his glasses, and intoned, "Dearly beloved, we are gathered here today to join this man and this woman in holy matrimony."

Heather devoured every detail of Morgan's profile. His black, wavy hair cascaded down over his eyebrow and ear and tumbled down over his shoulder. Her eyes lingered on his high cheekbone, his straight, proud nose, his bushy moustache.

Morgan looked like he'd been shipped directly from 1895; but what she loved best about him wasn't his high white collar or his black duster.

It was that Morgan was old-fashioned where it counted most. He was one of those rare men who lived his creed. He was a straight shooter, a hard worker, a man who put his family first. He was the man she'd always dreamed of and never thought she'd find.

She couldn't look away from his eyes; and when it came her time to murmur, "I do," she said it with all her heart. She and Morgan were still gazing at one another when the preacher announced *man and wife*, and the rest of the laughing room melted away for her when he took her in his arms.

Heather closed her eyes, and the love in Morgan's kiss transported her to a place where only the two of them could go. She hovered in that place for a moment, then descended as their laughing friends brought her back down to earth.

Heather released Morgan reluctantly, then took Morgan's hand as they marched down an aisle of smiling family and friends. Carson opened the front door for them as they walked out into the snow, and a grinning Luke was standing beside a flower-bedecked, horse-drawn buggy. He extended a hand and helped her step up into the front seat, then faded back as Morgan climbed up beside her to take the reins.

Buck walked down the front steps holding Kit in his arms; and as they watched, Kit raised his little arm and hurled a handful of rice at the buggy.

They all laughed, and Morgan called out to Kit as he took the reins. "Hold down the fort for us, buddy. We'll be back in a few days."

Kit waved and smiled, and Morgan shook the reins. The buggy slowly rolled down the cobbled courtyard, and Heather twisted in her seat to wave farewell to the smiling family standing on the front steps of the house.

She tossed her bouquet into the air and giggled to see Carson accidentally catch it, fumble it in horror, and almost drop it as his brothers laughed.

Heather giggled, then turned back to snuggle on Morgan's chest. He slipped an arm around her shoulder as their buggy clattered down the drive.

Morgan looked down at her, and bent down suddenly to plant a kiss on her brow. Heather received it in blissful silence as the snow swirled around them and blanketed the countryside.

Chapter 62

Buck walked back inside, carrying Kit in his arms. The wedding guests were still milling in the atrium and around the fireplace, and he set his squirming nephew down.

"Don't go outside the house," he called, and watched as Kit dodged through the murmuring adults and up the stairs.

A soft touch on his arm made him look down. Kate was at his elbow, smiling up into his face. She slid her hand into his and nodded silently to a small side room. It was a message that any husband would understand, and Buck led his bride through the laughing crowd to the little hideaway and closed the door behind them.

The lights were low in the paneled library, and snow was still drifting past the window outside. Kate turned, twined her arms around his neck, and smiled up into his eyes. "It was a lovely wedding," she murmured.

"Because of you," Buck told her, and brushed her smooth cheek with his hand. "Morg and Heather mostly just showed up."

Kate shrugged a smooth shoulder. "It was my wedding gift to them," she smiled. "After all they've been through, they deserved to just relax and enjoy it."

"Well, they did. It was a beautiful ceremony." Buck stared down at his wife in affection. Kate was like that. She was a generous woman who loved to do for people, and especially for people she loved.

"This reminds me of our wedding," she whispered, and smoothed his hair back from his brow.

A little smile curved his lips. "I remember. Maybe we could go back up to the old house sometime."

Kate gave him a peck on the cheek and whispered into his ear. "Just like old times."

Buck chuckled and slid his hands around her waist. "It hasn't even been a year," he teased. "It's not old times yet!"

Kate tilted her head in smiling acknowledgement. "I don't know," she murmured. "Six months."

"Yeah, but still," he objected. "Six months isn't all that..."

He broke off mid-sentence and looked at Kate again. The smile in her eyes deepened, and his mouth dropped open slightly.

"Wait just a minute," he stammered in surprise, and searched her face. She laughed and nodded, and he stared at her for an instant of stunned silence.

"The doctor says late May, early June," Kate whispered, and his arms tightened around her. He pulled her tight to his chest and buried his face in her neck. Emotion suddenly surged up in his throat, making it impossible to say the things he felt: love so strong that it choked him, excitement, pride, and a little fear.

Kate seemed to understand. She didn't push him to talk, and he was grateful as he stared over her shoulder and blinked back his tears.

She giggled and smoothed his hair back again. "You're going to be the most obnoxious father in the world, Buck," she told him in gentle amusement. "I can see you now, forcing everyone you meet to look at baby pictures."

Buck choked out a sputtering laugh, then suddenly grabbed her and spun her around in the air.

"What are you doing, you crazy fool!" she laughed, and clung to his neck.

"I'm going to be a father!" he yelled out, and swung her again.

"Buck, put me down!"

"I don't care who hears! I'm the happiest man in Texas, and I'll tell it to the world!" he laughed, and brought her back to his chest for a breathless kiss.

He pressed his cheek to hers fervently and closed his eyes. "We'll name him Russell Junior," he told her, and Kate opened her eyes and rolled them to his.

"Him?"

He laughed from the bottom of his stomach, and the loud, booming sound brought a curious face to the door. Kate cleared her throat, and Buck turned to see Carson staring at them quizzically.

"Sorry," he quipped. "I didn't know it was a private party."

Buck tightened Kate to his side and beamed at him. "It's not." He paused and turned to look down at Kate. "Is it?"

She gave him an exasperated look. "Not any more!"

Buck straightened to his full height and announced proudly, "We're going to have a baby!"

Carson's brows rose in surprise. "Congratulations, Kate," he smiled, and lifted his glass in toast. "You're a brave woman."

Luke's face popped up over Carson's shoulder. "What's going on in here?"

Carson turned to him. "Buck and Kate are going to have a baby."

Luke's tanned face split into a grin. "Hey, that's great! You'll have to name him Russ."

Buck nodded. "That's what I said."

Three more curious Spades crowded in at the door, and Kate turned to him and murmured in amusement, "You may as well announce it on the intercom, Buck."

He was struck by her suggestion. "Why didn't I think of that?" he wondered aloud, and started for the door.

"Buck!"

Chapter 63

Soft light leaped on the walls of the log cabin, and the faint, pleasant scent of wood smoke tinged the air of the bedroom. Heather snuggled on Morgan's chest, curled her fingers in his chest hair, and closed her eyes in perfect happiness.

Outside, the wind had picked up, and it moaned around the windows, but it was toasty warm under the covers. Heather drifted toward sleep, and only the slight motion of Morgan's breathing and his fingers on her shoulder kept her from dropping off into a velvet unconsciousness.

A series of mental images flashed through her mind, not quite a dream, because she could still hear the crackling of the fire and still feel Morgan's heart beating beneath her ear. But they danced before her eyes as she drifted between waking and sleeping: Arthur's bright eyes smiling at her gradually melted into Hank's freckled face and fringe of brown bangs; she saw Kit running across the grass, she didn't know where, and horses running free over a distant hill.

The scene and the mood of it shifted. Darkness fell down from the sky like a soft curtain. Snow began to drift down from the sky, and she saw herself in her beautiful party gown again. She twirled to make the skirts bloom out, and she saw Morgan stand up slowly with admiration gleaming in his eyes.

You're as beautiful as dawn, Heather.

When she whirled again, she was in the cabin with Morgan, and firelight gleamed off his bare shoulders as he took her into his arms. She closed her eyes and surrendered to the tickling pleasure of Morgan's kisses on her neck, and her delighted giggles teased out that rumbling laughter of his that she loved.

Heh heh heh heh heh.

Heather smiled in her sleep and turned slightly to slide her arm over Morgan's chest, but it wasn't there. She snuggled into the pillow, yawned, and drifted toward sleep again; but the scent of bacon and the crackling of the fire lured her awake.

She opened a sleepy eye, then stretched languidly. The lovely scent of coffee, bacon, and pancakes perfumed the air. Morgan was bundled up in a fuzzy housecoat and was kneeling in front of the fire.

The last few hours came back to her, and Heather smiled and stretched again. Morgan had taken her to a 150-year-old cabin near the ranch for their honeymoon, a lovely, historic B&B.

She sat up slightly and rubbed her eyes. Morgan had set up a little gridiron and trivet over the fire. There was a cast iron skillet on the gridiron, and a lovely aroma of frying eggs and bacon curled through the air. It mingled pleasantly with the scent of brewing coffee from the pot on the trivet.

"*Mmmm*," she yawned, "that smells wonderful!"

Morgan turned to smile at her. "You ready for breakfast?"

"Ready for two breakfasts," Heather murmured, and pulled the covers up around her chest. Morgan poured out a steaming cup of coffee and walked over to the bed to give it to her.

Heather reached up to take it. "Thank you," she murmured, and smiled up into his face as she took a grateful sip. It was just the way she liked it: hot as fire, dark as night, and strong as love.

Morgan puttered around the fire for a minute, then walked back to the bed with two trays. He set one down on the nightstand and leaned over to set the other on her lap, carefully and slowly.

"Yum," Heather approved, and took a deep, appreciative sniff of the plate. She had three crispy, luscious bacon strips, two perfect fried eggs, a piece of hot cornbread, and two slices of ripe tomato.

Heather reached for the fork and napkin, marveling, *He knows my love language already.*

Food.

But that was the wonderful thing about Morgan. He had a quiet, noticing way about him, and she'd already seen the way he showed love to his son.

With the sweet little everyday gestures.

Heather watched affectionately as Morgan crawled into the bed beside her, carefully and slowly. He reached for the other tray and set it down on his own lap.

Heather turned to him and mumbled through a mouthful of corn bread. "Is was sweet of you to make breakfast."

He tilted his head as he shook out his napkin. "Well, you were asleep. I didn't want to wake you."

Heather leaned over to kiss him, and he turned toward her to receive it.

"Now, don't mess with me, woman," he mumbled, as she leaned back again. "You don't want me to tip this tray over."

Heather shot him a teasing glance. "All right then, but just for now. I make no promises when this food is gone."

Morgan smiled under his moustache and the both of them addressed their breakfasts. Heather enjoyed every bite of the crisp, smoky bacon, coffee and corn bread, and she was finished long before Morgan. He ate with maddening deliberation, one leisurely bite after another, and she watched him in exasperation.

He seemed to sense her mood. "You're going to have to wait for me," he told her, without turning his head. He took a sip of coffee and smacked his lips.

"I eat slow."

Heather picked up her tray and leaned over to set it down on the nightstand. She sat up straight, smoothed her hair, and turned to her new husband.

"Kiss me, Morgan."

He rolled his eyes to hers over the coffee cup. "I would've thought you'd had enough of that for one day," he rumbled.

She snuggled in close to him. "Not hardly. Here, let me help you finish up."

She reached over, snitched a hunk of cornbread off his plate, and munched it expectantly as he finished his eggs. He wiped his mouth with the napkin, tossed it down, and to Heather's joy, removed the tray.

But instead of reaching for her, he grabbed a housecoat off the end of the bed and tossed it to her.

"Go ahead and put that on," he commanded.

She frowned at it. "Why?"

"You're going to be awful cold without it," he told her with a smile. "Come on, I want to show you something."

Heather pulled her mouth down. "I like it right here," she objected. "Come back to bed, Morgan."

He sank down on the edge of the bed and leaned on one elbow to murmur, "We didn't get to celebrate Christmas together, so I got you a present."

Heather's heart melted, and he reached for him. "You're the only present I want," she whispered into his ear, and kissed it. "Come to bed!"

But Morgan pulled out of her arms. "Come on," he beckoned; and he seemed so set on it that Heather finally sighed and reached for the housecoat. Morgan smiled down at her as she shouldered into it, and he helped her up.

"Put on your slippers."

"Where are we going?" she complained, but stuck her bare feet into the slippers beside the bed.

"Not far."

Morgan took her hand and led her out onto the back porch of the log cabin. To her dumbfounded amazement, a gleaming Palomino mare stood hitched to the porch rail, and tossed its glorious white mane in greeting. The mare was wearing a warm green blanket on its back with the inscription *Seven Ranch* stitched on one corner.

"*Morgan,*" she gasped, and walked up to put a gentle hand on the mare's nose.

Morgan's eyes gleamed with quiet pleasure as he watched her. "She's yours," he murmured. "I bought her last week. She's my Christmas present to you."

Heather went into his arms without a word, and he chuckled as she broke into tears. "What's the matter?" he teased, "Don't you like her?"

"Like her!" Heather sobbed.

Morgan kissed her hair and rocked her slightly in his arms. "I reckoned you weren't the kind of woman to want a lot of fancy jewelry. I figured you'd like a horse better."

Heather curled her fingers into his robe and shook her head. "She's beautiful," she hiccuped, and stared at the mare again over her shoulder. "She shines like silk!"

"I had Hank bring her over," Morgan smiled. "She's been out in that little barn over yonder all night, waiting for you."

Heather looked up to see a little log barn about fifty yards behind the cabin. She shook her head and looked up at Morgan with an overflowing heart. "I don't know how to thank you, Morgan," she whispered. "And I feel terrible, because I don't have a gift for you."

He tightened her to his chest. "You already gave me my gift," he murmured, and kissed her brow. "You kept Kit from being kidnapped. That was the best gift I could ever get."

Heather turned her face into Morgan's chest and held him; and the only thing in her heart at that moment was wonder.

What did I ever do to deserve such a beautiful soul? she marveled. She had no words to express what she felt; but she was sure to the bottom of her heart that she'd married the right man, the man she loved and would love for the rest of her life.

Morgan tilted his head to look down into her face; then smiled and turned her back to the cabin.

"Come back inside," he told her softly, "it's cold out here. I'll go put your horse up again."

Heather looked up at him. "She'll be all right out here for a while," she whispered. "I want you back inside with me, cowboy."

Morgan smiled and took her hand, and they drifted across the porch and back inside the firelit cabin; and Heather closed the door tight behind them.

Chapter 64

Nine months later Heather drifted to the huge glass wall of Buck and Kate's apartment. It was the last drowsy days of August. Flower petals swirled in the air and went dancing past on the wind, but they'd soon be replaced by the red leaves of autumn.

Heather bent down over a white bassinet, picked up the squirming baby, and smiled down into its bright blue eyes. The sturdy newborn boy was bundled up in a pale blue onesie and a matching cap.

"He's so beautiful," Heather marveled, and laughed to see the baby smile.

Kate bent in and gazed down into her son's face. "I think so, too. But of course I'm his mother," she sighed, and caressed the baby's silken cheek fondly. "Russell has Buck's eyes, and he's going to be big like him. I think he's going to have Buck's black hair, too," she added. "It's just fluff now, but what there is, is dark."

"How much did he weigh?" Heather murmured. She held out her finger and giggled to see the baby curl his little fingers around it.

"Eight pounds fourteen ounces," Kate sighed, and Heather goggled at her in sympathy; but she saw her own pity staring back at her from her sister-in-law's eyes.

"I hope you have an easier delivery," she said gently.

"I do, too!" Heather blurted, and put a hand to her stomach. She was four months pregnant, and she was healthy; but Morgan was almost as tall and broad-shouldered as Buck, and she gave Kate a *wow* look.

Kate laughed and hugged her. "Don't worry, you'll be fine," she soothed. "And once it's all over, you'll forget about everything except that sweet little face." She bent over the bassinet and gazed down tenderly at her son.

Heather looked down at the baby in mingled affection and dismay. She was fairly sure she wouldn't forget delivering a baby that weighed almost nine pounds; but little Russell was so cute that she could see herself getting resigned.

She glanced around the apartment. "Where's Buck?"

Kate pulled a little blanket up around her baby's chin. "Oh, he's in town shopping," she sighed. "He wanted a boy so badly, and now that we have one he's over the moon. Russell isn't two months old yet, and already Buck is buying horse toys and cowboy clothes," she explained. "He couldn't wait. He's going to have this poor child riding a pony as soon as he can sit up," she laughed.

The front door opened a crack, and Morgan stuck his head into the apartment. "Where's my nephew?" he asked with a smile, and Kate laughed and rose to greet him.

He took her hands and kissed her cheek. "You're glowing, Kate," he told her; and his eyes moved to the bassinet.

"Come and see him," Heather invited and pulled the blanket back just a little. The baby yawned and wriggled, and a smile dawned across Morgan's face.

"Well, will you look at that fine boy," he marveled softly. "He's the spit and image of Buck, all right. I think I see a bit of Big Russ in him, too." He turned to call to the little face peeping in at the door.

"Come in here, Kit, and say hello to your cousin Russell."

Kit slipped in and came over shyly. He peered at the baby's yawning face from behind his father's leg. Morgan rested a big hand on his shoulder.

"Soon little Russell here will be big enough to play catch with you."

Kate moved to take the baby in her arms. "Let's not rush things," she laughed, and pressed her cheek to the baby's little cap. "Momma wants a little time to enjoy him just the way he is."

The door opened again, and Morgan turned just in time to see Buck returning from town. He glanced at Kate laughingly.

"Well, it was a nice thought."

Buck set two big bags down on the floor and hurried over with another in his hand. "Look what I found in town, Kate," he announced, and held up a little Stetson hat.

"That's adorable, Buck," Kate agreed.

"You can't believe how hard it is to get a child's saddle in this town," Buck complained as he moved in to lean over her shoulder. He beamed down into his son's face and added, "There's a six month waiting list for a decent pony saddle!"

Heather stifled a giggle, and Morgan caught her eye and glanced toward the door. She rose slowly, gazed down at the baby again, and pressed her hand to Kate's arm.

"We don't want to tire you out," she smiled. "We just wanted to come up and see the baby."

Kate beamed at her. "I'm so glad you did. Come back tomorrow, and we'll have more time to chat."

"I will." Heather leaned down to give Kate a peck, and Morgan clapped Buck's shoulder.

"He's a fine one, Buck. We're so glad for you and Kate."

Buck beamed at him, and Morgan smiled and extended his hand. Heather took it, and the three of them walked out of the apartment. Kit went running down the stairs to dash into their apartment, and the two of them followed more slowly. Heather looked up into Morgan's face.

"I saw how you were looking at that baby," she murmured. "You want another boy, don't you?"

The corners of Morgan's mouth curled up a little. "I wouldn't say no," he rumbled. "But I wouldn't say no to a little girl, either. I'm gonna let the Lord decide." He looked down at her.

"You worried I'm gonna send the baby back?"

Heather broke out giggling, and Morgan joined her and kissed her cheek. "Surprise me," he told her.

She nodded and held his eye.

"Okay."

He gave her a curious glance out of the corner of his eye, and she giggled again as they walked into the apartment, arm in arm.

Chapter 65

"Are you sure you're going to be all right all by yourself?"

Heather sputtered and gave her husband an exasperated look. "Of course. I'm perfectly fine. Pregnant women go to the doctor every day, and they come back alive. Honestly, Morgan," she giggled.

Morgan gave her a worried sidelong look and rubbed his jaw. "Well…if you're sure," he grumbled. "It's your first big checkup. I thought you'd like me to be there."

Heather's heart melted, and she leaned over to give him an affectionate peck. "You sweet man," she murmured into his cheek. "But it's Kit's first day of kindergarten. He needs you more than I do. Run on."

Morgan hesitated in apparent reluctance, and Heather grabbed his shoulders and pushed him toward the door of their apartment. "Go on. You're going to make Kit late for his first day of school if you drag your heels any more."

Morgan sighed and looked back over his shoulder, but drifted off to the door. "Call me if there's anything…if you want me to come over while you're there."

"I will," she promised. "Hurry, now."

Morgan drifted through the door, and Heather giggled to herself and shook her head. She had never felt better in her life, and she was looking forward to her first ultrasound.

It was a bit disappointing that Morgan couldn't share that with her, but there was no way either one of them would let Kit go to his first day of school alone.

Heather moved to the glass wall of their apartment and stared down into the courtyard. She watched with a fond smile as Morgan climbed into the jeep, buckled Kit up, and slowly pulled away.

She picked up her bag, slung it over her shoulder, and prepared to follow. She locked the apartment door behind her and walked down the stairs just in time to see Carson skipping down ahead of her. He paused on the lowest step, looked up, and flashed a white grin.

Heather sighed and couldn't help thinking: *All of Morgan's brothers are so good-looking. Especially Carson. How on earth is he still single?*

"Morning, Heather."

"Good morning! Where are you off to, so early?"

Carson rolled one perfect sleeve up to his elbow. "I'm off to Dallas this morning, and I'm going to be late. *Ciao, bella.*" He nodded to her and launched off across the atrium.

Heather watched him hurry off and thought wistfully: *I'm going to have to talk to Kate about that one. Maybe the two of us can fix Carson up with some nice woman.*

Carson didn't look as he if *needed* help in that area; but just the same.

She stepped out in the sunshine just in time to see Carson's sleek silver Jaguar glide past, and she got a glimpse of his hand thrown up in a parting wave before the car zoomed off. Heather watched it go, sighed, and made a mental note to ask Morgan's opinion when she got back home.

She hit the button on her keyfob, and the lights on a massive black truck flicked on. Morgan had replaced her beat-up blue sedan with a Hennessey Mammoth 1000, surely the biggest truck ever made. She practically needed a ladder to climb up into it, and people in town always stared to see such a little woman driving such a big truck; but Morgan had thought that it would keep her safe, and when he'd added that it could pull any trailer she needed to haul, she'd thrown her arms around his neck.

Heather popped on her sunglasses, buckled up, and pulled the truck away. It was a bright, sunny summer's morning, and she was looking forward to a pleasant drive into town. She flicked on the radio and began humming along, and when she caught herself pressing the gas, she pulled her foot up.

Morgan had made her swear to drive slow before he gave her the keys, and most of the time she remembered. She'd been especially good since she'd learned she was pregnant; and she sighed a bit to think that it was another six months before she could loosen up a bit.

She pulled out onto the road and hummed to herself as she looked down on cars and over at trucks. The truck was so high that she was on the same level as semi drivers, and sometimes they nodded and waved.

Her doctor's office was right in the center of town in a building next to the courthouse, and Heather carefully pulled the truck into the parking space in front of the door.

She grabbed her bag, opened the door, and slid down onto the sidewalk. The cheerful sign on the office door read: *Dr. Colette Jenkins, the Baby Doctor.*

Heather breezed in and smiled at the receptionist as she approached the front desk, but she didn't need to introduce herself. The young woman beamed at her and chirped, "Good morning, Mrs. Spade! I'll take you right back."

The receptionist stood up and came out from behind the desk to escort her through a side door, through a narrow hall, and back to a big examination room. The girl gave her a bright look and nodded toward the table.

"There's a gown there on the chair for you to wear. The doctor will be here in a few minutes."

"Thank you."

The door closed behind her, and Heather undressed absently. She shrugged into the cotton gown and sat waiting with her fingers laced across her lap.

She wasn't sure if she was hoping for a girl or a boy. Morgan had been carefully neutral, and so far she couldn't tell if he had some secret preference; but as for her, she was hoping for a little girl.

But when she looked at Kit, she couldn't help imagining what it would be like to have another son. A boy who would have Morgan's dark hair, and her fair skin. Or maybe her blonde hair, and his dark blue eyes.

She and Morgan had already decided that if it was a boy, they were going to name him Cassidy, and if it was a girl, they were going to name her Bailey.

She was still mulling it over when the door opened, and the smiling doctor walked in. "Good morning, Heather! How are you feeling this morning?"

Heather smiled back at her physician. Dr. Jenkins was a large, beautiful blonde woman with perfect skin and an enviable updo. She cleared her throat.

"Feeling great, thank you."

The doctor placed her clipboard on the table and picked up a blood pressure cuff. Heather extended her arm as the doctor wrapped the cuff around it and pressed a button on the little machine.

She glanced at the reading. "Well, your blood pressure looks good," she murmured, and unwrapped the cuff. "Are you ready for your ultrasound?"

Heather gave her a hopeful, nervous look, and the doctor smiled at her. "Go ahead and lean back on the table." She opened a drawer and snapped plastic gloves over her hands.

"Let's have a look at your baby."

She pulled up a wheeled ultrasound machine and unhooked a plastic wand. "I'm going to put some clear gel on your tummy. It's going to be a little cold."

Heather pulled up her gown and yelped as the doctor squirted cold gel on her stomach. The doctor put the wand to her stomach and pressed it in slightly. She glanced at a black-and-white-image on a small computer screen, and her brows shot up.

Heather's eyes flicked to the screen, but she couldn't make any sense of the jumbled shapes.

The doctor circled the wand over her stomach, and over it again, as if she couldn't quite believe her eyes.

"Wow," she murmured, and Heather's eyes flicked to her face nervously.

"What? Is something wrong?"

The doctor shook her head. "I've never seen anything quite like this before," she mumbled, and moved the wand again.

Heather's heart jumped in her chest. "What do you mean?"

The doctor turned to look at her and took a deep breath. She set the wand aside.

"Well, I can tell you now or tell you later," she sighed. "Which do you prefer?"

Heather's eyes searched the doctor's face in painful suspense, and she licked her lips.

Lord, help me, she prayed.

"Tell me what?"

Her doctor stood up slowly, closed the door of the room, and settled back down into a chair beside her. She clasped her hands in her lap and met Heather's eyes; and Heather braced herself and prayed it was good news.

Chapter 66

Carson flicked on the radio and reached for a pack of cigarettes he'd stashed in the glove compartment. Smooth jazz curled softly through the elegant, leather-scented interior of the Jaguar, and he shook out a slender tube of tobacco, flicked a lighter, and exhaled smoke with a slow, deliberate sigh.

He'd been trying to quit, but the last few months had finally destroyed his resolve.

His exasperated glance flicked at the rolling green hills flashing past on the way down the long drive, but he wasn't seeing the lush Seven pastures. He was remembering the parade of indignities he'd endured since his wild older brothers had turned domestic.

Hey Carson, Luke had grinned and punched him in the ribs. *Saw you caught Heather's bouquet. No more 'always the bridesmaid,' huh?*

Buck's big arm had gone around his shoulder unexpectedly one day in the hall. *Say Carson,* he'd murmured, *I was hoping you could watch Molly and*

It'll be good practice for when you become a father!

Carson adjusted one shoulder. He'd been free that night, and he didn't mind babysitting as long as it didn't become a habit; but he couldn't shake the feeling that there was a big bull's-eye swinging on his back.

He'd seen the mischievous looks Kate and Heather were giving him, the twinkle in their eyes, and he was getting the feeling they were cooking up a romance with his name on it.

Kate's lips had curved up as she passed him a bowl of potatoes at the dinner table. *You'll have to bring your girlfriend over for dinner sometime, Carson,* she'd told him.

Rita and I broke up last month, he'd informed her; and he'd seen the smug look Kate had exchanged with Buck.

But they were all out of luck. He refused to become the object of some ridiculous campaign.

Carson grumbled under his breath and shifted into third gear. It was time for a break from the family. He loved his new niece and nephews, and he was glad for Buck and Morgan, kind of; but the ranch house wasn't a big, comfortable club for him and his single brothers any more. It was turning into a nursery, what with baby showers and laughing women and stacks of pastel-wrapped gifts.

Not his cup of tea.

It was convenient, then, that the thoroughbred yearling auction was coming up. It gave him an excuse to get out of town for a while, and would give Kate and Heather time to forget him and target one of his brothers instead.

Carson sputtered in amusement. *Maybe they'll find a wife for Luke. If he's sucker enough to hang around and get caught, that is.*

Carson paused at the front gate with his hand on the wheel. His cigarette smoldered lazily as he waited for the big gates to open.

I'll fly up to Kentucky a few weeks early, he thought with a sigh. *It'll give me a chance to settle in and get stabling all lined up for our horses. Maybe rub elbows with the early bird buyers.*

I'll send for the yearlings when it comes time.

The gates opened up at last, and Carson turned the Jag onto the road in the direction of the interstate. He'd drive to Dallas, catch a flight up to Lexington, and see what mischief he could get into up in bluegrass country.

It would be a real relief to be at an honest-to-goodness cocktail party again, among urbane people whose only one-year-olds ate hay and could outrun a deer.

An hour later Carson pulled the Jag up to the glittering front doors of the luxurious Texan Hotel. The Texan was a five-star resort a few miles from DFW, and it offered a comfortable hourly shuttle to the airport.

Or, in his case, private limo service.

A uniformed doorman came hurrying up to his window. "Welcome back, Mr. Spade!" he smiled. "We're glad that you're staying with us."

Carson grabbed his phone and his cigarettes and slid out of the car to hand his keys to a parking attendant. The doorman hurried on ahead to open one massive brass door for him, and Carson breezed into the deeply-carpeted hotel lobby to secure his usual: the executive suite on the top floor of the 15-story building.

The pretty desk clerk beamed at him as he walked up to the gleaming front desk. "Welcome back to Dallas, Mr. Spade! The executive, I presume?"

Carson winked at her and smiled lazily. "Thank you, that's right. I'd also like to reserve a plane ticket to Lexington tomorrow morning around ten, first class."

"I'll send the confirmation to your email address, Mr. Spade. Here are the keys to your room. Do you have any luggage?"

"No."

"Enjoy your stay, Mr. Spade," she purred, and Carson glanced at her in amusement before he sauntered over to the elevator on the other side of the elegant lobby.

He'd check in, enjoy a leisurely lunch, work the phones for a few hours to set up his own reservations and business contacts in Kentucky, then enjoy a relaxing spa massage and a nice hot shower before a pleasant dinner and a deep sleep.

A nice way to tee up his trip, and a convenient place to keep his car until he returned.

The elevator doors slid open, and Carson pressed the topmost button. The doors slid shut and the car began to move up so smoothly that its ascent was almost imperceptible.

After a few minutes there was a soft chime, and the elevator doors slid open to reveal a long, elegant hall with a pair of double doors at the end. Carson whistled and tossed the keys in the air as he walked toward them. The sophisticated atmosphere was like a balm to his soul. He was feeling better already.

He unlocked the doors to the suite and sighed happily to see a familiar panorama stretching out in front of him: a massive window showing him DFW's sprawling white buildings and dozens of planes landing and taking off, and beyond that, the blue skyline of Dallas.

The lines of the room were long and low in spite of its scale; the ambiance was elegant, modern, and sophisticated. Huge black and white photographs graced the walls, white and black leather furniture filled the step-down lounge area, and a small fountain whispered in the center of the room. A faint, pleasant whiff of sandalwood perfumed the air.

Carson's phone vibrated, and he reached for it.

"Hello?"

Buck's voice boomed through the phone, and it sounded faintly worried. "Where'd you run off to, Carson? Kate's been looking for you. She wants you to come to dinner tonight. I think she has somebody she wants you to meet."

Carson smiled, tossed his keys onto the couch, sank down into a leather recliner, and leaned back. "Oh, I'm sorry, Buck," he murmured, and reached for his cigarettes. "I'm on my way to Kentucky. Thought I'd get an early start on the auction this year."

Buck's voice sounded deflated. "Oh. Kate'll be disappointed. A friend of hers is having dinner with us, and she was looking forward to introducing you."

Carson stuck a cigarette in his mouth. "Well, thank Kate for me, but I'll have to take a rain check," he mumbled. "Maybe Luke can stand in for me."

Buck's voice brightened. "Hey, that's an idea! I'll have to go ask him."

"Yeah, better hurry," Carson murmured, and reached for the t.v. remote. "No telling what he might have planned."

"Okay, well I'll see you Carson," Buck replied. "Call me before the auction and I'll make sure you get those yearlings safe and sound."

"I will. Bye, Buck."

The line went dead, and Carson rolled his head back and laughed a long, evil laugh. Luke didn't know it yet, but he was about to have the most uncomfortable night of his life.

Better him than me, Carson thought in amusement. *And who knows, maybe Luke is looking to get married.*

But it'll be a cold day before I settle down. No ball and chain for this guy.

Carson blew a satisfied puff of smoke toward the ceiling and chuckled again, imagining Luke's horrified face.

Have fun, buddy, he sputtered.

I intend to!

Enjoy the next Spade brothers book

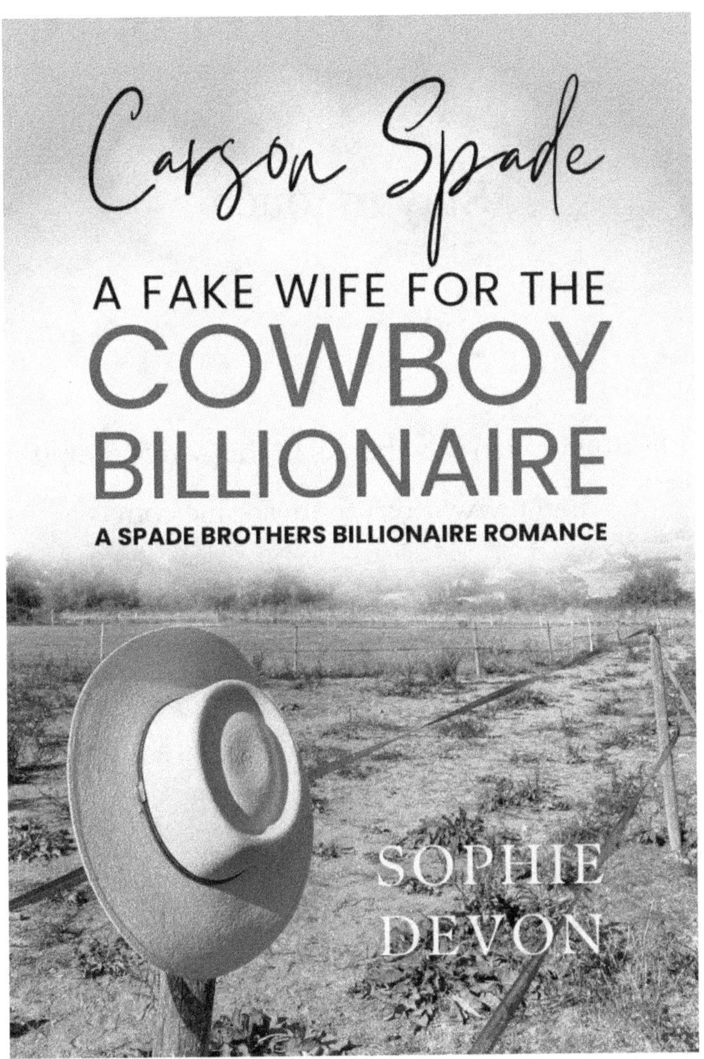

Stay in touch

Get notified when new books in this series are published here: www.writtenbysophie.com

Follow Sophie on Tiktok:

www.tiktok.com/@sophiedevonbooks